Burning RESOLUTION

STONEBROOKE SERIES

T.M. CROMER

BOOKS BY T.M. CROMER

Get your printable list here:

https://www.tmcromer.com/printable-booklist

CONTEMPORARY & ROMANTIC SUSPENSE

The Stonebrooke Series:

BURNING RESOLUTION

HIDDEN RESOLUTION

The Fiore Vineyard Series:

PICTURE THIS

RETURN HOME

ONE WISH

The Holt Family Series:

GOODBYE TO YOU

THIS TIME YOU

INCLUDING YOU

A LIFE WITH YOU

PARANORMAL ROMANCE

The Sentinels of Magic Series:

THE AETHER

THE DEATH DEALER

THE SEER

The Unlucky Charms Series:

PINTS & POTIONS

WHISKEY & WITCHES

BEER & BROOMSTICKS

COCKTAILS & CAULDRONS

WINE & WARLOCKS

HIGHBALLS & HEXES

The Thorne Witches Series:

SUMMER MAGIC

AUTUMN MAGIC

WINTER MAGIC

SPRING MAGIC

REKINDLED MAGIC

LONG LOST MAGIC

FOREVER MAGIC

ESSENTIAL MAGIC

MOONLIT MAGIC

ENCHANTED MAGIC

CELESTIAL MAGIC

EVERLASTING MAGIC

CAPTIVATING MAGIC

The Thorne Witches: Happily Ever Afters Series:

ENDURING MAGIC

BOUNDLESS MAGIC

The Angels of Legend Series:

LUCIFER

GABRIEL

To all the beautiful people, who don't see their own worth and who don't realize how lovely they truly are—both inside and out.

This one also goes out to my beta readers. Thank you, gang, for your willingness to help whenever I call. Love you bunches!

She contemplated her pudgy belly reflected in the full-length mirror, poked it a few times, and let out a heartfelt sigh. Until this exact moment, Erica Sutton had been able to ignore her emotional overeating. However, standing there, with her half-naked, overweight body on display, the truth was staring her in the face. Bad habits. They needed to be broken and fast! Her stretchy yoga pants were one pie slice away from splitting at the seams. The same ones she'd purchased last year, which were, at the time, too big.

The social media craze was another ugly truth she didn't want to face. She couldn't take a single selfie that didn't expose her double chin, regardless of practiced poses and filters. Recently, a fan mentioned she admired Erica and how she represented *real* women. Whatever the hell *that* meant. Women came in all shapes and sizes, and they held a variety of careers, from stay-at-home moms to small business owners to corporate CEOs. Writing from the privacy of her home in a t-shirt and lounging pants didn't make her representative of women in general. She was more of the swamp witch poster-child sort.

All she *did* know was she needed to get fit if she intended to have a long, healthy life. But damn, she hated to work out. Hated to sweat in any way, shape, or form. Vanity exacted a toll, requiring a woman to put up or shut up.

"Suck it up, Erica!" she scolded her mirrored self. "Enough is enough."

Still, she was unprepared for any drastic action, and she distracted herself with social media. Instant regret! She grimaced at the inundation of notifications. Apparently, all the stick-thin partygoers from last night's New Year's Eve revelry felt it prudent to tag her. Her fingers flew over the keyboard as she untagged herself from any photos or reels.

"That's what you get for going out without Shonda or Angela," she said aloud. "Now you have to pay the piper!"

She pulled her ex-boyfriend's overlarge t-shirt over her bulge and reached for her trusty laptop. After skimming through the online reviews for local gyms, she found what she sought. A month ago, Workout World opened its third location here in her hometown and, from what she read, maintained four- and five-star reviews for their personal trainers, staff services, and cleanliness.

Now, if her reluctant fingers would dial the damned number, she would be doing well.

Perhaps drumming up the courage after a coffee would be easier. The caffeine might chase away the last of her alcohol-overindulgence headache. She glared accusingly at the empty bottle of Moscato in her recycling bin. Why she'd continued to imbibe alone upon returning home was anyone's guess.

Wine.

Another crutch to prop herself up in the months since her split from the asshat who shall not be named. He'd certainly done a number on her, bringing forth all the insecurities she never knew existed until he'd entered her life.

Moisture burned behind her lids, and she blinked to dispel it.

Crying was akin to self-pity. Her bestie, Shonda, had assured her it wasn't allowed.

"Dickhead Dave"—oops, she mentioned him!—"doesn't deserve another second of your time," Erica reminded herself.

Still, unraveling the emotional knots he'd tangled her up in would take a serious effort.

Another social media notification popped up on her screen, and she pulled up the post with dread in her heart. Sure enough, another clueless acquaintance had caught her from the side in an awkward moment as she was speaking, thereby tripling her chin.

Not attractive in the least.

She groaned, hit the like button, to not hurt the woman's feelings, and clicked the hide-from-timeline option as she prayed to God the post wouldn't come back to haunt her.

With resignation in her heart, Erica dialed the gym's number.

Christ, this was going to suck.

Other people got a runner's high from working out. All she got was tired. Firming her resolve, she curbed the impulse to hang up when a man on the other end of the line answered. The deep, sexy timbre of his voice traveled the length of her body, forcefully shaking awake every cell between her brain and her pinky toes. They all shuddered with delight and high-fived each other. But since she'd solemnly sworn off men until the ripe old age of seventy, her body's reaction was not in the least little bit appropriate.

THE INCESSANT RING of the phone annoyed Zack Sharp. The main office of their newest fitness center was *supposed* to be closed for the holiday. However, his brother Mason, one of his two business partners and a marketing genius, had convinced him to open their doors.

January first equaled New Year's Resolution Day.

Mason had assured him that everyone and their brother, not hungover from the night before, would be calling to secure a membership. Of course, his brother hadn't been wrong. It simply pissed Zack off that half his staff hadn't shown up because they, too, had partied hard last night.

When his employees returned, there would be a come-to-Jesus meeting. The Sharps paid their team top dollar to be on time and professional. Human Resources would also receive a phone call about revising company policy. Zack had been too lenient for far too long. A few employees knew him from their old high-school football days. Because of their connection, they believed rules didn't apply to them. They were wrong.

"Hello. Thanks for calling *Workout World*. How may I help you?" he asked as he reached for a form.

"I need to set up a time to tour your facility and perhaps meet with a personal trainer. The sooner, the better. Preferably today if you have an opening."

The reply was lost, but the sex-kitten sound took the A-line straight to his groin, collecting his brain cells along the way. The husky phone-sex-operator voice brought to mind endless nights of dirty, delicious sex.

Holy hell!

That had never happened to him before.

With an attempt at concentration, he asked, "Is there a specific reason you would like an appointment today?"

"Yeah, I'm fucking fat and need to drop forty pounds," she retorted. "Why else does anyone join a gym?"

He pressed his lips together to contain an inappropriate bark of laughter. Her surliness was hell on his professionalism.

"We have many members who actually enjoy working out," he felt compelled to point out.

"Right." She scoffed. "Okay, well, I need an intervention. A left-over wedge of carrot cake is sitting on my counter, taunting me. I'm about to bury my face in the cream cheese frosting to show it who's boss." She sighed deeply. "Aren't you people trained to talk me off the ledge and not ask stupid questions?"

Zack's soon-to-be client was on the proverbial ledge. "We're at DEFCON ONE, but I know what steps to take for this level of crisis. Listen to me very carefully and do exactly as I say." He grinned when she snorted. "Slowly back away from the counter, run to your car, and make your way here. Don't stop for any reason. I'm planning to time you. How long would it normally take from your place?"

"Ten minutes if all the stoplights are green. I'm worried, though. Addie's Bakery is on the corner of 10th and Main. If you've ever had any of Addie's baked goods, you know my journey is fraught with danger. Getting to your place may be iffy." There was a lengthy pause before she spoke again. "And what's with the running comment? There's running? I'm not down with that."

He chuckled. The woman turned a shit day fun, and Zack couldn't wait to hear her complaints when he put her through her paces. He always took sadistic pleasure in seeing a reluctant newbie's wariness the first time they caught sight of the machines.

"We'll discuss your options after you're here. May I have your name, please?"

"Erica Sutton."

He frowned. Back in high school, he'd known an Erica Sutton. A skinny bookworm who'd agreed to tutor him in biology, and he'd taken considerable delight in teasing her during the human repro-duction lessons. She'd been such a cute, shy creature with large dark eyes, usually hidden behind her auburn bangs and oversized glasses. And she'd also been prone to blushing if they happened to make eye contact, which he strove to do for that exact reason.

The woman on the phone couldn't possibly be the same person. Mousy Erica would never think the word *fucking*, much less say it. Although, he wondered about the odds of two Erica Suttons in the same small town of Stonebrooke. Pretty slim, he'd wager.

"Okay, Erica. I'll see you in ten minutes. Twelve tops. I've activated a tracking device on your cellphone, and I'll know if you stop at Addie's. Keep in mind it'll go harder on you if you do."

"Nag, nag, nag. I'll see you in eleven."

Zack couldn't wait to meet this one.

CHAPTER

TWO

Erica girded her loins and forced herself to step through the double doors of the three-story building. About fifteen or so people occupied various stations, grunting and sweating their way through some routine or another. Glancing toward the front desk, she mentally groaned. A perky young woman in a low-cut sports bra was leaning across the counter, her goods displayed for the super jock across from her.

Freaking great.

As if Erica didn't already feel like a whale out of water because she had a double-digit dress size! Tugging the hem of her shirt over her ever-expanding ass, she made her way to the reception desk.

"Hi. Welcome to *Workout World*. Are you interested in signing up for a membership today?" Perky Chick's twin peaks bobbed with the cadence of her voice, and the jock's head followed suit. Really, his bobbing head *might* have coincided with her greeting, but he did seem distracted. It was too difficult to tell and well above Erica's general give-a-damn quota.

She sighed and faced the buxom twig. "I have an appointment," she said with patience she didn't feel.

The man of her dreams walked out of the office behind the dunderhead jock who was kicked back with his feet resting on the reception desk. One reprimanding look at said jock, and the guy dropped his legs faster than Erica could blink.

Delivering a nod of approval, Dream Man, then turned to her.

"Erica?" he asked with a smile and a lift of his perfectly groomed dark brows.

Zack Sharp.

She could hardly believe it. She'd know him anywhere. Having been in love with him for over half her life, recognition came swift. His near-black hair was shorter and permanently mussed as if he ran his hands through it multiple times per day. She recalled he used to do that when he was deep in thought. And damned if those piercing blue eyes didn't still make her heart beat faster! Good lord, the man had filled out and aged well, going from heartthrob to heart-stopping.

And wasn't *she* the true dunderhead? All she could do was gape and nod.

"Come on back," Zack said warmly. "I'd like to go over your long-term workout goals." He glanced at his watch and grinned. "You made good time."

Following him to his office, Erica had to concentrate on not staring at his perfect ass encased in tight three-hundred-dollar jeans.

Wait, what? Why was he in jeans?

He stopped short and spun to frown down at her. "Excuse me?"

The blood drained from her head.

She'd spoken aloud!

Erica jerked her gaze up from his crotch—now occupying the position where his fantastic ass had been—and gulped. Heat started at her toes and gained record-breaking velocity as it ascended her neck to her face.

"I... uh...y-you..." she stuttered.

"It *is* you! I thought so." Zack's smile was wreathed in delight. "Little Erica Sutton."

His comment brought her back to the reason she was here. "Not so little anymore. Can we get the torture over with so I can go home and drown my sorrows in a vat of wine?"

His bark of laughter had her closing her eyes and rubbing the spot between her brows. Once again, she'd forgotten to use her filter. She was glued in place, and if he hadn't thrown an arm around her shoulders to lead her the rest of the way into the office, she would've likely remained in place for the next hour, berating herself and praying for a sinkhole to swallow her whole.

"I'd forgotten how adorable you are," he said with a chuckle. "Come on. I promise to take it easy on your first day."

"But why *are* you wearing jeans?"

And why was she so obsessed with his ass?

"I'd only planned to work in the office today, but a few of my team members failed to show," he replied as he settled in the leather office chair behind his desk. "Let's start on the intake form, shall we?"

The next quarter of an hour was spent discussing her eating habits—she blatantly lied—along with her fitness goals. Afterward, Zack took her on a tour of the facility. He patiently explained the functions of each machine and showed her the rooms where they held the spin, Zumba, yoga, pilates, and blah-blah-blah classes. There were too many choices for her to process. Next, he brought her upstairs to view the inside track overlooking a basketball court, which doubled as a volleyball court.

"This place is incredible. You manage all this?" Erica was awed by everything *Workout World* had to offer. Not that she'd utilize any of it, but it was impressive.

"Own. Or rather co-own with my brothers Mason and Dane," Zack corrected with a self-satisfied smile.

"Is this a franchise, or do you own all three in the state?"

"I'm impressed you did your homework. Although, I suppose I

shouldn't be. You were always studious."

His admiring look, full of praise, made her want to preen. Nothing had changed since high school, that was for sure. She was putty in his hands.

He nodded toward an article on the wall. It showed him along with two other men at a ribbon-cutting ceremony. She recognized his oldest brother from their high school days.

"We own all three," he said. "And no, we haven't franchised yet, but we've been considering it."

"Zack, you've done an amazing job."

"That means a lot coming from you. I seem to recall it took a lot to impress you," he said with a half smile.

For what felt like a full minute, they stared at one another. The appreciative light in his gorgeous azure gaze made breathing difficult.

What could he possibly find to admire about her?

Flustered, she sought a distraction. Her eyes lit on the cardio equipment behind him and the joggers they contained.

"I thought you told me there would be no running," she lamented.

As he laughed and flung an arm around her neck for the second time in an hour, Erica's heart lightened and felt as if it had found its home. Lord love a duck, she was in major trouble.

"Come on, kid. Time to get started burning calories."

"God help me," she muttered.

His chuckle told her he'd misunderstood her remark and likely thought she was talking about the routine he had planned for her. In reality, being this close to him again had caused oodles and oodles of stupid schoolgirl feelings to resurface.

***

ONCE HE'D GOTTEN Erica situated on an exercise bike, Zack went to change into his gym attire. He instructed Todd and Lacey to continue handling the floor and not interrupt him if they didn't have to. His plan was to spend the next hour with his new client and get reacquainted.

Upon returning to where he'd last seen Erica, he saw the bike was paused and she was jabbing the display buttons. An irritated frown marred her brow, and he fought another smile. His ears, along with anyone else's within hearing distance were assaulted by her colorful curses.

"Wow! When did you develop such an extensive vocabulary?" he asked with a laugh.

"Screw you. And screw this stupid bike. It tried to kill me. Did you know these things speed up on their own?" she demanded.

"It's a function of the unit. It simulates uphill, flat roads, and downhill." Tamping down his amusement, he compressed his lips into a straight line.

"Well, I don't like it. They should come with a warning label." Jumping off, she dusted her hands as if she'd finished an odious task. "What else can I do?"

Zack pinned her with a hard stare. In fitness circles, he was known for his stern, no-nonsense approach, and he planned to set her straight from the beginning. Just because they had shared history, it didn't mean he'd let her walk all over him.

"I don't care if you don't like it." He gestured to the bike. "You have ten more minutes of cardio. Get busy."

Her eyes narrowed. "I don't like *you* very much, either."

"Too bad."

"Do you speak to all your new members this way?" she demanded.

"Only the ones who need tough love."

As he waited for her to finish, he sorted through his email and gave her a stern stare whenever she slowed down. As soon as the timer sounded, Erica hopped off the bike like her ass was on fire.

"What's next, coach?"

Twenty minutes later, Zach wanted to quit the fitness business forever, and he'd never felt that way before.

"You can't say 'fuck you' whenever I propose an exercise routine you don't want to do, Erica." His frustration grew and made him short with her.

"Yes. I. Can."

Her stubborn chin jutted up, and her mouth pursed into a pout. If she didn't look so damned kissable, he would have strangled her.

Kissable?

Where had *that* thought come from?

Fixing her with a stony glare, the one he reserved for belligerent clients, Zack gestured with his thumb to the weight rack behind him. The stubborn wench glared right back.

"I'm tired," she whined.

"Look, all you have left is free-weight bicep curls. You've got this. Finish those, and I'll give you a donut," he lied.

"Really?" Hope and doubt fought for the prime spot on her face.

"No. Get moving." He nodded toward the rack.

"I hate you."

"Whatever. You have two sets of fifteen reps."

"I'm *never* coming back. This is your only chance to torture me."

He rolled his eyes so hard he glimpsed brain matter. "You've paid for a year's membership in advance. Besides, I *will* come and drag your happy ass in here if you don't keep to the schedule we set. I know where you live."

"I hate you."

"You've already said that. Three more curls... Switch arms... Good," he encouraged. "Okay, Grumpy Pants. Your workout is officially concluded for today."

"Thank you, Baby Jesus!" Erica wiped the sweat from her brow with her sleeve and cast a concerned look at her upper arm. "Are my arms supposed to twitch like this?"

"It's not uncommon. We have a smoothie bar downstairs. Let me treat you to a protein shake."

"It had better taste like chocolate cake, or I won't be happy with you," she warned.

They placed their order and selected a small two-person table. Zack discovered it was difficult to take his eyes from her flushed face. He developed a burning desire to know how she'd fared in the interim since they last saw each other.

"Are you married?" *Where the hell had that question come from, Zack?*

She snorted out protein shake.

"Um, no. I would have thought the Sutton name would tell you as much." The arch look she gave him lost its effectiveness as she wiped the chocolate from her face.

"Some women keep their maiden name," he replied with a sheepish shrug.

"Valid point. Okay. What about you? Are you married with any little rugrats running around?"

"No to the marriage. I was close once. But I do have a son. He's eight."

"Why didn't you marry his mother?"

She'd breezed right over the fact he had a child and focused on his marital state. *Interesting.*

"What? The residents of North Carolina don't hold shotgun weddings anymore." His lips twitched at seeing her pique. "I figured I was safe enough simply paying child support and getting dual custody."

"You don't have to be a sarcastic ass. I was only wondering."

Abruptly, he didn't feel like kidding around anymore. Better to be honest with her right off the bat.

"His mother, Christie, and I dated for a few months. She thought it was great fun to lie about birth control. I was the idiot who believed her when she told me she was on the pill." He shrugged, and to avoid her searching gaze, he surveyed the workout area beyond her shoulder. "We called it quits, and six months later, she presented me with my son, Jacob. When I saw him, I fell instantly in love. He's honestly the best part of my life."

"Did you try to make things work... for his sake? I know some people do."

Zack played with his drink, stirring it with the straw, as he considered the question. How did he tell her Jacob's mother was deranged and had been committed to a sanitarium two years after he was born?

"I'm sorry. I didn't mean to pry," Erica said softly. There was a wealth of understanding in her voice, and his heart contracted in response.

He sent her a sharp glance and noted her contrite expression.

"It's not that. I don't talk about it to anyone. Not even my family, if I can help it," he said. "Christie had a psychotic break a couple of years after Jacob was born. Her parents had her institutionalized when they finally understood none of us could help her on our own. They're active in Jacob's life, though." He took a deep breath and went for gold. "Three months ago, there was a fire at the hospital. Christie didn't make it."

"Ohmygod! I'm so sorry, Zack."

He stared down at the hand gripping his, marveling at Erica's compassion. "Yeah, no worries. If you don't mind, would you keep it to yourself? I don't tell many people outside my immediate circle."

"Of course." Flustered, she fumbled her keys. "I'd better go. I still have edits to apply tonight."

"Edits? What do you do for a living?" he asked, weirdly desperate to find out more about her current situation.

"I'm an author."

He raised a brow to encourage her to elaborate.

"Yeah, I... um... well..." Erica paused to clear her throat and sip from her water bottle. "I'm a romance writer."

"Seriously?"

The thought of shy, constantly blushing Erica writing steamy romance novels had him grinning broad enough to split his face. As he watched, she toyed with the lid on her water bottle, pressed the plastic bubbles on the lid covering her shake, then traced a pattern in the condensation on the table.

Yep, she was adorable, nervous as hell, and just as fun to tease as she had been in high school. "So you write mommy porn, huh?"

Her dark mocha eyes burned with pure fire as they locked with his.

"We don't use the term 'mommy porn' in the industry," she snapped.

"No? I was sure that's what I've heard it called…" He tapped his chin like he was attempting to solve a puzzle. The self-control it took to contain his laughter was significant.

"You've maintained your punk-ass status all these years later, I see."

"You like me anyway," he taunted. The sweep of color tinging Erica's cheeks sent a cheap thrill through him. He hadn't expected to get that type of reaction from his teasing.

"Whatever. I've got to go." She gathered her things and threw the empty cup in the trash. "Thanks."

"I'm heading out, too. I'll walk you to your car."

"You don't need to. I'm a big girl."

"It's getting dark. Even though we built in a safe area of town, you can never be too careful." When she would've argued, he gave her a cajoling smile. "Humor me, and let me walk you out. Please?"

Only a handful of cars were left in the parking lot as they made their way to her white sedan. Her gasp encouraged him to pay close attention to her car.

"He's mine, whore!" was carved into the driver's door. It also looked like Wolverine had a vendetta against her tires. The destruction sent his heart into overdrive.

He'd seen it before.

CHAPTER

THREE

"Do you have any idea who might've done this, ma'am?" The policeman writing the report had already asked twice and thought he'd score a trifecta.

Erica threw up her arms and glared. "*No*. Like I said the other *two* times, this is my first visit here. I came out and found my car mutilated by Freddy Krueger." She gritted her teeth. "Also no, I'm not currently dating anyone, I live alone, and I work from home. Clearly someone mistook my car for someone else's."

One good look at her highly irritated expression encouraged Zack to step in. "Look, officer, your partner reviewed the security tapes, and Erica has given her statement. Please let us know if you discover anything. Otherwise, I intend to escort her home."

"Are you two an item?"

The question momentarily stunned them into silence. Before he gathered his wits to answer, she burst out with, *"Hell no!"*

He shot her a sharp glance. Did she have to act horrified by the officer's question? Talk about a direct hit to the ego.

"Jesus, Erica, you don't need to make it sound like I'm a plague carrier."

"Oh! No! I didn't mean to. It's just, well, the question surprised me. I don't date jocks, is all."

"You're digging yourself in deeper." Zack raised his brow, noting with no small amount of satisfaction the color sweep up her neck and into her cheeks. "Come on, I'll see you home."

"You don't need to. I can manage."

He refused to argue. With a nod for the officer, he escorted Erica to the passenger side of his vehicle. After he closed the door behind her, he made one last visual sweep of the area. The niggling sensation in the back of his mind told him this whole incident wasn't a case of mistaken vehicles.

As he drove, he checked his rearview mirror. To his relief, nothing appeared out of the ordinary. He hadn't mentioned it to Erica or the police, but things like this had happened in the days prior to Christie's diagnosis. She'd made life difficult for him and any woman he chose to have a relationship with after her. There hadn't been any issues after she was institutionalized, and since she was deceased, it ruled her out in this particular instance.

Hell, maybe it had nothing to do with him and everything to do with someone associated with Erica.

"What's with the heavy sigh?" she asked.

"Nothing. I was thinking."

"About?" Erica drew the word out to indicate she expected a response. The impatience in her tone had him fighting a chuckle. He hadn't forgotten her constant need for answers.

"About how difficult it's going to be to get you back to *Workout World* when you wake up sore tomorrow," he prevaricated.

"Pfft. I know an evasive maneuver when I hear one. What aren't you telling me, Zack?"

They pulled into her driveway. After cutting the engine, he half turned in the seat. Everything in her expression said she expected the truth and wouldn't set foot outside the car until she got it.

"This kind of thing has happened to women I've dated in the past."

Her brows clashed together in a deep frown as she tried to make the connection why those past threats had anything to do with her.

"I don't understand. Do you know who's responsible?"

"No. Previously, it was Christie. Or at least, I believed it was," he said. "But I don't know." He sighed and shook his head. "Having seen it again, knowing she's gone, I'm compelled to consider I might've been wrong in accusing her. Or perhaps it's a different stalker this time."

Erica paled. "Do they pop up frequently?"

"No! Poor choice of words on my part. And don't worry. I won't let anything happen to you." Zack clasped her hand in his, hoping to reassure her. "I promise."

"I don't understand why anyone would think you're interested in *me*, of all people. Today was the first time I've seen you since our high-school graduation. Even then, it was only to have you walk me through your torture chamber."

A grin split his face. How did she always make every situation funny? "You're a nut, you know that?"

"So I've been told." She eased her hand from his. "I'll get the dealership to tow my car tomorrow. Thanks for the ride."

"I intend to see you safely inside."

"Why?"

"Because I can't shake the weird feeling something's off, and you have to deal with the consequences. My overprotectiveness is a side effect." He checked the yard through the window behind her back.

She snorted. "You planning to look under my bed, too?"

As soon as the words left her mouth, she sucked in a breath and blushed.

Her telling reaction suggested she was flustered by the idea of him in her private space. If she was half as obsessed with him as he was with her, sex was consuming her thoughts.

"I suggest we start in other areas of the house and end in the bedroom," he said in a low, smooth voice, eager to test his theory. Her deep inhale told him all he needed to know—Erica was hyper-aware of this bizarre attraction.

Sweet.

"I-I don't think th-that's necessary."

"Oh, but it is," he assured her with a wicked chuckle.

As he exited the car, he caught sight of her through the windshield, frantically fanning her face. She stopped as he approached, and he hid a grin as he opened the passenger door.

A short while later, after all the windows and doors had been secured, Zack entered the kitchen, where she'd darted off with an excuse about coffee.

"Everything is locked up tight," he said.

"Thanks again. I could've caught a ride with one of the officers. You didn't have to do all this."

"I did." His tone was firm, and he wanted her to understand he took his responsibilities seriously. "I wasn't comfortable with the idea of you returning home alone."

Their gazes locked.

Erica pressed her lips together and nodded before busying herself with a spoon and mug. He had no way of knowing what conclusions she'd drawn, but he wasn't prepared to broach the subject at such a sensitive juncture.

The awkward silence had him casting about for a new topic, and he finally gestured toward the coffeemaker. "I would've thought someone living by themself would have one of those single-brew machines."

As her auburn brows flew skyward and her mouth rounded in an O, he realized how terrible his statement sounded.

Open mouth, insert foot.

Next, he'd be mentioning that she needed a few more cats. Involuntarily, his eyes shot to the fat feline on top of the refrigerator. The Goliath beast had been giving him the evil eye since he walked in the door.

"I write at night," Erica said by way of explanation. "I need a full pot of coffee to see me through the wee hours of the morning."

"Fair enough. Do you mind if I have a cup?"

Going back to his empty house didn't appeal to him. Jacob was with his grandparents in Florida and wouldn't return for another three days. The extended quiet of his home made Zack's nerves raw. Everything felt off-kilter when his eight-year-old wasn't banging around.

"Uh, sure. How do you take it?"

"Black."

"Figures," she muttered.

"Excuse me?"

"I-I... It's just... *Oh hell.*"

He leaned against the opposite counter, legs crossed in front of him, and waited her out. To keep from laughing again, he bit the inside of his cheek.

"I load my coffee with flavored creamer and sugar. You take yours black," Erica finally said.

Zack easily guessed where she was headed, but teasing her was great fun. "Annnndddd?"

"I just meant, it figured you would choose the healthier alternative."

She appeared uncertain and yet thoroughly annoyed, and the urgent need to kiss her preoccupied his mind. His desire for Erica had been building since their first phone conversation today, and at that precise moment, it went beyond necessary. If he didn't taste her—and soon—he would regret it.

Zack closed the distance and crowded her against the granite surface, lightly pinching her chin and angling it for perfect mouth-to-mouth contact. For what seemed like a lifetime, he stared into her wide, expressive eyes. He fancied he saw burning curiosity and matching desire in their depths. What he didn't see was fear or hesitation.

He dropped his gaze to her full, red lips—red because she had been gnawing on them in her nervousness throughout the night's events. One last time, he met Erica's soulful dark eyes and sought permission. Her slight nod encouraged him to dip his head and claim that much-anticipated kiss.

Ever so softly, he teased her lips apart with his own. Her breathy gasp allowed him to slide his tongue inside and explore the warm recesses of her mouth. She released a strangled cry, and he felt a smile start. Never before had he wanted to laugh and make love at the same time. With her, he did.

The fingers digging into his biceps unfurled and slid up over his shoulders to tangle in his hair. Her mutual desire was gratifying and filled him with hunger, an aching need for more. Erica tasted like honey, heaven, and heavy addiction. The tone of their kiss quickly turned serious, and getting enough of her was impossible. It would take little encouragement to get carried away. One come-hither smile and he was done for.

Zack pulled back and gazed down into her flushed face. Raw desire transformed her features. Her lids were heavy, her mouth slack, and her lips were glistening, waiting—nay, begging—for more.

He gave it to her.

Only when his hand worked its way under her top did she protest and give him a forceful shove.

"What's wrong?"

"I think you should go," she said, actively avoiding his gaze.

Her about-face was disconcerting. Had he misread the signals? Christ, he hoped not!

"Erica, if I've overstepped, I'm so sorry. Please accept my deepest apologies."

Desire remained in those warm, chocolate eyes of hers, and the knowledge made him long to dive back in. The hand applying pressure to his chest was telling a different story, and he was a strong proponent of consensual sex.

"You didn't. Overstep, that is," she replied, quick to reassure him. "It's a bit fast for me. I'm also not comfortable being naked with someone who looks like you."

WHEN ZACK'S JAW DROPPED, Erica could have bitten off her tongue.

Good grief!

Why the fuck did she say that?

Way to look pathetic, Erica!

Wasn't it bad enough she lived with a mammoth attack cat as her only companion? Did she have to throw her insecurities out there, to boot?

His gaze intensified. "We need to clear up a few things. If you're exercising to get into shape or to feel better physically, that's one thing. But if you think, for one split second, you aren't beautiful the way you are, then I have news for you, babe."

She was too dazed for words.

"I don't want to hear things like that out of your mouth, Erica. *Ever.*"

Zack's anger startled her. Seemed to surprise him, too. He jerked back as if he'd been electrocuted and shook his head. With one last lingering glance at her mouth, he stalked toward the door.

"I'll call you in the morning, and we can decide what time I'm picking you up," he said over his shoulder. "Lock the door behind me."

After he'd gone, Erica pressed her fingers to her kiss-swollen lips. Oddly, she didn't feel an ounce of irritation at his high-handed comment. A slow smile started somewhere in the deepest part of her soul and quickly bloomed on her face.

Zack Sharp, the all-star golden boy from their high-school days and current super-sexy entrepreneur, had kissed the living daylights out of her. *Her!* Erica Sutton, nerd extraordinaire.

He hadn't acted like he wanted to stop, either. If her body wasn't screaming in pain from her earlier exercise, she would dance her way to the bathroom for her post-workout soak. Instead, she limped in and rested against the rim of the tub as it filled.

As she eased down into the steaming water, she moaned. Dear God, was there anything as lovely as a hot Epsom salt bath when your whole body ached? She rubbed her index finger over her lips. Yeah, most likely sex with Zack. If she were comfortable with her physical self, she'd be all over him like a fat kid on cake.

Groaning at the thought of cake—her kryptonite—she slid under the water to submerge her entire head. She had to stop sugar—*STAT!*

A crash sounded from her living room, launching her heart into her throat. The noise seemed louder than anything McFatty could make. Erica scrambled out of the tub, slipped on the wet tile, and fell on all fours.

"Sonofa*bitch*, that hurt!"

She remained there, trying to calculate the best way to stand when her muscles were screaming and twitching like a marionette with every movement.

A secondary crash brought her head up, and an involuntary scream erupted from her throat as a shadowy figure loomed large in the doorway.

CHAPTER

FOUR

Z ack was four blocks away when he caught sight of Erica's gym bag in the passenger's seat. He whipped into the parking lot of the closest business and snorted. It happened to be the pastry shop she'd mentioned this morning.

With a chuckle at the coincidence, he rifled through her bag, checking if there was anything she couldn't live without. He pulled out her wallet and cell phone. Both necessities. Returning to see her wouldn't be a hardship.

After a second's deliberation, he swung out of the car and into Addie's Bakery. Although he was giving into Erica's addiction, he felt she deserved a treat for how hard she'd worked out. Obviously, he had no intention of allowing her to get away with too many cheat meals, but he could be generous for a first-timer.

He grinned in anticipation of her reaction.

As he waited in line, the freaky sensation of being watched woke the fine hairs on the back of his neck. Like miniature antennae seeking danger, they rose and vibrated, sending shivers along his spine. A quick glance around the restaurant assured him the feeling hadn't been triggered by anyone inside the establishment, and Zack brushed off his body's heightened reaction to the day's events.

With a smile of thanks, he received his order and turned toward the glass doors. A person was huddled beside his rear tire, and a sense of wrongness kicked in.

"Hey!" He rushed for the exit.

He was quick, but the hooded figure possessed the speed of a gazelle on crack.

"Dammit!" As he stomped around his car and surveyed the damage, customers milled about and watched him. "Did any of you get a good look at the person who slashed my tire?"

A chorus of "no" and shuffling feet were all he received from the late-night donut crowd. Today's society hated to get involved. Their heads were either bent over a phone or stuck up their asses.

Huffing out a breath, Zack withdrew the card from the officer who'd responded to the vandalism at his gym. The two incidents were related. They had to be.

Within five minutes, a patrol car was on the scene, and like before, the officer jotted down his statement, repeating questions already answered as if trying to trip him up. Luckily, the crazed knife-wielder only had time to vandalize one tire before Zack charged out, and swapping it for the spare was done with minimal fuss.

As he was tossing the jack into the trunk, Zack jolted. Whoever was responsible for their vehicle mishaps had to have followed them from the gym to Erica's house, and him to here. Sweat dotted his forehead, and fear for her sent his heart into overdrive. He possessed her phone and had no way to contact her.

Breaking every driving law known to man, he sped back to Erica's.

Not soon enough.

Flames were consuming the main room and licking the roof from a shattered front window. In horror, he watched as the conflagration spread higher and wider. Braving the heat, he tried the door.

Locked.

Of course, it was! Hadn't he heard her slip the deadbolt when he'd left earlier?

"Erica!"

Three powerful kicks later, he'd managed to gain entry to her house. He continued shouting her name, doubting she could hear over the crackling and eardrum-splitting pops.

A sixth sense propelled him toward her bedroom.

Her bloodcurdling scream drowned out the sound of her name spilling from his lips. He found her sprawled on the bathroom floor, gorgeous round ass mooning him as she peered over her shoulder. If fire wasn't licking his heels and smoke hadn't permeated the air around him, he'd have done his damnedest to persuade her to take advantage of the position.

Reason intruded by way of the blistering heat at his back. Zack whipped a towel off the closest rack, wrapped her up, and hustled her toward the hallway door. Unfortunately for them, the way he entered was now blocked by the raging inferno.

He swore a blue streak.

"This way!" she shouted, and he followed without question. "Wait! Zack, I need something to wear. I can't go outside in a towel!"

"Are you fucking kidding me right now?" He shoved the window open and punched out the screen. "Let's go!"

The paint began to peel on the far wall. They had a minute, at most, until this room was engulfed. Worried as he had never been before, he wrapped an arm around her waist and prepared to stuff her out the window.

"No! No!" she screamed, clawing at the frame in an attempt to stay in the room. "McFatty!"

"Goddammit! You are not fat, and no one cares if you're in a towel!"

"*No!* McFatty is my *cat!*"

A black streak shot by them and out the window.

"McFatty's safe. Move your ass," he barked.

Thick, choking smoke filled his lungs and stung his eyes. The overbearing heat was a precursor to the ball of fire breaking through the drywall. Without another word—and Zack would bet it was because her self-preservation had finally kicked in—Erica unceremoniously climbed through the window. He wasted zero time diving out after her.

They raced to the front yard. Their arrival coincided with the first fire engine. Close behind was the same patrolman he'd talked to not once but twice that day. The poor bastard would be filing one helluva report before his shift was over.

Erica ducked behind Zack, using him as a human shield, and he assumed she was trying to hide from the gathering crowd. In an effort to preserve her modesty in addition to keeping her warm, he removed his jacket, drew it around her, and zipped it up to her neck. The watery smile she gave him squeezed his heart.

"I'm sorry about your house, babe," he said softly, wishing he could've somehow prevented it all.

She nodded, lips compressed.

Sympathetic to her plight, he opened his arms, and it was all the encouragement she needed. His tight hold offered minimal comfort in a situation like hers.

Lingering in his mind were a multitude of horrifying questions. The two at the forefront haunted him. What if he hadn't gotten to Erica in time? And what if she'd charged into the main room to look for her stupid cat?

He shuddered. Those bleak images would give him nightmares.

Zack squeezed her tighter.

The firefighters worked diligently to extinguish the flames as he and Erica stood by, helpless and exhausted from the day's events. For the third time in as many hours, he gave his version of the personal attack by the sick individual who had it out for them.

Erica was devastated. Everything happened so fast that she hadn't had a chance to process it. Grief, for all the lovely things she'd worked hard to obtain, consumed her, and she desperately tried to shut it away. Breaking down in front of a bunch of random strangers would be humiliating.

Zack had encouraged her to leave the scene, but leaving without McFatty was a no-go on such a chilly night. Indoor cats didn't typically fare well outdoors, but because of his size, he likely wouldn't go far. As soon as the activity died down and McFatty was less fearful of his surroundings, the search could begin. In the interim, she agreed to sit in Zack's toasty vehicle. Anything to be out of the open, wearing nothing but a bath towel and his jacket, freezing her nips off.

The continued deluge of water on her blackening house hurt her stomach, and she shifted her attention to the interior of Zack's sports car. Running a hand over the conditioned leather, she marveled at its buttery softness. Perhaps she'd treat herself to a new vehicle after her next book release. Might as well, since she'd never be comfortable in hers after it had been carved up by someone's hatred. At the first opportunity, she'd take it to a body shop, have the damage repaired, and trade that sucker in.

For something with buttery-soft leather.

A flash of white caught her eye. Without a second thought as to whether she should or shouldn't, the ravenous beast inside her recognized and reached for the pastry bag. She hadn't eaten in hours, and she was almost certain her body had gone into fat-storage mode. Next time she was in front of a computer, she'd google how quickly it could happen. She was positive fat storage was a thing, and her body might be setting a speed record.

Zack opened the driver's door and slid inside as she tested her willpower by sniffing the lemon-filled donut. She'd swiped along the side to ascertain the flavor seconds before he joined her, and now, she was deeply ashamed of her lack of control. How innocent could she possibly appear with powdered sugar down the front of his jacket? It looked like a kilo of cocaine had exploded in her face!

"Go ahead. I bought it for you, anyway." His smile was kind, the complete opposite of judgy. "You left your gym bag in the car. I was returning it, along with bringing you the now-cold latte and the donut."

Not thinking of consequences, surroundings, or audience, Erica lurched forward and planted a big smacking kiss on his lips.

"My hero," she murmured.

His wolfish grin was hot enough to reheat the latte.

"If I received a response like that for a single donut, I wonder what a dozen would get me."

"Laid," she replied without conscious thought.

His shout of laughter set her cheeks ablaze.

Dammit.

When would she stop blurting out whatever popped into her head? Sure, it was effective when writing, but in real-life circumstances, it spelled trouble.

Averting her gaze, Erica caught movement and squinted at the bushes to the left of her garage. "McFatty!"

As she twisted to open the passenger door, the towel caught on the gear stick, revealing her girl garden. With a strangled cry, she slapped the donut bag on her lap. The flimsy bag burst and an explosion of powdered sugar filled the car's cabin. Cold lemon filling splattered the tops of her thighs and found a home in her crack.

"Ohmygod!"

Sugar particles tickled the back of her throat, and she coughed, blowing powdered sugar through the cabin and onto the windshield. Mortification complete, she snuck a peek at Zack's face. His eyes were glued to the spot where her hands shielded her mound, and he seemed to be oblivious to the destruction she'd wrought on the previously pristine interior of his vehicle.

"Two dozen," he whispered hoarsely. "We're getting get two dozen, and I'll cover you in filling, then eat—"

A sharp rap on the driver's window interrupted him.

A godsend.

Dizzy from the rush of blood to her head, Erica sat back. His sexy suggestion replayed in her mind and sent that needed blood flow to various parts of her body, causing her extremities to tingle uncontrollably. Was it possible to faint just thinking about Zack going down on her?

Talk about inappropriate timing!

They were surrounded by the entire Stonebrooke fire brigade, along with her nosy-ass neighbors, all rubbernecking to see the latest drama. Could she be any more harebrained? Erica scrambled to detangle and readjust her towel as she silently praised Zack's gloriously broad shoulders for blocking the fireman's view.

"We're all through here for now. Is there anything your girlfriend needs out of the house? It's pretty unstable, but if she tells me what to look for, I can try to find it. Only the half of the garage and a single room off the north section remain intact."

Leaning over the console and partially across Zack's lap to peer out the driver's window, she addressed the firefighter. "I'd love to retrieve some files from my office. Possibly the first print copies of my books if they survived the fire?"

The guy's eyes locked on her semi-exposed breasts about the time Zack cleared his throat. Erica sent him an inquiring look. He, too, was fixated on the gaping neckline of her borrowed jacket.

Gasping, she slapped a hand over her chest and sent up a poof of dust. Zack's sneeze broke the spell the two men had been under. He opened his mouth, then closed it with a regretful glance at her covered neckline.

Christ alive! There wasn't a part of her anatomy he hadn't seen or that she hadn't exposed to the first responders of Stonebrooke. Asking if this day could get any worse would be tempting fate beyond its limits, and she'd surely be struck by lightning or sucked into a sinkhole, never to see the light of day again. Although, the last one would be more of a blessing than a curse. Hadn't she wished for exactly that at the gym?

Avoiding direct eye contact, Zack squeezed her hand and informed her he'd be back with whatever was salvageable. Her conclusion? He'd rather breathe in smoke-filled air than be stuck another second with a disaster magnet like her.

Erica wallowed in misery as she hand-swept all the donut dust into a pile. Minutes ticked by into what felt like hours, and those who'd grown cold or bored wandered off. The noise settled down enough for her to catch snippets of a nearby conversation.

"So, she was in the bath when it happened, huh?" Man One asked with a laugh.

"Yeah. Did you see those legs?" Man Two's voice was raspy and admiring. "God, what I wouldn't give to have those babies wrapped around my waist while I use my hose on her forest fire."

She sat a little straighter and leaned forward to catch a glimpse of the speaker. He was prepared with a bold stare and shot her a Chester-molester wink. Her gag reflex activated.

For fuck's sake! The guy was old enough to be her father!

Face hot, she averted her gaze and stared straight ahead, keeping watch for Zack. McFatty had long since disappeared, and she prayed he hadn't gone far.

Within five minutes, boredom set in again, and Erica fidgeted with the stereo, hoping to drown out any additional lurid conversations. Weary down to her bones, she reclined the seat back and closed her eyes, hoping beyond hope that this was all a bad dream and she'd wake up in her bathtub to an un-torched house, with her cat sitting on the counter, blatantly ignoring her instruction to get down.

It wasn't to be.

CHAPTER

FIVE

Two hours later, McFatty was found and firmly ensconced in the carrier Zack had retrieved from the undamaged section of Erica's garage. Crime scene tape encircled her house, and anything remaining of her belongings reeked of smoke.

Although the firefighter had informed her the fire hadn't reached her office, he failed to mention the water damage from the high-powered hoses. Her laptop, notebooks, and pictures were ruined. Any hope of meeting her current deadline was gone if she couldn't pull a backup from the cloud.

Erica was at a loss as to where to go. Her parents had relocated to Florida the year before, and her bestie, Shonda, was on vacation and unreachable. Prior to taking off for Aruba, she swore her cell phone would be off the entire time. Clearly, she wasn't fooling. But it wasn't as if Erica couldn't have stayed at her apartment anyway. McFatty was a real bastard about other animals and refused to live in harmony with them. An attack on one or both of her friend's cats was a distinct probability. Her other close friend, Angela, had disappeared from town recently. No one had heard from her, and the assumption was she'd taken off with her son, leaving her unsuspecting husband of seven years distraught.

"Where to?" Zack asked as they pulled away from her place.

Unable to come up with a single destination, she promptly burst into tears.

"Aww hell. Babe, please don't cry."

"I'm sorry. I... a hotel should be fine," she said through her sniffles.

"A hotel? Don't you have family in the area?"

"No."

"A friend?" he asked, somewhat desperately.

"No." The tears, once started, refused to stop. "I'm not... very... social." She hiccuped a sob.

"Erica, I can't dump you at a hotel. It wouldn't feel right. Besides, the closest one is Sagefield."

Meaning it was a pain in the ass to drive twenty-five minutes out of his way, but he'd do it if she insisted.

"It's okay. Really." She scrubbed at her eyes and tried to put on an air of strength, failing miserably. Her wobbling chin and nonstop waterworks gave lie to the statement.

Zack heaved a heartfelt sigh and reached for her hand.

Turned out he was a really great guy, and she felt shame that she'd ever shoved him in the category of 'jock.'

A long-forgotten memory reemerged. His heavy sigh was reminiscent of the one after she rejected him.

"Zack? When you asked me to prom all those years ago, you were *serious*, weren't you?" It was a weird-ass question to pose considering their current situation. Yet the sweet man beside her was probably the same as a teen, but she'd been willfully blind, believing he was toying with her.

His left hand tightened on the steering wheel, and his white-knuckled grip was a clear indication she'd struck a nerve.

"Yes." His voice was raspy, and she suspected it had more to do with the emotion he was keeping in check than any smoke inhalation.

Feeling like a first-class idiot, she shut up, and they sat in uncomfortable silence as they waited for the light to turn green.

Guilt got the better of her. "I had no idea you wanted to go with me."

"Really?" He didn't try to laugh it off as he had back then. "Why not?"

"Honestly?" At his nod, she confessed, "I thought it was a prank or dare. That I was being set up for a scene from *Carrie*. I didn't want to be the butt of a joke."

Her heart stuttered in her chest when he lifted her hand and kissed her palm. Closing her fingers over the spot his lips had touched, he said, "It bothers me you thought so. I would never have done something so mean to anyone, and especially not you, Erica." Zack appeared undecided for a moment, then with a fleeting frown, said, "I had the biggest crush on you in high school."

"*Shut. Up.* You did not!" Lord, if she'd only known. How she'd fantasized about being his girlfriend in those days! So much so it was difficult to look him in the eye. Too many times to count, she'd practiced what she'd say, and the fevered love words she whispered to her frilly throw pillows made her blush to recall them. She'd never revealed her secret to Shonda. If anyone suspected, then or now, she'd die of mortification.

Zack's hand tightened over hers. "Why do you find it so hard to believe?"

As Erica stared at their entwined fingers, she asked herself the same thing. For his honesty, he deserved her truth.

"In what world would someone as gorgeous and popular as you want someone as nerdy and plain as me?" she asked.

He didn't answer, and Erica's ever-present insecurity ratcheted up.

Zack pulled to a stop in front of his stately home and placed the car in park. Untangling their hands, he twisted across the console to peer deep into her eyes. Gently cradling the back of her head to keep her from shying away, he continued to watch her. What those gorgeous electric blues searched for, she couldn't begin to know.

His focus dropped to her lips. He smiled, slow and sure. "In this one," he assured her, claiming her mouth.

Shocked, she sat like a petrified toad on a log. Not deterred in the least, Zack stroked feather-light kisses along her jaw to her ear and back.

"You're beautiful, Erica, and your intelligence is hot as fuck. Believe it."

As he drew away, her stupor wore off, and she launched herself forward. He met her halfway.

Their tongues danced a delicious tango. He tasted of fresh coffee—Erica's favorite—and she savored the rich flavor of him. Hands, both his and hers, explored with wild abandon, brought on by her unexpected burst of passion. Body aflame, she trailed her hand down his abdomen, marveling at the plethora of ridges and hard planes.

A sharp tap on the window startled a scream from her, and Zack echoed it with a shout.

"Jesus, Erica! You almost gave me heart failure," he croaked. His hand tremble was slight but noticeable as he pressed the button and lowered the steamy pane. That small tell spoke to how their mini make-out session affected him, too.

From his stupid smirk, the officer on the other side knew exactly what he'd interrupted.

"Hey, Zack. Heard you were having a bit of trouble tonight and thought I'd do a routine patrol past your place. I see you have everything *handled*."

"*Bucky?* Bucky Whitmore? Is that you?" Erica gaped at the round face in the opening. He'd been in their science group back in the day and was voted class clown. Bucky in law enforcement boggled the mind.

"Erica Sutton? Holy shit! I didn't realize you and Zack were an item. It's good to see... uh..." He registered her dishabille and frowned as his gaze dropped to the towel smeared with donut filling. But rather than make a sexist comment, concern transformed his heavyset face. "You were the one whose house burned down?"

Word spread fast in their podunk town. Between the firefighters and the officers, her appearance had to be quite the joke, but Bucky didn't treat her like one.

An onslaught of self-pity mixed with gratitude burned her eyes and clogged her throat. "Um, yeah," she choked out.

Zack, her Johnny-on-the-spot, cut off the expected line of questioning. "If you don't mind, Buck, it's been a really long day. I want to get Erica settled so she can get some rest. If you're on tonight, can you keep an eye out for whoever's targeting her? I can run a bite out to you."

"Oh, sure. Sorry. No, I'm good on the food front. If you'd like, I can cruise by a few more times during my shift."

"That'd be great, man. I really appreciate it."

They shook hands, and Bucky sauntered off.

Zack gave her a once-over. "You really are a hot mess, babe. Let's get you inside."

"Can we not use the word *hot* after the fire?"

"Too soon?"

"Much."

A LONG, scorching shower washed off the worst of the smoke clinging to her hair and restored Erica's equilibrium. Ready to face the world again—or at least Zack—she exited the bathroom and discovered a pair of sweats and a T-shirt. The front displayed the logo of their old school.

Had he given it to her on purpose, or was it simply the first shirt he'd grabbed?

With a shrug and a nostalgic smile, she slipped it over her head. Looking as she did, she wouldn't be winning any beauty contests, but at least her breasts were still perky without a bra. She grinned, recalling how Zack had fondled them. Fortunately, there was nothing for him to complain about in *that* department. The boob fairy had blessed her right about the time she graduated high school and went off to college. She experienced profound relief when she retired her "flat is beautiful" t-shirt.

With an encouraging pat for the girls, she opened the door and stumbled into the object of her thoughts.

"Oh!" she squeaked, one hand still cupping her ladies.

"Yeah, sorry. I was about to knock." His full attention was on her chest, and his lips twitched. Seeming to recover his wits faster than her, he shook his head and held up a bag of toiletries, then graced her with a bone-melting smile. "I thought you could use these."

"You could use a month in bed with him," the devil on her shoulder quipped.

"Get it together, Erica!" snapped the warring angel on the other.

"Shut the fuck up," she ordered them both.

Clearing her throat, she accepted his offering. "Thanks. You must've read my mind. I was about to come looking for you."

Realizing how it sounded, especially considering the firm grasp on her breasts when the door opened, she froze. Heat rose in her cheeks as she shook her head and ducked into the bathroom.

"I'm gonna brush my teeth," she mumbled, slamming the door in his face.

By the time she re-emerged and was headed for the kitchen, she'd given herself a stern lecture and had her wayward desire under control.

The mouth-watering fragrance of home cooking greeted her as she stepped into the room, triggering an audible response from her abdomen.

"My god! What is that? It smells divine."

"Steak fajitas. Hungry?"

"Hell, yes. You couldn't tell by my stomach's monster growl?"

"I thought it might be another donut craving." He gestured to the breakfast nook. "Have a seat. It'll be ready in two minutes."

Erica ignored the comment disparaging her pastry habit. "Can I do anything to help?"

"Nope. Got it covered."

"Keep this up, and I'll be on bended knee offering you my heart forever."

"Got to love a woman who appreciates my culinary skills, but you may want to wait on the proposal until you've sampled the food," he suggested.

She laughed. The wine and table layout gave the impression of being intimate but tasteful. Smiling for the trouble he'd gone through for her, she slid into her seat.

"Shall I pour?" she asked, needing to be helpful. At his nod, she filled the glasses two-thirds full and, going a step further, placed a warm tortilla on each plate.

"Do you want to keep McFatty in the carrier, or is it okay to let him loose in the house?"

She jumped up. "Ohmygod! I forgot about McFatty."

"Erica, it's okay. You've had a stressful night. He's in the far corner of the guest room. I threw a towel over the top, assuming he might feel safer," he explained. "While you were in the shower, I had my brother Dane pick up the makings for a litter box. I went ahead and set it up close to the carrier." Zack cast her a wry glance over his shoulder as he turned off the burner. "Since McFatty seems to dislike me, I thought you might want to be the one to free him. I didn't care to lose a finger."

"Zack, I can't believe all you're doing for me. Thank you. From the bottom of my heart, thank you."

He paused next to her and set the sizzling steak, red peppers, and onions on the table. With a grin, he dropped a quick kiss on the tip of her nose. "Not a problem. This is still hot. It'll give you a minute or two to set that vicious beastie of yours loose."

The meal, the sweet affectionate buss on her nose, the level of comfort she felt with him—it all spoke to what she craved from a relationship, and she wanted to bask in the intimacy of the moment. The lack of many, if not all, of those things, had been a prime reason she'd bailed on her last boyfriend. There was never any true closeness, to say nothing of the abuse.

Not caring to think about what Zack's kindness meant to her love-starved soul, she left to release her cat from his temporary cage.

CHAPTER

SIX

Zack wasn't ignorant to the fact he'd spooked Erica with the few kisses they shared, but she'd been so lovely, staring up at him, wonder in her chocolate eyes. What had her previous relationships been like if every single thing he did brought effusive gratitude? She must've dated some real losers if he was a prince in comparison.

As he waited for her to return, he sipped his wine. Who the hell was terrorizing her? Somehow, she'd made an enemy. Not only her. The tire on his coupe had been a casualty, which meant whoever was attempting to frighten or harm wasn't strictly after Erica.

"Why so serious?" she asked as she sat down.

Covering his brooding mood with a smile, Zack served up the food. "No reason. I have a lot on my mind. McFatty doing okay?"

"He's pissed off at the world, but he'll be fine."

"Well, dig in," he said with a gesture to the food. "After dinner, we can make a list of things you'll need to replace immediately. Tomorrow, we'll go shopping."

"You don't have to go. I can rent a car to run my errands," Erica protested. "You shouldn't have to miss a day of work. Besides, I need to apartment hunt, too, and I'm sure it will be incredibly boring for you."

"Yeah, about that..."

Her expression shifted to guarded, and an uncomfortable light entered her eyes. As if she were bracing herself, she leaned back from the table. Once again, her reaction struck him as odd.

"I want you to stay here, Erica." As the denial formed on her lips, Zack held up a hand to forestall an argument. "Only until the police find the person responsible. I hate the idea of you being alone while a whack-job is on the loose."

"I appreciate the offer. Truly. But I can't."

Irritated by her stubborn refusal, Zack huffed out a breath. "Why the hell not?"

Surprise lit her face as if she hadn't expected him to push the issue. As Erica searched for a viable excuse, Zack could almost see the wheels turning in her head. Contrarily, her rebuff made him want to dig his heels in and insist. Twelve years ago it probably would've worked, but the Erica across from him was a helluva lot tougher and stubborn than the shy girl she'd been. Although he had a soft spot for Young Erica, Zack respected the hell out of the new-and-improved version.

"It wouldn't be appropriate for your son to see a strange woman in your house when he returns from his trip. What kind of example would we be setting?" she asked, her voice filled with concern.

"Since you would be staying in the guest room, I think it would show him it's important to help a friend in need. It might be a different conversation if you were planning to sleep in my bed with me."

Color high, Erica lifted her chin. A rush of pleasure shot through him, similar to how he'd felt when he managed to fluster her in the past. Maybe he was twisted in receiving delight by making her blush. He'd be damned if he could stop, though.

"*Were* you planning to sleep in my bed with me?" he asked with a faux frown of speculation.

"No!" Her denial was swift and fierce, causing her flushed skin to darken.

He lifted his glass to hide his grin behind another sip of wine and immediately saw it was empty. Reaching over, he refilled both their drinks.

"So, you *don't* want to sleep with me?" he asked.

"I-I..." It clicked that he was toying with her, and she scowled. "Dammit! Not funny, Zack. Not funny at all."

"It totally is." He chuckled in the face of her indignation.

Pointing with her fork, she said, "That right there is the prime reason I don't want to stay here. You enjoy baiting me. Isn't it enough you're allowed to torment me at the gym?"

"I get my jollies where I can."

"Mm-hmm. I'm not talking to you." She frowned down at her plate after taking a mouthful of food. Her eyes widened with pleasure, and she hurriedly scooped up more. "Hush, and let me eat this delicious meal."

He barked a laugh, and she grinned around another forkful.

Zack loved her smile. Always had. It was a bit shy and twisted to the left, indicating she was trying hard not to laugh outright.

"If I promise not to harass you, am I allowed to make dinner conversation?" he asked around another sip of wine.

She eyed him warily. "I suppose."

He clamped his lower lip between his teeth to stem another wave of laughter. When he had the urge under control, he picked up his silverware and dug in. "Why did you choose romance as your genre?"

"Technically, it's romantic suspense. I like to throw in a little mystery here and there," she said. "After graduating college, I free-lanced for a local newspaper. It didn't take long before I decided traditional journalism was boring as fuck."

"That's the wrong analogy. Fucking is far from boring if done properly." He grinned when she laughed. "So, why romantic suspense? Why not murder mysteries or children's stories?"

His interest was genuine, and she seemed to sense it. Giving him a considering look, she nodded absently. "Thrillers and murder mysteries take a great deal of plotting and research. They're extremely well thought out—much more than standard contemporary romance, in my opinion. Every sentence, every word, needs to be perfect and not give anything away too soon."

"But suspense doesn't?"

"It does, but not in the same way. It's difficult to explain the nuance. Regardless, I can complete a novel in roughly eight weeks, have it to my editor, and self-published within six weeks after receiving it back. A thriller or mystery would take me forever from sheer obsessing alone."

"Fair enough, and children's books?"

"Eventually, I would like to try my hand at one, but not yet. It's taken me years to become established as an indie author and create a decent following." She shrugged. "I'll never say never. But enough about me. How in the world did you get started in the fitness business? Was the goal to always open a chain of centers?"

"I blew out my knee playing ball in college. ACL tear. During the endless months of rehab, I went through rigorous training and found I actually enjoyed it. The challenge of transformation appeals to me."

"Transformation?" she snorted. "What did *you* need to transform? You've always been hot."

Expression arrested, she looked like she wanted to bite off her tongue, but then threw back her shoulders as if to stand by what she'd said. Zack didn't give weight to her comment about his looks. There was a time in his life when he believed he was hot shit, but the incident had humbled him.

"After my knee injury, I fell into depression. I'm not sure if you knew or not, but I was at college on a sports scholarship. When my chance was destroyed, I was no good to anyone, or so I thought. I went into a funk, turning to booze and junk food. Essentially eating my feelings. Fifty pounds later..." Zack shrugged, letting her come to her own conclusions.

"No freaking way do I believe you were *ever* overweight." Based on his current physique, her skepticism was warranted but misplaced.

"Believe it. It's what drove me to help others."

IMAGINING Zack as anything but stacked, even for a second, taxed Erica's brain. Yet it made her feel marginally better about herself. Emotional overeating wasn't exclusive to her, but maybe it had been his intention to tell her about his journey.

"You really don't judge," she said softly.

His brows rose. "What made you think I would?"

She shook her head, unable and unwilling to explain how much his good opinion meant. "Never mind."

"When we discussed your fitness goals earlier today, you mentioned losing forty pounds. I tried to tell you then, and I want to reiterate you don't need to." Zack clasped her hand and gave it a small shake. "I mean it." When she remained silent, he sighed and released her. "It strikes me that you want to return to your high school size. You were too skinny, and I can't see you losing more than fifteen pounds, twenty at most."

"You don't understand."

"Then explain it to me because I really don't."

With a frustrated sigh, Erica rose, intending to take her plate to the sink. Zack stretched and placed a hand on her arm to halt her retreat.

Raw self-hatred clogged her throat, and the sharp sting of defeat burned in her chest. She tried to will away the bitter emotions threatening to consume her. How did she account for how her ex's hang-ups had become hers? How she'd fallen victim to some fucking jerk's abuse? So hard, in fact, it had undermined her confidence and left her feeling less of a person than almost everyone around her.

"Hey, what's this?" Zack asked gently.

Mortified he'd so effortlessly picked up on her distress, she attempted to pull away.

"I'm sorry, Erica. I didn't mean to hurt your feelings. I've told you before, you *are* beautiful."

"You don't have to flatter me to make me feel better," she mumbled, head down.

"I'm not. I'm being honest. To me, you're stunning. I wish you could see yourself through my eyes." Zack removed her plate from her hands. After he'd captured her attention, he cupped either side of her face and gazed deeply into her eyes. "I'm never going to lie to you. Not as your trainer and not as your friend. Got it?"

Zack's sincere promise lightened her heart. There was no doubt he was telling her the truth as he saw it.

"Thank you," she whispered past the lump in her throat.

He waited a beat as if he understood her need to compose herself. With a nod toward the counter, he said, "There's a notepad and pen. Why don't you make a list of your must-haves, while I clean up?"

A short while later, she'd completed two full pages. With any luck, the insurance company wouldn't screw her around. She had a small nest egg, but not enough to replace everything if they wouldn't pay out.

Of course, Erica's number-one priority was a new laptop. The deadline for her latest novel loomed, and she didn't want to push the release if she didn't have to. Present Erica sent a mental *thank you* to Past Erica for backing up all her manuscripts to the cloud. Barring any complications, she should be able to retrieve the files.

"How's it going?"

She glanced up to see Zack filling the kitchen entryway, towel over one shoulder and hands on his lean hips. A girly sigh tap-danced its way up her windpipe, but she shoved that shit back down. Good grief, the man was hot as fuck and hell on her system. If she wasn't careful, she'd be sighing and pining like a teenager with her first crush!

Oh, who was she kidding? He *was* her first crush. Her *only* crush, if truth be told.

It was never being told.

She didn't plan to give another man power over her.

"I think I've got a decent handle on the basics," she replied.

"It's been quite the New Year for you so far, huh?"

She snorted her agreement.

As Zack sauntered farther into the room, the words carved into the paint of her car came to the forefront of her mind.

He's mine, whore!

Whoever held this vendetta against her wanted Zack for their own. Erica couldn't blame them, but seriously, did they need to go all Rambo and burn down her house? What kind of twatwaffle does shit like that?

"Zack, have you thought any more about who's behind all this? An ex-girlfriend? A woman whose advances you've rejected? A female employee?"

His black brows dipped and creased his forehead. "None I can think of."

"But you see this *has* to be about you, right?" As his frown deepened, she asked, "How often do you act as a personal trainer? Do you normally take the new clients coming in, or do you pass them to your staff?"

"Why is it important?"

"I'm establishing a motive. If it's standard practice for you to work with new members, then our car-carving arsonist should already know that. It means our training session, in and of itself, shouldn't have set her off—I am assuming it's a her, but in all actuality, it could be a him." Erica leaned into the cushions and drew a pillow in front of her as she got comfortable with her working theory. "However, if it's out of the norm for you to act as a PT, then maybe it *was* the trigger. Otherwise, I believe it had to be about us spending time at the smoothie bar."

The slow nod of his head suggested he followed and agreed with her reasoning.

"Working with new clients is purely random, and only when we're short-staffed. Usually, it's left to one of the other certified trainers," he clarified. "I emailed a digital copy of the recording to Bucky earlier, by the way. He's going to review it personally. Hopefully, he'll find something the others didn't."

"Good. Do you mind if I take a look, too? Another set of eyes couldn't hurt."

He flashed an appreciative smile. "If you hadn't already told me you specialize in suspense, I might've guessed it when you went all Sherlock Holmes."

"My deductive reasoning is more in line with Watson, I think."

Zack chuckled as he exited. Within minutes, he was back with his laptop. After rattling off the login info, he left to refill their drinks for the second time.

"Ah, a man after my own heart," Erica sighed as she accepted the glass.

"You mentioned something earlier about a vat of wine. Just trying to do my part," he quipped.

"Yes, well, stop being so perfect. You're ruining it for other men."

"That's the plan."

Her heart thudded in her chest.

If only!

Shaking her head, she played the video.

Painstakingly, they rewatched it three separate times, determined no small detail would be missed. All they received for their efforts was eye strain. The recording showed a hooded figure from behind, but no identifiable marks were visible.

Zack couldn't even say if it matched the person he saw at Addie's Bakery.

Finally, Erica shut down the program and started her fourth glass of wine. Was her tipsiness part of the problem? Here she was, in front of a warm fire, wrapped up in a fleece sofa throw, a fine vino in hand, and sharing the company of the only man who'd ever lit her fuse. Granted, she was a teenager when she'd last known him, but it appeared nothing had changed. Her body reacted to his nearness without any encouragement, and she was feeling too good to worry about the night's events anymore.

"Why have you never married?" The question was out before her filter could contain it.

His finely groomed brows shot up in surprise an instant before a sardonic smile tugged the corners of his mouth up. "Never met the right woman, I suppose. You?"

"Never met the right man, I suppose." To avoid his probing gaze, she concentrated on the hearth and guzzled her drink.

"You've never been tempted?"

"To get married?" At his nod, she shook her head. "Nah. Not once." As he continued to watch her, she found herself opening up. "I've had boyfriends. Some I'd lived with. But mostly, by the time they moved on, I was more than ready for it to happen. You?"

Zack's grimace was so fleeting that she'd have missed it if she wasn't completely focused on him. "I've had a few girlfriends. But I was too busy raising Jacob. Between my son and business, there's little spare time for anything else. A partner doesn't like to come third on the list."

"Yeah, I get it. It's how I am about my writing. Most men didn't care to come in second to my career."

Their gazes locked in shared understanding.

"Their loss." The low timbre of his voice caused her stomach to flip.

His intimate look convinced her he meant what he'd said, and a shiver of awareness coursed through her. God, what she wouldn't give to be thirty pounds lighter and a fitness bunny. If she was, she'd feel a helluva lot more comfortable with his blatant invitation.

"I mean it, Erica. It was their loss."

She nodded and avoided glancing in his direction again. Deep down, she knew he was right, or at least thought she did. When a person's self-esteem was in the toilet, it was hella hard to believe in themself.

"Thank you," she said softly.

"I'd better turn in." Zack climbed to his feet and tossed the pillow he'd been holding onto the couch. "I have a few things I need to take care of in the early morning. I know your laptop was damaged, but if you want to use mine until yours is replaced, feel free."

"I keep finding myself saying thank you, like a broken record. It doesn't feel like it's enough anymore."

Bending over, he cornered her with his arms and shifted to within an inch of her lips. "I'll tell you what. One day, when we've eliminated all your insecurities, I'll give you leave to thank me any way you want. Until then, this will suffice."

He closed the gap and pressed his lips to hers. The kiss was butterfly-soft, and he only lingered for three solid heartbeats before he straightened to leave.

The distance restored her sanity. "Is that why you're helping me? For sex?"

She didn't want to think she'd misjudged him, but she needed to know.

"*What?* No! Jesus, Erica. What do you take me for?" His anger was tangible.

Hurting his feelings hadn't been her intent, but his immediate reaction put her mind at ease.

"Please don't be offended, Zack. I don't want there to be any misunderstandings. Not to drag my personal baggage into the mix, but there have been way too many in my past."

After a brisk nod, he left her to her own miserable thoughts. Her primary one? Boy, she'd royally screwed up.

CHAPTER
SEVEN

The following day, Zack's alarm tripped at five a.m. For the first time in his fitness career, he was tempted to ignore the incessant beeping. He'd spent most of the previous night tossing and turning, unable to sleep. The thought of having the one woman who'd gotten away under his roof mocked him endlessly.

She'd stayed up late. The faint glow from the living room light had been visible from beneath his door. He'd waited for what seemed like hours, willing her to join him but knowing she wouldn't. His white-hot desire for her left him with a case of blue balls until he took matters into his own hands. The singular experience was less than satisfying. What he wished for was out of reach until she admitted she wanted him, too, and found a way to deal with her self-image issues. No red-blooded heterosexual man would look at her and not desire her, a few extra pounds or not. She was a goddess. Only she didn't realize it.

But perhaps it was good she didn't. Otherwise, with her sharp-as-a-tack brain, she'd rule the world, and he'd be one of a million SOL guys, falling at her feet.

Dragging himself out of bed, Zack threw on his running clothes and took off on his usual early morning jog. The chilly air cooled his heated skin, warm from last night's fantasy of making love with Erica. He shifted his mind off her and to the matter at hand. There was a nutbag out there willing to do her harm, and neither of them could afford not to be diligent.

Should he leave her without anyone close by?

The thought made him stumble during his normal stride, and he barely avoided a face plant. Pivoting, prepared to turn back, he noticed a police cruiser easing to a stop. Zack waved and hustled over.

"Hey, Buck. Do you mind keeping watch on my house for about a half hour? Can you catch up on a report or two? After everything that's happened, the idea of leaving Erica alone makes me nervous." He smiled, certain Bucky would understand. "I'm hoping to kill some of this restlessness with a jog."

"No problem. My shift ends in fifteen, but I'm happy to stay as long as you need me to."

"Thanks, man. In that case, I'll do my normal route and be back within the hour. Come by the gym this week, and I'll extend your membership." Zack grinned. "Maybe this time you'll use it."

Bucky laughed in his standard good-natured way and waved him off for his morning run.

From the safety of her vehicle, the person responsible for Zack's current stress watched as he jogged by, oblivious to the fact his new whore's life could be snatched away in a mere instant.

In her hand, she flicked a lighter open and closed, keeping her eyes trained on his backside. She didn't bother to duck down as the cop passed.

What an oblivious buffoon!

More than once, she'd watched in disgust as Bucky Whitmore

patrolled the area. If the criminals around this small town discovered how inept he was at his job, they would have a field day with their larcenous activities. Her maniacal laughter rang out, echoing within the confines of her sedan. Soon, she would enact her plan and have her long-awaited revenge on Zack.

Stupid men! They loved their routines.

This one would cost him.

Cost them all!

FORTY-SEVEN MINUTES LATER, Zack thanked Bucky and entered the house. Not that he expected Erica to be awake after staying up half the night, but the quiet unnerved him. Stealthily, so as not to disturb her, he cracked open the guest-room door. Like a kingpin surveying his empire, McFatty lay with his back against the headboard, tail flicking to convey his irritation. All he needed was a cigarette and a tumbler of booze to complete the picture of indolence.

The woman herself was sprawled on her stomach, her head shoved halfway under the pillow. For someone who was wound so tight when she was awake, she certainly let loose while she slept.

Zack grinned.

In a weird way, her idiosyncrasy delighted him. He was tempted to smack her protruding rump to see her irate reaction. Damn. She could say what she wanted about having to lose weight, but he would nibble on that ass all day long if she'd let him. She was delicious. He'd always been a butt man, and Erica's was top-notch.

With a respectful nod to her furry guardian, Zack backed out of the room and went to shower. His next order of business was to get Human Resources on the phone and deal with his lackadaisical employees. Some days, he felt like a glorified babysitter.

Showered, shaved, and dressed, he headed to the kitchen for

his standard morning omelet. He halted inside the doorway when he noticed Erica by the island, confusion clouding her face. From the shadows, he watched as she swung left, then right, as if searching for something. Suspecting he knew precisely what that something was, he stepped farther into the room, careful to keep the counter between them.

"Where is it?" she growled.

"It?"

"The coffee pot, espresso machine, French press—anything of that nature. You know—*it!*"

"Ah. Yeah, about that—"

"Don't you *dare* tell me you don't have anything resembling coffee in this house!"

For personal safety's sake, Zack contained his amusement.

"I don't."

"Jesus, Mary, and Joseph! *You're dead to me,*" she spat.

His laughter broke free. Oops.

"Really?" Her outrage was a living thing. "You're seriously going to stand there and bray like a jackass in my hour of need?"

Bent double, he was out of breath. It didn't help that her hair was sticking out in all directions, leftover mascara encircled her eyes, rumpled clothing was twisted around her torso, and a thunderous scowl pulled her features tight. Erica looked like she'd been on a three-day bender.

"Babe, if you could only see your face. I've never seen anyone so enraged over the lack of coffee before," he finally managed.

"Because you don't know any authors, you dolt!"

"Is it safe to assume you're not a morning person?" he asked, circling the island and cautiously moving to within striking distance. Her fiery glare gave him serious reservations about his current path. What was it John Wayne said? *Courage was being scared to death and saddling up anyway.*

Zack inched closer. The Duke would be proud.

"Okay. I'm forgiving you for calling me names—I'm pretty sure you mumbled a few choice words under your breath—and offering to go on a coffee run for you. Will an added donut soothe the savage beast?"

Her nod was grudgingly given.

Placing an arm on either side of her, Zack leaned in close and attempted to kiss her pouty lips. All he received for his effort was a hand shoving his face away.

"Seriously? I haven't even brushed my teeth," she grumbled. "Keep it in your pants, Romeo."

He changed trajectory and nibbled her neck. As he trailed small kisses along her jaw to her earlobe, she softened and sagged into him. Something *other* than coffee helped to calm the monster within.

"How do you take it?" he murmured against her throat.

"Ohdeargod!" she croaked.

Zack leaned away to see her expression, biting back a grin.

"Wait!" She scowled. "What?"

"Your *coffee*, Erica. How do you take it?"

Her mouth formed an O as she realized he wasn't referring to sex.

Chuckling, he bussed her forehead and stepped back.

"I hate you," she grumbled.

"You keep telling yourself that." He snickered and dodged a flying fist.

"Cream, three sugars. And don't come back without at least a gallon of it."

"Bossy much?" he teased. "Oh, and by the way, you're now down to cream and one sugar."

"Huh?"

Her confusion was endearing, and Zack let it sink in as he grabbed his wallet and keys off the bar.

One, two, thr—

"*Oh, hell no!* You're not denying me my constitutional right to have sugar in my coffee. It's a medical necessity."

"It is *not* a medical necessity," he stressed from a safe distance.

"It is for *you*," she retorted, breathing fire. "Because if you don't bring me coffee the way I like it, I'll cut you. Is your insurance up to date?"

"Let me put it another way. Donut or three packets of sugar?"

Almost positive he'd heard what constituted a rabid animal growl, Zack hightailed it straight for the front door. Erica was hot on his heels, fist in the air.

It was one way to make her exercise.

Luckily for him, she was out of breath with a hand to her side before she got halfway across the lawn. He was securely tucked behind the wheel of his car, with the doors locked, when she shot him the bird and stormed back into the house. The knock on his window started a yelp from him.

Christ, he was getting jumpy.

"Jeez, Bucky! What the hell? I thought you left."

"Sorry, Zack. I was about to when I decided to do one last drive around the neighborhood." He crossed his arms on the doorframe. "Saw you hot-footing it away from Erica. What the heck did you do to piss her off?"

"Personal-trainer mode before her coffee."

"Yeah, I can see where that would do it. You going to get her coffee now and make it up to her?"

"How'd you guess?"

"I was married for a number of years, remember?" Bucky replied.

Zack stared in wide-eyed wonder at his front door. "I'm pretty sure she was possessed there for a moment."

"It happens. Want me to stay for another ten minutes?"

"Nah. I think she'd kill anything or anyone who comes at her without her fix. I suspect she's safe for now." Zack offered him a wry smile. "Thanks, man. You really are awesome."

With a double pat on the driver's side door, Bucky shuffled off to his car. It became obvious he planned to sit tight for a time when he shut off the cruiser's engine.

Zack smiled.

Bucky was a fantastic friend.

CHAPTER

EIGHT

"Oh, Evil Spawn of Satan, I'm home," Zack sang out as he reentered the house thirty minutes later.

Torn between anger and a warped sense of humor, which apparently matched his, Erica gave in and laughed.

"You're *so* pushing it," she growled with a jab of her index finger against his six—no, make that *eight*-pack—abs. She knew this because her fingers, of their own accord, continuously felt him up. Catching his stunned stare, she blushed. "Uh, sorry?"

"Did you brush your teeth?"

A giggle rose up, and she bit her lower lip. "Nope. Not yet."

"You are a cruel woman, Erica Sutton," he said with a hearty sigh.

"So I've been told." She stretched for the to-go cup he was holding up and out of her reach. "You're ransoming my coffee and donut, aren't you?"

"Yep."

"State your demands."

His wicked grin took her out at the knees. With her best casual air, she steadied herself by placing her hands behind her on the quartz counter. The movement displayed her braless breasts to full advantage. Her girls gained his undivided attention.

Booyah! She still had it.

Effectively distracted, Zack lowered the carrier, providing the perfect opportunity to steal it.

"What the—"

"You snooze, you lose, big boy," she taunted with a smug-ass smirk.

"How'd you know I'm a big boy? Girls' locker-room talk?"

"Oh please, not before the nectar of the gods touches my soul. I don't want to hurl on an empty stomach," she returned over her shoulder as she spread her goodies out on the table. An unexpected slap on her ass brought her around. "It's a good thing I already—"

His too-tempting mouth cut her off as his capable hands plunged into her wild morning hair and angled her head to receive him. Zack's tongue swiped across her parted lips, then delved into her gaping mouth. Again and again, he kissed her. Teasing yet urgent and seeking. Slow, languid strokes designed to taste, followed by faster, masterful strokes to stoke her fiery passion. And damned if it didn't.

God, the man could kiss!

She'd give him about an hour to stop before she reasserted her need for coffee.

"Christ, woman." He was panting—deep, lungfuls of air scissored in and out of his chest—when he finally drew away. "Please say the word, and we'll spend the day in bed."

She was tempted.

Oh. So. Tempted.

Reality intruded in the form of his ringing phone.

"Crap. I have to take this. Hold that thought," Zack commanded. He'd taken only two steps before he spun back and gave her a narrow-eyed look.

Liar, he mouthed, putting the phone to his ear.

At her frown, he pointed to his teeth.

She laughed and snagged a cup with her name along with the bag of donuts. As she headed for her room, she began humming under her breath. *Of course* she'd brushed her teeth. What was the Girl Scout motto? Always be prepared.

Erica had earned *all* her badges.

ZACK SOUGHT her out to tell her his business was finished and ask if she was ready to go shopping.

"You don't have to chauffeur me around."

"In case you forgot, this dot on the map we call a town doesn't have rideshare. The closest car rental is twenty-five miles away," he replied to her expected protest. "I went ahead and had Todd contact Stan's Garage to tow your car and refit it with tires. He'll check if they can buff out the worst of the scratches until it can be repainted."

"You didn't have to do that. It was on my agenda for today."

"I know, but I had to coordinate the employee schedule with him anyway." He shrugged and gave her a small smile. "I hope you don't mind that I took the initiative."

"I should probably be annoyed with your high-handedness, but I'm not. You saved me additional work, and I'd hire you as my assistant if you didn't already have a job," Erica assured him. "Thanks for making the arrangements. My brain is still about thirty minutes from kicking into high gear, and I didn't want to think about all I had to do today."

She groaned dramatically and flopped back against the pillows.

"You realize it's almost noon, right?" Zack sat on the bed, his hip butting up to hers, and offered her a second cup of coffee.

"What's this for? I don't want to take yours."

"I actually drank mine on the way back. Both were for you. I seem to recall there was a threat to my life if there wasn't at least a gallon in my hand when I returned," he said.

"You are a god among men." She sipped and sighed her contentment.

"I bet you say that to all the boys."

"Nope, just the gorgeous ones who bring me two cups of joe and lemon-filled donuts."

"You think I'm gorgeous?" He didn't try to hide his grim. She'd commented on his looks more than once, and it thrilled him that she found him attractive.

"Oh, stop. As if you don't already know you are." Rolling her eyes, she chugged her drink.

"So, about our earlier conversation..." He traced the comforter's edge.

Slapping a hand over the cover, she gave him the stink eye. "No."

"You can't be persuaded?" The question was accompanied by his fingers trailing along the neckline of her borrowed t-shirt.

"I can *definitely* be persuaded. It still doesn't mean I don't have a million things requiring my immediate attention."

He wrinkled his nose to show his fake ire and dropped his arm. "Fine."

Erica caught his hand and squeezed. "No one has ever made me feel as desired in my whole life as you have in the last twenty-four hours," she said, suddenly solemn. "Thank you."

For whatever reason, she'd thought it important to tell him, and he didn't know what to do with her unguarded honesty.

"Well, that's a crying shame, and it also proves the males of our species are dumber than rocks." Seeing he'd made her uncomfortable, he let his sincerity shine through his steady gaze. "I mean it, Erica. If a person doesn't find you incredibly attractive, they're an idiot."

She cupped his jaw and kissed his cheek.

"My hero," she declared.

The hint of adoration in her eyes discomfited him. He didn't want her to see him as anything other than the flawed human he was. If she put him on a pedestal, eventually he'd topple it. Just as he always had. "I'm nobody's hero."

Another awkward silence hung between them, but she quickly filled the gap. "Really? Because I'd say you are for fetching us coffee."

"Well, I suppose I did save lives from your explosive temper."

"Hardy-har-har," she mock laughed, causing his real one.

"Come on, babe. Let's get this show on the road."

"I'm ready."

Her breathy response struck him hard and fast. Certainly, she didn't mean what he wanted her to. Involuntarily, his gaze dropped to her erect nipples. The thin cotton did nothing to hide the firm, perky tips. His fingers twitched to touch. Erica folded her arms across her chest, and a creeping blush spread up her neck, straight to her hairline. For once, he didn't tease her, and he became wildly territorial about her being seen in public, looking delightfully rumpled.

In a low, fierce voice, he said, "You can't go out like that. *Without a bra!*"

"Pfft." Her dark eyes danced with humor.

"What's so damn funny?" he demanded.

"You. Women go braless all the time, Zack."

"Not you!"

"Before yesterday, you hadn't seen me in twelve years. How would *you* know?" she asked. There was a snap to her tone and sharpness in her narrowed eyes.

Sure, he'd been a bit overbearing, and she had every right to be annoyed. It wasn't as if he was her boyfriend.

Yeah, but you want to be, his inner devil taunted.

Scrambling, Zack sought any excuse to keep her from the outside world a while longer, but he couldn't come up with a single one.

"Look, I just know. Okay?" Scowling when she rolled her eyes, he continued. "What's your bra size, and where's the best place to find one for you?"

"Ohdeargod! I'm not doing this with you right now." When she saw he intended to be stubborn about it, she blew out a breath and changed her brisk tone to soothing. "Zack, don't you have a sweater or jacket I can borrow? It's January, and layers are a necessity."

A memory tickled his brain, and he jumped up to check the guest room closet.

"I wonder if that's a no," he heard her mutter as he foraged.

Less than thirty seconds later, he found what he was searching for. Returning to Erica, he tossed a bulky, pink sweater and a woman's tan leather jacket next to her.

On a dime, she turned downright pissy.

"I'm *not* wearing any of your ex's clothes. You can put them right back where you found them. Or better yet, donate them to a shelter."

His smirk sparked fire in her. This spirited side was one he fancied, and the hint of jealousy shining from her expressive eyes gave song to his soul. Zack didn't intend to question why she made him feel so alive, but he enjoyed the feeling.

"Dane roomed with me for a few years. His ex left them behind after one of her many trips up from Charlotte." He smiled. "I forgot her things were here, to be honest. But you're roughly the same size."

"You'd better not be lying. All I need is some chick out for my blood."

Her statement sobered them both. A chick was *already* out for her blood.

CHAPTER
NINE

Their shopping excursion lasted the rest of the day and well into the evening. Zack couldn't recall a time when he'd had such fun. Nearly every situation with Erica was packed with humor. She'd also taken the loss of her beloved home in stride, remaining upbeat, as if she were excited to purchase replacements for the things she needed. Her resilience impressed the hell out of him. No one in his circle would've taken the destruction of their house as well.

The one trying moment came during their late lunch. He didn't want to appear as the bad guy, always cracking down on her poor eating habits, but Erica had zero discipline when it came to sweets. She'd ordered dessert first, claiming she could be firebombed at any moment. The waitress had blanched when she realized Erica was earnest in her claim, especially when the news popped up on the flat-screen television behind their table, and the top story was the previous night's events.

With a shrug and a grin, Erica ordered key lime pie to go with her cheesecake.

After they arrived home, she suggested reheating the leftover pizza from lunch.

"What is wrong with you?" Zack demanded. "Did you, or did you not, come to my gym yesterday, intending to get fit?"

"Guilty as charged. But are you saying members sign a pact with the devil or something? They aren't allowed a cheat day?"

"A cheat *meal*, maybe, and only after they've been at it for a while. *Not* the second day into the program." His reply was sharp, and frustration leaked from every pore in his body.

"Pfft. Well, it's either feed my endorphins with sugar and carbs, or I cry. I'd rather not be a blubbering baby."

There was tension in the smile she flashed, and tight lines around her tired eyes. How had he missed that her behavior might be a front? Hoping to distract her from her troubles, he gave her a sensuous smile. "We can feed those endorphins another way."

Desire snaked through him as she fanned her warm face. Damn, he loved her blush.

"You're relentless, you know that?"

"Is that a no?" he called to her retreating back.

She paused mid-stride and whirled to glare. "I have work to do, you horn dog." After delivering her haughty insult, she spun to walk away.

"Yeah, well, I still didn't hear a no."

Her giggle pleased him. It indicated she wasn't offended or opposed to a fling with him.

He busied himself with putting groceries away and a phone call to Jacob. When his son's voice came over the line, Zack exhaled his relief. The list of rides, food, and stories about Jacob's experiences was endless. As his son's excitement wound down, he asked to speak to Christie's father, Charlie, who had been the police chief of their small town until he retired last year.

"Okay, lil man. I love you. Can you put your grandpa on the line? I'll see you soon."

"Sure. Bye, Dad!"

A moment later, Charlie's mature voice came through the

connection. "Hello?"

"Hey, Charlie. I wanted to run something by you. Do you have a minute?"

"Sure, son. What's going on?"

It took no time to bring him up to speed regarding the threat. As a veteran of the force, he hoped Charlie might provide a detailed profile of the kind of person they might be looking for. Any insight would be helpful.

"I can cut our vacation short," Charlie said, his voice heavy with worry. "We can head home as early as tomorrow morning."

"No. I'm actually wondering if you shouldn't extend your stay to keep Jacob out of harm's way. I can clear it with his school when they open again on Monday."

"I'll tell you what. Judith wants to visit her sister while she's here in Florida. Why don't I get them settled with her and come back? Then we can work out a plan to trap this stalker of yours."

"You wouldn't mind?"

"Not at all, Zack. You're like a son to me, my boy. Anything I can do to help, I will," Charlie said gruffly. "I'd like to think if Christie had been mentally stable, you would've worked things out between the two of you. As it is..."

"I know, Charlie. Me, too. And thank you," Zack replied, humbled by the love. "Are you flying or driving?"

"I'll text you tonight and let you know if I can catch a flight. If not, I'll rent Judith a car and drive home."

"Fair enough. Give her my love. I'll see you tomorrow."

After signing off, he whipped up two chicken Caesar salads and went to seek out Erica.

"Ready for dinner?" he asked her.

She glanced up from her new laptop, giving him a startled look. Her bewildered expression suggested she'd been too engrossed in her task to consider eating.

Come hell or high water, he would help her revise her diet, and not for the weight, but because skipping meals and eating crap was harmful. She was the first woman he wanted to hang around for the long haul.

"You know, *dinner*," he mocked. "The pesky meal that doesn't contain a donut, unlike breakfast and lunch."

"Oh, yeah. Want me to reheat the leftover pizza?" Her attention was already drifting back to the screen in front of her.

Sighing his frustration, Zack picked up her laptop, shifted to set it on the coffee table, and saved her document. In the middle of her protest, he hauled her to her feet, dipped to put a shoulder to her stomach, and straightened.

"What the hell?" she exclaimed. "Why are you manhandling me?"

"Quiet."

"The hell you say!"

"Quiet," he ordered again.

Before she thought to struggle, he was setting her on the counter, wedging his hips between her splayed legs, and grabbing a plate he'd set on the island. He held a forkful of salad to her mouth. "Eat."

"Dude. What's with the caveman routine?" Erica grunted a few times and pounded her chest. Deepening her voice, she said, "Man. Wo-man. Tarzan. Jane."

Laughing, Zack pressed a fast, friendly kiss to her lips, then offered up the fork. "You're a damn trip. Now, *please* eat."

"Only because you asked so nicely," she said in a prim tone, then consumed the bite he offered her. "Mmm, this is good!"

"See? Healthy can taste good."

She gave an exaggerated eye roll and a snort, promptly choked. Tears streamed down her reddening face, and she struggled to draw a breath without coughing.

"Erica!"

Waving him off, she croaked, "Wrong pipe."

"You are a hot mess." He rubbed her back. "But damn me if you aren't the most compelling one I've ever seen."

Zack left to get a damp washcloth, only to return and find her rooting through the fridge. With a triumphant cry, she emerged with the leftover pizza box.

"Babe, what the hell are you doing?"

"Your health food tried to kill me. It's time to return to what has my back," she replied flippantly.

"No," he stated firmly.

"You can't tell me no!"

"I just did."

"Let me phrase it a different way. Who the hell are *you* to tell *me* no? I'm a grown-ass adult. I'll eat whatever I want."

"Erica, you're a carb junkie, and I'm your personal trainer, as well as your friend. *You* came to *me* for help. If you don't think that gives me license to be on your ass about making healthier choices, you can think again. Now, put down the pizza, and no one gets hurt."

Her mulish expression hinted at her desire to make a run for it.

"Don't do it," he warned. She squinted, weighing the consequences. It tickled his funny bone, but he suppressed the laughter. "You won't make it out of the kitchen with that box, Erica Sutton."

The moment to strike was when she contemplated the cardboard container. Darting around the counter, he reached for her just as she recognized his intent. Her piercing squeal was deafening, and he slapped his palms over his ears. The tactic allowed her to get the jump on him.

He had to admit that when she wanted to, the woman could move.

But he was faster.

Zack caught her in the breakfast nook as she was reaching for the door handle to make good her escape. Gripping the box, he wrapped an arm around her, getting an unintentional handful of boob.

They both froze.

"Oh!" she squeaked.

"Oh, shit! I'm sorry," he gasped.

Shifting, she looked up at him, and calculation flashed in her eyes.

The little witch planned on taking advantage. He knew it as surely as he knew his own name.

Erica turned and pressed against him, chest to chest. The thrill of having her body flush against his turned his brain to mush.

She tiptoed her fingers across his pecs. "If you give me the pizza, I'll allow you a peek to go along with the feel you copped," she purred.

His cock twitched, one hundred percent for the plan. And although he refused to give in to her demands, it didn't mean he couldn't have fun with her.

"Really?" He shifted his hand from the small of her back to her ass, urging her closer. "What would you do if I warmed it up for you? And for the record, allowing me to look without touching is cruel."

"Something might be arranged."

"You must really want *it*," he said softly, suggestively.

Her sultry chuckle sent blood rushing to his dick. Erica was a fucking pro at the flirting game. Who knew? Her shy high-school self was certainly cheering from the bleachers.

"I'll go take care of it," he told her, unable to resist a squeeze of her butt.

She didn't bother to hide her triumphant grin.

He didn't intend to heat the pizza, but as she leaned across the bar, unbuttoning the top two buttons of her shirt, Zack experienced a moment's pause.

Maybe it's worth making her happy, his throbbing dick suggested.

With firm resolve, he shook off the lust and moved to the other side of the island. Before she registered what happened, he'd opened the box, dumped the contents in the trash, and slammed the lid.

"No!" She charged him, fists raised for battle. "You did *not* just throw away my food."

"Yeah, I did. The first step to recovery is admitting you have a problem," he said.

In her anger, she twisted his nipple, and he bellowed his pain. Goddess or no, she was mean as a rattler when things didn't go her way.

"Jesus Christ! You're a crazy bitch, you know that?"

She sputtered her outrage.

Zack ducked the hand intent on grabbing his junk.

"Knock it off, Erica. You're going to get hurt," he warned, shielding his balls.

"You won't hurt me. You'd rather torture me and deny me food."

Dammit, she was right. He wouldn't harm her; that wasn't his thing.

"I wouldn't want to, but I'll damned well defend myself if you go for the family jewels again," he retorted.

Their combative gazes locked, and seconds ticked by until the ridiculousness of their situation struck. They doubled over with laughter.

"Your face!" she crowed.

"And *yours*! I've never seen anyone so enraged, like *ever*." He sighed and wiped his eyes. "Well, minus this morning and your coffee tantrum."

"Let this be a lesson to you."

"I don't give in to terrorists. You want to play hardball, missy, we can play hardball."

"Pfft! Whatever. Can we order a pizza now?"

He stared at her incredulously. "What part of 'no' didn't you understand?"

"Well, you don't need to be rude about it." She grabbed what remained of the grilled chicken salad and sailed out the door.

CHAPTER

TEN

The next week passed without any major incidents from their stalker. Zack didn't kid himself that their tormentor had moved on, the odds leaned toward them waiting for Erica and him to lower their guard before striking again. Either way, he was enjoying her stay.

Her hours were the polar opposite of his, but the in-between times, when they shared a meal or watched TV, were fun-filled. Her quirky view of life was refreshing and unique. Maybe it was her artistic nature, or perhaps life had shaped her differently, but he enjoyed her perspective. Their discussions were always laced with challenge and laughter, and Zack loved the hell out of any time spent in her company.

With an endless amount of complaining, she'd agreed to all of his health-improving rules. The exception being her morning coffee. The first cup was the way she preferred it, but any she drank afterward were reduced to one sugar. It wasn't to say she didn't try to barter sexual favors when she wanted something. Being on the receiving end of her creative come-ons amused him.

She did it as a joke, or so he assumed, but in reality, he'd cave in a New York minute if he believed she was serious. What would she do if he said yes? The question kept him awake at night.

Their more intimate moments came in their everyday actions. A glance over dinner, a brush of shoulders as they prepared a meal together, or hand-holding during a scary movie. Each day, their necking turned a bit more heated, and they pushed the limits farther and farther.

Erica had him tied up in knots like a horny teenager, and Zack wanted to ditch the extended foreplay to consummate their budding relationship. If things had been different all those years ago and she'd taken his interest for what it was, it may have played out this same exact way, but sooner. Perhaps they'd be in a lasting relationship by now. He'd like to think so.

That evening after they finished setting the table, he passed her a glass of wine. "I've been meaning to ask. Why do you write at night as opposed to standard daytime work hours?"

"I find I'm more business-minded during the day and creative in the evenings. From noon to three, I tackle marketing, emails, and the administrative side of my job. I work through plot lines and character development from about three until dinner. In the evening, I write the meat of the story." She paused to consider her next words. "There's a freedom and sense of timelessness as the rest of the world sleeps. It feels like I tap into a collective creative energy."

"That makes perfect sense. I run in the early morning before the world wakes up, and there's a freedom in the stillness. As if I'm the only one moving and getting a jump on the day."

"I want to understand, but my mind shut down when you said *run*," she replied with a saucy smile.

"You're impossible. Come help me in the kitchen. You can put the salad together while I finish up the rest of the meal." Zack dropped an arm across her shoulders and led her to the island. "By the way, Charlie's popping by for dinner tonight. He's been checking on a few things down at the PD for me. If everything is okay, Jacob will be returning with his grandmother tomorrow."

"Oh."

Her tone alerted him something about his statement bothered her. He drew back to look at her.

"What's wrong?"

"Nothing. I didn't realize all this was coming to an end so soon. Somehow, I'd forgotten I needed to look for a place to stay."

"Why would you? Aren't you comfortable here?" Zack asked, alarmed by her willingness to abandon ship so quickly.

THERE WAS an odd quality in Zack's voice that grabbed Erica's attention. Whereas, initially, she'd thought he was trying to give her the hint to leave, it became more apparent his intention had been the opposite. Relief exploded in her chest.

"I'm perfectly happy here, Zack. But I worry I'm cramping your lifestyle," she confessed.

He laughed. "Don't be silly. I don't have a lifestyle to cramp. Single dad, remember?"

And just like that, Erica felt adrift again. Was he using her because he was bored? Old insecurities banged on her door. The feeling of not being good enough, like in school with the cool kids or with past relationships, returned.

Sighing, she shook her head. "I should just move in with Shonda." She and Erica had been fast friends from the time they were small children living next door to each other. They were practically inseparable if one didn't consider Shonda's vacation blackout. "She should be back from vacation by now. It's odd I haven't heard from her, though," she said.

"You intend to move out?"

"I think it's time, don't you?" *Please ask me to stay.*

He shrugged and looked away. "Sure, if that's what you want."

"Fine."

His casual dismissal hurt. She'd been convinced they were developing a deeper connection. Apparently not. Her body overheated, and the need to be alone for wound licking hit her. "Um, I'm not really hungry, Zack. Why don't I leave you to talk to Charlie?"

Without waiting for his reply, she placed the chopping knife next to the board and escaped to her room. The crushing weight in her chest attested to the fact she'd once again set herself up for a fall. Her inability to connect with men sucked donkey balls. The bonus was they hadn't had sex. Erica wouldn't ever recover from doing the deed with Zack. If she'd already fallen this far, this fast, then making love with him would've only added to her problems.

ERICA's abrupt departure was disconcerting. Somehow, some way, Zack had misstepped. He replayed the scene in his head—twice. Was it possible she was pissed he *hadn't* argued in favor of her staying? Sure as shit, he'd wanted to. Still did. But she'd seemed insistent.

He vaguely remembered her blonde best friend as the outgoing of the two, and Shonda had stood up for her at every turn. Whenever Erica was bullied, her best friend had been there with a cutting comeback, able to flay the offender alive if Zack hadn't gotten to the offender first. For that reason, he liked Shonda. No-nonsense and loyal deserved appreciation.

Staring gloomily at nothing and feeling miserable, he knew he had to broach the subject. Erica responded to his knock immediately, and the abject sadness in her eyes gutted him.

"What's this about, babe?" he asked softly. "Please tell me where I screwed up. I need to fix it."

"If you don't know—"

"Erica, I'm a guy. To make it worse, I'm a meathead jock. We're constantly clueless. Cut me a break here. Please."

Her lips twitched, and humor brightened her eyes. "You didn't do anything wrong, Zack. Truly."

"What didn't I do right?"

She shrugged and studied the collar of his t-shirt.

"If you don't tell me, I won't give you any of the key lime pie I brought home today," he cajoled.

Her head whipped up. "You got me pie?"

"Mm-hmm. The best key lime in three states."

"With those interrogation skills, you should work for the FBI," she muttered as she moved to pass.

Sidestepping, he blocked her path "Nope. First, you tell me what I said to hurt your feelings. Then dinner and dessert. In that order," he added in a stern voice.

Her lips twitched again, but almost immediately, she sobered. "I guess I didn't want you to so easily agree with me. I like spending time with you. It's nothing more than that, I swear."

Relief made his entire being feel lighter. He drew her into his arms. "Babe, you can stay forever if you want. I've already told you, I'm in no hurry for you to go."

"Really?" She tilted her shiny auburn head back and searched his expression as if she didn't quite believe him.

"Really."

Later that night, long after Charlie dined, delivered the disappointing news that he'd been unable to uncover any additional clues regarding their arsonist, then dashed, Zack cuddled Erica close. They sipped their wine in comfortable silence.

The rightness of her in his arms wasn't lost on him, and he wondered if she felt the same. He hoped like hell her earlier reaction was an indication she did.

"I like having you here, Erica," he said.

She twisted to meet his steady gaze. "I like being here."

"Really?"

"Really."

Their matching grins spoke all the truths they couldn't confess.

The turning point was now, and the beginning stage of their relationship had begun. Zack only knew he'd never experienced such a sense of home and well-being with a woman before.

"But I need to find a long-term rental until my house can be rebuilt, Zack. Disrupting your life with Jacob isn't fair."

His good mood vanished. Was trying to tell him she didn't like kids, or she couldn't see a future with a jock like him? Either way, her hurt had shifted his way, and he was the one feeling suddenly salty.

CHAPTER

ELEVEN

Searching for a rental in a small town was an exercise in futility. A few duplexes boasted long-term lease options, but contracts were already in place. The waitlist was eleven months.

Erica needed to expand her search, but she hated the idea of living elsewhere. Stonebrooke had been her hometown for her entire life, and she was beyond comfortable here. The grocery store cashiers knew and accepted her bagging quirks. They no longer got upset when she demanded they double-bag the meat and eggs separately or complained vegetables didn't go under the condiments.

And where the hell was Shonda? It was as if she'd disappeared off the face of the earth. Considering Angela was missing, too, Erica's friend list was dwindling. Countless voicemails were left for both women in addition to blowing up Shonda's phone with text messages.

She needed to take action fast. Zack's son would return home today, and she didn't want to be a third wheel during their reunion. Faking a dinner date had potential. It allowed her the excuse to leave the house without a lot of rigamarole. With no leads on a residence, Erica returned to Zack's.

"Honey, I'm home!" she called out to McFatty.

She jerked to a halt when she saw Zack sitting in the living room with his son, game controllers in their hands.

"Oh. Crap. I'm-I..." What could she say that wasn't damning in front of his kid?

Awkward.

As if he guessed her dilemma, a mischievous gleam lit Zack's eyes. She fought a fiery blush and lost.

"Sorry. You must be Jacob. Hi, I'm Erica," she babbled. Having no experience with children, she was clueless about what to say.

"Hey," Jacob muttered. He couldn't be bothered to meet her eyes and continued playing his video game.

She assumed he was one of those kids who thought all adults were dumber than a box of rocks. "Okay then. I'll just leave you guys to it. Have fun."

"Erica, wait."

Zack's deep, commanding voice was hard to ignore.

"Why don't you join us?"

"I'm not sure how to play. I'd only slow you down," she hedged.

"We can teach you. How 'bout it, Jacob?" He received a shrug for his efforts.

A dark frown settled between Zack's brows as he continued to stare at him. What he was trying to accomplish with his glare was beyond her, but she could easily tell Jacob was oblivious to anything but the TV screen and the action going on there. He certainly didn't care if an adult he'd never met hung out with him.

The best thing was to drop the excuse bomb and get the hell out of Dodge. "I appreciate the offer, but I have plans. Maybe another time."

Zack's glare shifted to her. "Plans? What kind of plans?"

"A date, if you must know."

"A *date*? You are going on a *date*?" His furious expression drove her back a step.

Jacob, the little shit, pressed the pause button to watch as the drama unfolded.

"Yeah, I… uh… It was set up weeks ago. Before my house caught fire," she fibbed, unable to look him in the eye. The heavy silence prickled her skin, and she finally glanced up. The coldness on Zack's face made her heart clench.

"I see," he said, ice dripping from those two small words.

Erica bit her lip, torn between wanting to confess the truth and letting him believe she'd scheduled a date. If she didn't know any better, she would have sworn he was hurt. Perhaps she should clarify it was a girls' night? She doubted he'd believe her since she'd already said she had no friends other than Shonda and Angela, both MIA.

"Don't let us keep you."

Unable to bear his anger, she sliced a glance at Jacob. Their gazes locked. He watched her, eyes narrowed slightly as if he knew she was lying. With a shrug, he turned to the television. She'd been dismissed in his eyes. Yet his apathy bothered her, too. What the hell was wrong with her? Had she expected the kid to welcome a total stranger with open arms?

"Well, good night. Have fun with your video game," she said.

Lame, lame, lame.

She couldn't leave fast enough.

Since she wasn't very hungry, Erica decided to take her time preparing for her fake date. A nice, long bubble bath was the ticket. She hoped it would help ease her tension from fabricating a whopper of a story. She'd never been good at making up lies, but the author in her recognized there was irony in there somewhere.

She'd just relaxed in the water when a knock sounded on the outer bedroom door.

Shit!

Had she locked it? What if the kid decided to barge in?

"Erica?" Zack's low voice drifted to her.

"Um, I'm in the bathroom, Zack," she called, hoping he would take the hint and leave.

No such luck.

He joined her without a by-your-leave, and his cool eyes raked over her suds-covered form. Even knowing he couldn't see below the bubbly surface, she experienced a chill.

"What made you think it was an invitation?"

No humor showed in his frosty blues. "Where are you going, and who are you going with?" he asked.

"*What?*"

"I asked—"

"I know what you asked, Zack. I'm curious why you think it's any of your freaking business?"

"Seriously? You have a fucking stalker, Erica, or did you forget in your rush to date another guy?"

"How can I? I'm homeless because of some maniac's obsession with destroying my life," she retorted, ignoring the verbal jab.

"Regardless, I think you should cancel your *date*." He spat the last word, indicating he was a helluva lot more bothered by the thought of her being out with 'another guy' than by some phantom attacker.

"Are you *jealous*?"

"No!" he hotly denied. "Why the hell would I be jealous?"

"You totally are! You're jealous!" she crowed, elated he cared.

"I am *not* jealous," he snapped. "Whatever. Do what you want. You intend to anyway."

As he spun on his heel, Erica called him back. He didn't leave, but he also didn't turn around.

"I don't have a date," she said softly.

Whirling, his all-to-perceptive gaze locked on her. After a long moment spent studying her, relief flashed across his face. "Oh, thank God!"

Two strides brought him close, and he lifted her from the

water. With little regard for his clothing getting soaked, he pulled her flush against his hard body. His lips hovered over hers, and he growled, "Don't ever put me through that again."

His kiss was masterful. Erica didn't care to think about where he'd learned *that* particular skill, but he certainly excelled at it. The way his mouth worked hers, his tongue tasting and exploring, as his hands held her—one banded around her waist and the other cupping the back of her head—stirred her juices and made her forget her name. His was the kind of demanding kiss women dreamed about and was why she wrote the steamy stories she did.

"Dad?" Jacob's voice tore Erica from her seductive splendor.

"Jesus, Mary, and Joseph," she swore, jerking out of Zack's embrace. Her heels slipped. She landed flat on her ass, sending a tidal wave of water, bubbles and all, over the porcelain edge to drench Zack from the crotch to feet.

Thoroughly mortified yet also terrified his son would catch a glimpse of her bodacious bobbing tatas, she plastered her arms over her chest and ducked under the water.

"Get out, Jacob," Zack bellowed, loud enough for her to hear him from below the surface. "You know better than to walk into an adult's room without knocking." But there was laughter in the sound, and she wanted to maim him.

ONCE HE'D REDIRECTED his overly curious son, Zack assisted Erica. She resembled a drowned rat. Unable to contain his laughter, he collapsed on the rim of the tub and let loose.

She retaliated by arching a wave in his direction, splashing his lap, but it did nothing to dampen his ardor. His humor died away, but not for any reason she might suspect.

In this time and place, Zack was standing on a precipice, and falling was the only way forward. The problem was Erica and her unfailing ability to tie him in knots. When he wasn't on the verge of strangling her, he wanted to screw her brains out.

"Put me out of my misery and sleep with me already." It came out as more of a demand than a request, but he wouldn't apologize.

The hitch in her breathing and the heat in her unblinking eyes told him he didn't need to. She wanted to make love as badly as he did.

"It's Jacob's first night home, Zack. You need to spend it with him," she said, regret thick in her voice.

"After he goes to bed, then."

Her gaze, ever so slowly, trailed over the tent in his slacks before meeting his.

"Yes," she said huskily. "Come to me tonight."

If Zack was dreaming, he never wanted to wake up.

He didn't dare touch her again. Not now. Not if he wanted to retain control and kill his erection. After a lingering look, he left her to finish her bath. He stopped and adjusted himself before heading into the next room. The extra time it took to change his clothes helped ease matters somewhat. He purposefully switched his mindset from feasting on her delectable curves to the video game. Jacob would expect his full attention.

Erica joined them about fifteen minutes later. Dressed in jeans and a hoodie, she sat on the other side of the room, in a side chair, and observed their play. Her bare toes, with their bubble-gum pink toenails were curled over the cushion's edge as she hugged her knees to her chest. Oddly, she seemed unsure of her welcome.

"What's the objective of the game?" she asked.

Jacob surprised Zack by answering first. "You have to avoid the monsters. And you get to build things."

"Is it difficult?"

"Nah."

Silence reigned for a bit as the two of them leveled up, broken only by Erica's next question. "Did you guys already eat?"

"No." Zack cast her a side glance. "I was considering pizza. You know, for a cheat meal."

He would've sworn pure love shone from her eyes. The probability was high it was for the pizza and not him.

"I can call it in," she said, quick to jump up. "My treat."

"You don't have to do that," he protested.

"It's the least I can do after disrupting father-son night."

A stray thought occurred to him that the made-up date might have been her way of gracefully bowing out and allowing him to spend quality time with Jacob. Of course, the way she went about it wasn't the wisest, but he couldn't fault her for the sentiment. It pleased him that she'd considered his son's feelings on the matter.

"Erica, were you trying to make it so Jacob and I had alone time? Is that why you came up with the date excuse?"

Standing there, uncertainty written all over her, Erica struggled to form an explanation. In the end, she sighed and nodded.

"Thank you. Although you didn't need to do that. Lil man and I have lots of guy nights."

"Yes, but it is his first night back. He hasn't seen you in two weeks."

"You're a rare breed, babe."

Her blush broadened his grin if it was at all possible.

Man, he adored her.

"Okay, what do you fellas take on your pizza?"

He loved it when she changed the subject. Another wonderful thing about her was the lack of conceit. She honestly didn't know how beautiful she was.

"The number for Tony's is on the fridge. Jacob and I usually order pepperoni. But whatever you want on it is fine."

"Do you mind if we make it half-pepperoni, half-cheese?"

"You can order two. I love pizza," Jacob piped in.

"Marry me," she blurted.

Jacob turned the shade of a ripe turnip, causing Erica and Zack to chuckle.

"Sorry. I'm invoking the thirty-year-minimum age requirement for any man of this household to get married. You're stuck with me since I'm the only one fitting the bill," Zack joked, flashing her another grin.

"But you won't let me have pizza every night. Jacob will," she retorted before sashaying toward the kitchen.

As his normally quiet son laughed, Zack told himself, right then and there, he would be marrying that woman. He only had to convince her. Time to come up with a game plan.

CHAPTER

TWELVE

"Okay, lil man. Time for bed."

"Aww, Dad!"

"Nope. You have school tomorrow, and you've stayed up later than normal. Move it."

Jacob's internal struggle played out on his face. He clearly wanted to hang out with the adults, but it appeared once his father called bedtime, no debate was allowed.

"Say good night to Erica and thank her for the pizza, please."

Jacob did as he was instructed and went one step further by throwing his arms around her. "Thank you, Erica."

Her heart melted.

Jacob was a mini version of his father. She remembered when Zack was the same age in school. He'd mercilessly teased her on the playground. Nothing too terrible, just standard bratty-boy stuff. But there were countless times she cried to her mother because he'd pulled her braid, thrown dirt on her dress, or raced off with her books to make her chase him. Typical boy, unable to simply tell her he liked her. Yet he'd been sweet, too, not allowing any other kids to bother her.

In his son, Erica saw the same sweetness. She squeezed Jacob tightly, knowing how rough it was at his age. What was it like to be as young as him without a mom?

"You're more than welcome, Jacob. Anytime you want pizza, you let me know, and we'll gang up on your dad. Two against one. Majority rules, right?"

His enthusiastic grin said he was all in. Zack, however, didn't appreciate their game plan.

"Oh, no! You two will *not* be in charge of the menu in this house. How will it look for the owner of a gym to be out of shape from eating pizza every night?"

"Nag, nag, nag," Erica teased with a wink at Jacob. "Good night, kid."

"Will you read to me?"

"I'd love to if it's alright with your dad."

As one, they turned to Zack for permission.

"Sure. Am I banished, or can I listen in?"

In his eagerness, Jacob grabbed both their hands and dragged them to his room. Once they were all situated on the bed with him snuggled squarely between them, Erica started the story of *Harry Potter and the Chamber of Secrets*. They had gotten through two chapters before he fell asleep.

"Was it something I said?" she asked, easing off the bed.

"No. Two chapters are his limit. Especially when he's had such an eventful day. Thank you for being kind to him," Zack said. "It's tough without his mother. I try my best, but sometimes..."

He didn't need to explain. Being a single parent was rough.

"I get it. Come on." She threaded her arm through his. "I'll help you clean up."

"Have I told you how awesome you are?"

"Only about five times today. I think you have another five to go before I believe you're sincere."

"That will come later," he said suggestively.

She wanted to warn him not to get his hopes up. It

wasn't as if she was an exemplary lover or anything. Yet the truth refused to come. Soon, he would find out all on his own. She was a poor excuse in the bedroom—or so she'd been told.

The words of her ex haunted her. *"You'd think someone who writes hot sex scenes wouldn't be such a dud in bed."*

A spark of anxiety expanded inside her until her thoughts became a raging inferno of doubt. What if she wasn't good enough? What if Zack laughed at her pathetic attempts? Her insides froze even as her skin heated. The rhythm of her breathing increased, and her palms grew clammy.

"What's wrong, babe?"

Zack could stand to be less attentive. Sometimes it annoyed her how quickly he noticed her slightest mood change.

"About that..."

"You've changed your mind," he stated flatly.

"No!" she practically shouted. Shaking her head, she sighed her resignation. She needed to tell him. "No, I..."

The confession locked in her throat, and she gave him a helpless look.

He studied her for a moment before coming to an internal decision. Wordlessly, he scooped her up in his arms and headed for his bedroom.

"Zack! What are you doing? Put me down. You'll break your damn back."

"Pfft. Hardly."

"I mean it. Stop. I don't want you to carry me." She struggled against the steel bands holding her.

He halted but didn't put her down.

"Erica, look at me," he commanded, gently. His voice was full of understanding, and his warm gaze admiring. Why did he have to be so perceptive and sweet? "We're not doing anything you don't want to. You call all the shots here." After another considering pause, he said, "I suspect your self-confidence has taken a major beating. I don't intend to assume or question why. But if you care to tell me, I'll listen."

Her tears began and streamed in earnest. Giving in to her need to cuddle, she wrapped her arms around his neck and buried her face against his warm skin. With maximal care, he set her on the bed and crawled in beside her. Holding her, he stroked her hair as the events of her past tumbled out.

"My last boyfriend was abusive. I didn't realize it until too late," she said haltingly. "Looking back, I don't know how I didn't see the red flags. It started with minute emotional manipulations, eventually, graduating to verbal digs. Gaslight, undermining... all the narcissistic things a person does to control another. I kicked him out when he backhanded me."

Zack inhaled sharply. And she received no satisfaction in shocking him.

"Did you press charges? Tell me you did," he said roughly.

"Yes. I was blindsided. Unbelievably naive for someone who writes psychologically driven plots and creates well-developed characters." She released a shuddering breath. "But, yeah, I refuse to be anyone's punching bag."

He kissed her temple. "How long did this go on?"

"We dated for a handful of months before he found an excuse to move in. It was another four before he struck me. The whole disaster lasted less than a year, but it was enough to trash my self-worth. Hence, the emotional overeating. Losing myself in the sweet bliss of dessert is easier than remembering what a dumbass I was to let that happen in the first place."

"No. You don't get to blame yourself for what he did, Erica. Some people are skilled at manipulation and concealing their true nature until it's too late. Believe me, I know. I went through the same thing with Christie."

"The logical part of my brain knows you're right. It's harder to get the rest of the gray matter on board."

"True enough."

Seconds ticked by, then minutes. He seemed content to hold her, not demanding anything from her.

"Zack?"

"Hmm?"

"I don't want us to be a one-night stand." Her voice was barely above a whisper, but he still heard her.

"Is that what you really think is happening here?"

"I don't know. I've been wrong before."

"If you believe we're developing a healthy long-term relationship, then you're not wrong. Not this time," he assured her.

ERICA WOKE to the sound of voices drifting to her from the kitchen. Opening one bleary eye, it registered she was tucked all safe and snug in her own bed. Zack must have carried her back to her room in the early hours. She smiled in remembrance of being held securely in his embrace and the sweet things he'd said, indicating he wanted more than a quick lay.

It was difficult to fathom. Zack Sharp wanted a relationship with *her*. Ridiculously happy, Erica jumped out of bed with more energy than she'd had in years. After a quick face scrub and brush of her teeth, she sauntered out to join the guys.

Seeing them sitting on the island and eating cereal, her heart lurched. The picture was perfect: father and his nearly identical son with dark heads bent over their bowls, legs swinging in sync as they chatted about their morning plans.

Zack glanced up, and his welcoming grin brought an answering smile to her mouth.

"Look at you. No coffee yet, and you're not scowling. Has something miraculous happened, or are we special?" he teased.

"Something miraculous *did* happen. Yesterday, I met a wonderful boy by the name of Jacob. *He* doesn't deserve my surly attitude. As such, I've decided to be on my best behavior," she said, chin in the air. "When he leaves for school, all bets are off until I've had coffee."

Zack jumped off the counter and retrieved the dirty bowls. "Brush your teeth."

"I already did," Erica replied.

He laughed, and she resisted the urge to smack her forehead.

He'd been talking to Jacob.

When she would've fled, he curled an arm around her waist and drew her in for a soft, nibbling kiss.

"Aww, Dad!" Jacob protested the mushy stuff with a scowl and an eye roll.

"Go finish getting ready for school. I have to wish Erica a good morning."

"Can I say good morning, too?" Jacob asked.

Both Erica and Zack sputtered their disbelief and amusement, certain he didn't mean what his father had.

"Of course you can," Erica said, squelching her desire to laugh. She spread her arms, and he rushed into her embrace. As he wrapped his thin arms around her, she dropped a kiss on the crown of his head. "Good morning, Jacob."

"Good morning, Erica. Will you take me to school?"

"How do you usually get there?"

"Dad or Grandpa. But *you* can drive me today. They won't mind."

Over his head, she sought Zack's permission by lifting her brows in question.

He nodded.

"I'll tell you what. You finish getting ready, and I'll throw on something other than my PJs." Erica glanced at the wall clock. "We'll meet back here in about five minutes, and I'll ride along with you while your dad drives. Fair enough?"

His happy shout could be heard downtown, and Jacob ran to prepare for his school day.

"You've made him ecstatic."

"He's great, Zack. You've done so well."

Erica wasn't prepared when he pulled her back in his arms for a second, deeper kiss. Her head was spinning when he finally released her.

"Thank you."

"If I'm rewarded for compliments like *that*, you can be sure I'll come up with them more often," she said.

He chuckled and hugged her. "And you can be sure it's no hardship doling out those rewards."

"That's what I hoped you'd say."

"Go get dressed. We have just enough time to hit the drive-thru for your morning coffee."

"You keep this up, and I'm going to fall in love with you."

"You've figured out my plan."

"Don't let your mouth write checks your ass can't cash, my friend."

"Oh, Erica," he growled. "I have much better things to do with my mouth."

Her audible gulp drew another chuckle from him.

He gave her a quick tap on the butt to set her in motion. "Go."

THIRTEEN

Two days later, Erica's sedan was sporting a fresh paint job and four new tires. She'd enjoyed the luxurious rental, but having her own vehicle back put her in a better frame of mind. If one didn't count the hatred attached. She'd been in contact with her homeowners' insurance agent, and they'd assured her all damages to her house, minus her deductible, were covered. Thank goodness for full-coverage policies!

Life was looking up—for the most part.

She'd spent the better part of the morning picking through what was left of her belongings, all the while fighting back frustration and fury. Her home had been cozy. Perfect for her in every way. Yet now, with the exception of half her garage and the room directly behind it, the structure was a blackened shell.

After placing the last boxes in the trunk, Erica stretched to reach the overhead door. A hard push drove her to her knees. Thankfully, she hadn't tugged the garage door hard enough to close all the way, or she'd have been decapitated.

Swearing akin to a drunken sailor who'd tumbled into rough

seas at high tide, she struggled to her feet, weirdly out of breath from the impact. She looked up in time to see her assailant booking it down the sidewalk. There wasn't a snowball's chance in Hades Erica was in good enough shape to catch up, and the knowledge made her surly as hell.

An internal debate ensued. Did she inform the police or ignore the incident? She chose the latter. What could she say? A medium-sized person in a gray hoodie shoved her? Determining the sex of the person was out of the question. Instinct said female, but she couldn't be sure.

Erica intended to get serious about training with Zack. Had she been fit, she might've easily run the mad cow down. And she definitely would've. These personal attacks were pissing her off, and her inner chicken shit was all for taking a back seat to her rage. She would only be pushed so far before she snapped and fought back.

Her new ninety-dollar jeans were torn at both knees. Forget the money, these ruined pants made her ass look fantastic. A bitch needed to die! Preferably not her, but it was open season on that twatsicle, and she'd cheerfully play the huntsman!

The air burned her open scrapes and strengthened her resolve. Zack would be ecstatic about her new drive to become Miss Fitness USA. She'd need self-defense classes, too, and she was certain he'd be able to steer her toward an excellent class. But first, she needed to research if there really was a Miss Fitness USA or if she made it up during her get-fit fantasy. No point in trying to achieve a goal that didn't exist. Because there would be running involved. She was sure of it.

As Erica once again reached to close the garage door, a razor-sharp pain in her side let itself be known. She looked down to find blood soaking her sweater.

What the actual hell?

Easing up the hem, she exposed a raw, angry wound.

Good Christ Almighty, she'd been stabbed!

How had she not felt the blade go in? Yes, she felt what equated to a punch to her side, but it hadn't begun to hurt until she moved. On the errant thought, she made a mental note to deep dive into what a knife wound felt like. If she'd been describing it wrong in her novels, her readers needed to know. Erica chided herself for her ludicrous musings and applied pressure to her side.

She stumbled to her car, hollering for assistance. If someone was outside, they would certainly hear. As she collapsed in the driver's seat, two of her closest neighbors approached.

"Erica! Ohmygod, honey! You're bleeding!"

Leave it to Mrs. Wilson to state the obvious. Her elevator didn't go to the top, and she relished a good gossip about the neighborhood drama. She'd be eating on Erica's misfortune for weeks.

"Yes, Mrs. Wilson. Would you please dial 911 for me?"

"I'll do it." John, from across the street, whipped out his cell and made the call.

Why Erica hadn't thought to use her own cell was a mystery. Perhaps the blame lay with blood loss and the lightheadedness it had wrought.

"They're on their way. Is there anyone else you want me to call, my dear?" he asked.

As she gazed up into his compassionate gray eyes, she was reminded of Zack and his many kindnesses to her. Both men had quiet confidence, and it reassured a person everything would be okay.

"Thank you, John. Do you mind calling *Workout World* and asking for Zack Sharp? I don't have the number, and you'll need to look it up. Ask him if he'll meet me at the hospital, please." Doubts set in. Did she really want to lay another problem on his doorstep? If it was a simple matter to have her side patched, perhaps waiting was the better option. "On second thought, maybe you shouldn't call him. I don't want to bother him at work."

John's bushy brows shot up, and his bewildered expression was the last thing Erica registered before the lights went out.

She came to in an ambulance. A paramedic with a gentle bedside manner encouraged her to remain calm. "Everything will be fine."

Trusting the medical team had it covered, she let her lids drift shut. Resting couldn't hurt, right?

The second time she woke was in the emergency room. A range of hospital staff asked the standard questions of name, date of birth, if she had insurance, and allergies as they wheeled her gurney toward the surgical unit. Sounds blended together, but one angry male voice stood out above the others.

"I'm her fiancé," he shouted. "I need to see her."

Poor guy.

Whoever he was, he was having an emotional crisis.

"Erica Sutton."

Her name carried, and she struggled to concentrate. She painstakingly concluded the overwrought visitor was Zack.

"Zack," she croaked. Against all odds, over the plethora of hospital noises— intercom announcements, humming or beeping machines, and people milling about—he heard. When she turned her head, he was jogging to keep up with the team pushing her gurney.

"Hey, babe." His greeting was as haggard as his appearance.

"I told them not to bother you."

"Why the hell would you say such a thing? Do you really think I wouldn't come after hearing you were stabbed?" he demanded, tone incredulous.

"Just a knick," she murmured, closing her eyes against the glaring overhead lights.

"Not so much," inserted another voice. "While I'm ninety percent certain the knife missed any major organs, it's no small cut, Erica. We're taking you to the O.R." Erica faded in and out as he explained the process, but she grasped the basics as he continued on. "The wound needs to be opened, explored, and irrigated. Then you'll require quite a few stitches and a whole lot of rest until it heals completely."

"You sound like a doctor." Erica bestowed a pained smile on him.

"Yes, ma'am. Doctor Trace Montgomery at your service," replied the cute, dark-haired thirty-or-forty-year-old physician. She absently noted he'd make a splendid hero for one of her books.

"Are you single?"

"Babe," Zack scolded.

"She's had a lot of blood loss. Don't hold it against her." Doc Montgomery chuckled. "I get asked frequently."

"Arrogant much?" Zack snapped.

The chuckle turned into an all-out laugh.

"Wait! No! It wasn't for me," Erica clarified as she squeezed Zack's hand. "My friend, Shonda, is single."

"Good, because you aren't available."

"Okay, fake fiancé." She giggled as she flirted with oblivion.

He groaned after she'd unintentionally blown apart his lie.

"Sorry, this is as far as you go. Someone will find you when she's out of surgery. I'll make sure they know you're allowed to be with her during recovery," Dr. Montgomery said.

"I'll be here when you wake up, Erica," Zack told her tenderly.

"Okay."

The kiss he gave her was light and comforting. Reluctance to let her go was etched in the lines of his face.

"I'll be fine, Zack. Promise," she said. He required reassurance more than she did. "You should see about Jacob."

"Charlie's got him. I'm staying." His resolve was firm and brooked no argument.

As she met his determined gaze, Erica's heart was full to over-flowing. Beyond any shadow of a doubt, she loved him. He was the type of man every woman dreamed about having in her life. Strength, compassion, caring, and protectiveness rolled into one.

She poured all the unexpected emotion she was experiencing into her wobbly, adoring smile. And in her delirium, she thought maybe his smile mirrored hers.

Dr. Montgomery slapped a button to open a set of double doors. "We have to go."

FOURTEEN

Zack paced the surgery waiting room, praying to a God he wasn't sure he even believed in. He hoped, with every fucking fiber of his being, the stab wound was as minor as the good doctor had indicated.

Enraged by the attack, he beat himself up for letting his guard down. He was also pissed Erica hadn't told him she planned to go off on her own again today. Pissed he couldn't seem to protect the incredible woman he'd come to care for.

Perhaps he should've been surprised by how fast he'd fallen, but he wasn't. She'd taken his life by storm, and he had no regrets. Okay, maybe one—they hadn't made love yet. Getting horizontal was the least important area of their relationship, and it didn't matter in the entire scheme of things. He'd be content to snuggle her in his arms every day for their entire lives if it was all he could have, but he wanted those lives to be long and healthy.

Zack needed the constant reassurance she was safe, and if he were able to convince her, he intended for Erica to sleep in his bed from here on out. Touching her, knowing she was protected within the circle of his arms, was the only way he'd sleep soundly at night.

He needed to wake up and have her beside him, breathing and well. Persuading her might be the hardest part.

He placed a call to Bucky and provided the details of the attack. Of course, the PD had already been informed about the incident and was amping up the patrols around Zack's residence along with Charlie's, which was three doors down and where Jacob was currently.

Next, he called Mason. His brother had been MIA since his scheduled return from the Caribbean three days ago, and with the chaos surrounding him, Zack was beginning to get itchy. "Mason, I *really* need you to get back here soon. A close friend's been stabbed and is in surgery. I need time off. You and Dane... Fuck it! *Call me!* I need to know you're okay."

After disconnecting, he dialed Dane and filled him in on everything that had happened to date. Dane silently listened to the entire tale, then proceeded to chew him out for not telling them everything earlier. The Sharp family was annoyingly overprotective of one another, and it was the primary reason Zack hadn't said anything. Who wanted the drama of it all when they were already in the thick of things? He left it up to his brother to inform their mother or not. The fifth degree from Connie Sharp would be too much to handle, and she'd be a damn pit bull with a bone.

Within twenty minutes, both of his brothers were charging into the waiting room, followed by a vaguely familiar blonde.

"What happened to Erica? Is she all right?" the woman demanded, anxious to the point of trembling.

"I'm sorry. *Who* are you?" he asked.

"Shonda. Erica's best friend. I—"

"How the hell did you even hear about this? Did the hospital call you?"

"Yes. I'm her emergency contact. Have been since her parents moved to Florida."

She burst into tears. At a loss as to how to deal with his own emotions, much less hers, Zack's panic set in. The hand he raised to comfort her shook, and he chided himself for allowing her fear to feed his.

Mason elbowed him aside. "Don't cry, love. She's going to be fine. Promise."

The shock sent his eyebrows skyward. Dane showed his equally stunned disbelief. Their astonishment was warranted. Ninety-nine of a hundred times, Mason abandoned ship if a crying female was aboard. The only constant he desired or required was the business. Women, especially the clingy variety, were interchangeable and meant to be bedded and quickly discarded or avoided altogether. Deeper emotions gave him hives.

"How is it that you're here? I didn't expect to see you again." Shonda's visage was one of pure wonder.

Zack ignored his curiosity and the urge to lean in for Mason's reply. Watching his older brother closely, he witnessed the pained expression flash across his rugged, tanned face.

Although Mason's eyes were the same color as Dane's, they always seemed an icier blue. Perhaps it was the constant calculating look or the self-imposed distance, but a single glance from him was intimidating as hell to anyone who didn't know him. Dane possessed a softer appearance, and he was always brimming with good humor. His lighter hair set him slightly apart from Mason and Zack, and it was a less severe style than the shorter, carefree dark cuts they preferred.

Zack studied his two brothers objectively.

Mason, only a year older than him, and Dane, a little over a year and a half younger, could never have been mistaken for twins. Yet their pale eyes and tall, gym-perfected bodies set hearts aflutter their entire lives. While Zack's own hair was blacker, his eyes a darker blue, and his height about two inches shorter, he'd never been excluded by them, which sometimes happened with the middle child. They were a unit, the three of them, especially when it came to their shared business.

Their personal lives were a different matter, and they each kept their affairs as private as possible. None cared to overshare, and there was always a real risk their mother would meddle if she learned any of her boys were dating someone she deemed important.

Shonda's question, directed toward Mason, required privacy, and Zack didn't want to bear witness to histrionics when his brother crushed her heart, as he was bound to do. Racking his brain for an excuse, he touched upon caffeine.

"Anyone need coffee? I was about to hit the kiosk in the lobby."

"I'll go with you," Dane offered.

The words were rushed as if his younger sibling wished to be gone from the ugly scene about to unfold as much as he wanted to be.

"We'll both take a cup. One black, the other with two creams, no sugar," Mason said.

"You know how she takes her coffee?" Dane blurted tactless and clearly taken aback.

At Mason's black look, Zack dragged their younger brother from the room.

"I saved you from a beatdown. You should thank me."

"What?" Dane protested. "It was a legit question."

"Maybe. But his expression was screaming she's different. I wouldn't tease him until he's ready to talk about it."

All he received for his warning was a careless shrug.

Oh well, Dane had to make his own mistakes. It might be the diversion Zack needed to see the two of them square off.

"You're pretty serious about the chick in surgery, huh? Wait! She's not *the* Erica? The one from high school? The girl who turned you down for prom?"

"Shut up."

"*She is!*" Dane said. His smugness tempted Zack to slug him.

"Keep your voice down, idiot. We're in a hospital."

"Ha! I wonder if Mason remembers."

"No, because I never told him. I wouldn't have heard the end of it," Zack groused. "I didn't tell *you*, either, if you recall. You just happened to hear me pouring my heart out to Mom."

"That's right. You were moping around the house for months after she said no."

"I really liked her," Zack said quietly. "I still do."

All teasing left Dane's face as he flung an arm around his brother's neck. "She'll be fine, bro. Don't worry."

"Yeah." He gave Dane a tight smile. "Let's go order our coffee."

It was another hour before Dr. Montgomery appeared in the doorway of the waiting room. The doctor zeroed in on Zack as he popped up from his chair.

"How is she? When can I see her?"

"The surgery went well. Erica was lucky to find help as quickly as she did. She's in recovery for the next half hour, then we'll move her to a private room. You'll be able to see her after she's settled."

"How soon before she's able to go home?" Shonda asked.

"I'd like to keep her for the next day or two. I want to be certain she doesn't experience a fever or infection. If everything looks good in a few days, she'll be discharged." Dr. Montgomery smiled in the face of their relief. "She's going to need to rest for the next ten days. We'll go over everything when we discharge her, but I expect Erica to make a full recovery."

Overcome, Zack merely nodded and pumped the man's hand in gratitude.

"She'll be fine, Mr. Sharp."

"Thanks."

"If any of you plan to hang around, the cafeteria food isn't half bad."

"Are there donuts?" Zack asked.

"Excuse me?"

"Erica's going to want donuts when she wakes. It's her go-to food for stress."

The doctor chuckled and shook his head as he exited the room.

"I'll make a bakery run," Dane offered. "Text me what everyone wants."

"You guys don't have to stay." Zack was grateful for their support, but worry and amped-up adrenaline had taken a toll. Currently, he preferred the peace and quiet of an empty room. He needed to chill until he was allowed to see Erica.

"Three musketeers, remember?" Mason replied.

"The three musketeers," he repeated, but his response lacked the standard enthusiasm. Addressing Dane, he said, "Since everyone is staying, pick up a dozen. Four need to be lemon-filled. The rest can be whatever you guys want."

"You know Erica's favorite flavor?" Delight edged out the amazement on Shonda's lovely face. Her mossy green-gray eyes were lit from within from thoughts he wasn't party to.

Zack's brows pinched together. What was the fuss about? "It's not like she's kept her donut addiction a secret."

"Uh, *yes*, she normally does."

"Right. The woman is all about consuming carbs and would kill for a slice of cake, pie, or pizza. Not necessarily in that order." He scoffed. "I hardly think her love of lemon-filled donuts is something she'd be able to hide for long."

"You don't understand. Not even her last boyfriend knew what she liked. She's actually very secretive and shy." Shonda shook her head. "She rarely speaks up for herself."

"Are we talking about the same Erica here? She swears like a sailor and grumbles every time she has to go to the gym. She threatened my life once because I couldn't produce coffee fast enough."

"She only gets testy about coffee when she first wakes up... *Oh!*"

"Oh? Oh, what?"

"You're sleeping together," she exclaimed, with rounded eyes. The lively sparkle in them showed her excitement over their situation—which was none of her business, thank you very much. "It's the only way you would know that."

Not sure how much Erica wanted known, he didn't volunteer any additional information other than to say, "She's been living at my house since hers burned down two weeks ago."

"*What?* Her house... Oh, God! She loved that house." Shonda clutched his wrist. "How did it happen?"

"A screwball fire starter who happens to have a hard-on for hurting Erica," Zack replied, anger heavy in his voice. "It's why she's here."

"How—"

"Look, I'm sure she would've explained it if you'd bothered to return her calls. As it is, you'll have to wait to talk to her. I don't care to go into it right now." Tired and testy, he wasn't prepared to spill his guts to a virtual stranger.

"Zack!" Mason barked. "Don't speak to her like that. She hasn't done anything wrong."

His hard-won control snapped. "No, nothing you didn't do, right? You've avoided me for the last three days. If you'd have returned a goddamned text or call, this might have been prevented. I could've been with Erica today while you ran the office." As abruptly as the rage had washed over him, it dissolved. The outburst had been a result of the building stress, and like a pressure cooker, he needed to release the steam. Shaken, he ran a hand through his hair and blew out a breath. "I'm sorry, Mason. I..."

"No. You're right. There's no excuse to avoid responsibility. It won't happen again." Mason was exceedingly consolatory and understanding.

It served to make Zack feel like a total shit. But indulging in small talk was beyond his capabilities. They waited in awkward silence for Dane to return with burgers and pastries. Each lost in their own thoughts.

"Mr. Sharp?" They shot to their feet as a recovery room nurse entered. She addressed Zack as he rushed forward. "Ms. Sutton is being wheeled to room three-twenty-three. You can head there now. We ask you to keep it to only two visitors at a time."

"Thank you." He turned to Shonda. "Do you mind if I see her first?"

Her agreement was a soft smile.

In the part of his brain where puzzles were sorted and solved, it became apparent why his brother was attentive to her. If Mason had a type, Shonda Grant was it. His brother was in deep shit, and Zack couldn't be happier.

Feeling oddly lighter, he grinned and gave her a tight hug. Bending to speak directly in her ear, he was careful to keep his voice whisper quiet. "Play hard to get. He won't be able to resist you."

He followed his advice with a lightning-fast kiss. His grin widened when Mason jumped up to object, a scowl pinching his dark, slashing brows together.

With a wink in the direction of his brother's new obsession, Zack exited the room and took off at a run. He intended to be there when Erica woke up.

CHAPTER
FIFTEEN

Dull, nagging pain penetrated the darkness and prodded Erica to wake. Before she opened her eyes, she felt for the area producing her discomfort and encountered a bandage. Cottonmouth was the second thing to register. For once, she wanted something more than a donut—*water*. She'd kill for one sip.

Cracking her lids to mere slits, she winced at the brightness. She hadn't fully taken in her surroundings before sleep beckoned once again.

"Erica? Erica, it's time to wake up, hon."

The nurse's words penetrated her foggy mind, and she attempted to comply. Unfortunately, her eyelids refused to cooperate. One single-minded thought loomed, and she whispered, "Thirsty."

"Can she have water?"

The pleasant tone of Zack's voice fluttered through her consciousness, and she turned her head toward the sound. If asked prior to that moment, she would have said he had a deep voice, but hearing him speak now brought to mind Mexican hot chocolate, made with fresh whole milk, topped with homemade whipped cream and a dusting of cinnamon. She'd tasted it once in Cancun, and the creamy richness was a flavor she constantly craved. She dreamed of that damned chocolate and was determined to recreate the recipe. To date, she wasn't able to. Listening to Zack speak was the next best thing, and she savored the delectable sound of each spoken syllable.

"Ice chips only. Too much, too soon will make her sick."

"We ordered her something to eat. Will that be okay?"

"If she holds down the ice, she can drink water, then move on to small bites as she's able to tolerate it."

Like a baby bird awaiting a worm from its mama, Erica opened her mouth. She sighed her appreciation as he rubbed ice against her cracked lips. After a few seconds spent moistening her mouth, he slipped the chip onto her tongue. She released a happy moan. Was there anything as delicious as that first taste of liquid when one's mouth was drier than the desert?

"More."

As he had before, he moistened her lips and slipped a chunk of ice into her mouth. This became the pattern for the next few minutes.

"I think you've had enough, babe. Try to wake up, okay?"

The soothing sensation of his warm fingers stroking her hair back from her forehead was divine, and Erica wanted to stay that way forever. If it wasn't for her wound, she could've.

Her wound!

Her eyes flew open as she recalled the attack. She locked onto Zack's concerned visage, and the second their gazes connected, his expression reflected relief.

"Hi. Welcome back."

"Hi," she whispered, following it up with a wince. Her throat felt like she'd swallowed a lemon—whole. And not the puny kind —one of those giant mofos the size of a baseball.

"You had us pretty worried, babe."

"Us?" She frowned, unable to remember anyone else prior to surgery.

"Shonda and my brothers are in the waiting room," he explained. "She called your parents after the staff gave us the first update. They're searching for a flight."

"Where are they staying?" In her drugged state, the sleeping arrangement logistics escaped her.

"I figured they could take your room. You can move into mine."

"What about you?" she asked, confused and suddenly worried about putting him out. Her entire crew was too much, too soon.

His light chuckle made her smile. Although she was in the dark about what had amused him, she would happily listen to his laughter forever. It heated her from the inside out and chased away the chill making itself at home deep within her bones.

"I was hoping you don't mind me sharing."

"I don't mind, but I think the queen bed in the guest room might be crowded with my parents," she joked, secretly amazed she was able to. "They might have something to say about it. Well, Dad might. Mom will take one look at you and kick my father to the curb."

"Funny, but I meant you and me sharing a bed."

Bliss settled in her heart. She'd love nothing more, and she told him so.

"Good. Then it's settled." Leaning in, he brushed her nose with his. "On a more serious note, I spoke to Bucky. The PD received conflicting descriptions of the incident from the handful of people present. He wants to know when you're up to making a full report. Do you remember what happened?

"Yes. You can tell him to head over at any time." She accepted more ice with a grateful smile. When her throat was less parched, she said, "I didn't see much, but I can tell him what I do know."

"Fair enough. Second order of business, I have a special delivery for you." Zack opened a bag and waved it under her nose.

The divine fragrance of Addie's Bakery teased her olfactory glands, taunting her with the promise of sweet delights.

"Think you can keep down a bite of food?"

Erica sighed happily. "If that's what I think it is, damned straight I can. I'll sell my soul for it."

"*Reallllllyy?* Good to know how much a soul is going for on today's market. But I'll let you keep your soul if you indenture yourself to me for sex."

"Done. Hand over the donuts."

"You're so easy," he smirked.

"Pfft. Only *you* know my kryptonite. One day I may have to take you out, Lex Luthor, but not today." She bit into floofy, lemony goodness and moaned. "You are a prince among villains, Lex."

Whatever Zack would've responded was cut off by the arrival of another person.

"Erica?" Shonda's tentative voice broke through their teasing.

"Well, if it isn't my long-lost friend. You don't call. You don't write," Erica joked tearfully.

Seeing her bestie sent her into an emotional spiral. Suddenly, everything—the fire, the vandalism of her car, the stabbing— became an inescapable reality, and her two worlds collided. Until that exact moment, she'd been content to pretend it was all a bizarre dream. The ugly truth was that someone had set out to kill her.

Multiple times.

And they were scary close to succeeding with each attempt.

"Can I hug you?" Shonda asked.

"Yes, if you're careful of my right side."

As Shonda got comfortable, Zack excused himself. The next thirty minutes was spent catching up. Finally, when Erica was sick of talking about her troubles, she changed the subject.

"So, where the hell have you been? I thought you were only supposed to be gone a week?"

"Ten days," Shonda corrected.

"Okay, ten days. It's been fourteen. You couldn't shoot me a text to say you were alive and well?"

"I'm sorry, E. I met someone on the flight down." Shonda's eyes sparkled, yet the light in them faded as she added, "He's amazing."

"I sense a *but* coming on," Erica said, searching her friend's face. Noting the unhappy frown, she squeezed her hand. "What's up?"

"He's not interested in long-term. I'm crazy about him, but I can't say he didn't clarify from the get-go that he wanted nothing more than a holiday fling."

"You're pining away for a guy you hooked up with in the islands? It should help that you're home, right?"

"It should." Shonda sighed, and the ragged breath sounded distinctly glum.

"But it doesn't," Erica concluded with a crinkle of her nose.

"He lives in Stonebrooke."

"You're shitting me!"

"No. And I should mention he's the brother of your new boyfriend."

Nonplussed, Erica stared. "What? Which one?"

"Mason."

"Ah." Crap! She wished Shonda had referenced Dane because Mason had heartache written all over him.

"'Ah'? What do you mean by 'ah'?" Shonda demanded hotly. She'd jumped up to pace but paused to glare from the foot of the bed. "What do you know?"

"Don't you remember him from school? He was the most earnest one of all the Sharp brothers back then. If I recall correctly, he was dating Melanie Simms," Erica explained.

"Melanie Simms? You mean the girl who died in the car accident up by Hurricane Ridge, the make-out spot? But wasn't she there with Tony Travers?"

"Yep. Can you imagine discovering your one true love was cheating on you after she died in a wreck with another guy?" Erica asked. "Zack told me Mason developed a ruthless devil-may-care attitude ever since. The only thing he doesn't play at is business. Supposedly, he's a marketing phenom."

Seeing her friend's downcast look, she reached for Shonda's hand again and gripped it tightly. No words were necessary between them. They were as close as twins, each able to read the other's mood without needing to discuss an issue to death. Both respected when the other needed time to regroup, as Shonda did now.

"Are you planning to stay with me?" she asked after a time.

Feeling weirdly exposed, considering she'd just pried into her friend's love life, Erica gazed out the window and struggled with a response.

"It's like that, huh?" The amusement in Shonda's voice prickled.

"Like *what?*"

"Don't try to pretend with me. I know you better than I know myself. You're the queen of avoidance if you don't want to answer."

Erica's helpless look was met by Shonda's smug laughter. Heaving a resigned sigh, she leaned forward to check if the door was closed. "Fine! I'm completely and hopelessly in love with Zack. I should move out—I know that—but I want to stay."

"Do you think it's wise? How does he feel about you?"

"That's just it. I'm not sure. The way he acts toward me, how caring he can be, how protective, leads me to believe he sees me as more than a convenient lay."

"I suspected as much, but holy shitballs! You've been sleeping with him? With Zack Sharp? Mr. All-Star Jock? *You?*" The volume of Shonda's voice rose with each syllable she uttered. Her screeched response beckoned Zack, and there was panic on his face as he swung the door wide.

If not for being trapped in bed, Erica could've cheerfully murdered her.

CHAPTER

SIXTEEN

Upon charging in and skidding to a halt, Zack realized he had overreacted. He'd responded to the excitement in Shonda's tone, not the actual words. When they sunk in, he'd already interrupted.

Fury radiated from Erica with the intensity of solar flares from the sun—all directed at her blonde friend. They were fortunate she didn't have a weapon handy.

"Everything okay, ladies?" he asked innocently.

"Fine," she snapped.

He paused and replayed the snippet of conversation he'd overheard. They'd been talking about him, he was sure of it. Erica wasn't thrilled he'd overheard, either!

He was.

If two best friends were discussing a guy with the emotional intensity of these women, it meant one of them—Erica—was invested.

Lighter in heart, Zack strode to her bedside, delivered a scorching kiss, and stole her half-eaten donut. Grin smug as fuck, he tore off an enormous bite and strutted toward the door. Shonda sputtered behind him, and he offered up a salute with the last bite of powdery goodness, leaving the two women to their privacy.

Oh, to be a fly on the wall after his exit! Erica wouldn't find it easy to explain away the kiss. On his return trip to the waiting room, he whistled a happy, off-key tune. Both of his brothers raised their brows in question.

"This is an about-face," Dane said.

"Erica's well on her way to a full recovery if her yelling at Shonda is a sign," he said with a light laugh.

Mason smiled, and it looked good on him. "Should I be concerned?"

Zack's elated mood crash landed. "I don't know. You tell me. What's going on there?" If Mason broke Shonda's heart, it might impact his relationship with Erica. Friends were quick to take sides.

"Nothing," his brother snapped. "Jesus. First Dane, now you. It's called a *private* life for a reason."

"Don't break her heart, man. I don't need the fallout. I have enough shit on my plate without navigating your trail of broken hearts," he warned.

"Look, she knew the score going in. We met on the plane, had some mind-blowing sex for the week we were there, and parted ways when we got back home. No hearts were involved."

"Bullshit, Mason. You're looking everywhere but at me. Where were you these last three days?"

A flush stained his brother's neck. "Okay, fine. I followed her home, and we spent another few nights together. But that's it."

"That doesn't explain why you're both here together," Dane interjected.

"Actually, I was sleeping off the aftereffects when you called. I bumped into Shonda again in the parking lot." The truth shone clearly in Mason's eyes. "I didn't expect to see her again, but she came walking up the same time we did." To Zack, he said, "Dane was the one who picked me up this afternoon."

Zack groaned. "Erica is going to hate you, and maybe me, because you're an ass."

"Her friend is an adult who knew the score. I'm not taking the rap for someone reading more into a casual fuck—" An oh-shit grimace replaced Mason's arrogance.

Shonda was halted outside the doorway, and her stricken expression distressed him.

Backpedaling, Mason spouted one ridiculously lame apology after another, attempting to soothe her feelings.

With a wince on his brother's behalf, Zack said, "Dude, your groveling is painful to witness. Stop before you dig any deeper than you already are."

"Idiot," Dane muttered on his way out.

Copying a page from his youngest brother's book, Zack left to give his clueless older sibling an opportunity to tiptoe through the minefield he'd stumbled into.

Erica appeared to be dozing when he entered her room, and he shifted to retrace his steps.

"Don't go," she murmured.

"I'm here for the duration, babe. But you should rest."

"No. I don't want to be alone."

Perching on the bed, he massaged her scalp, and the repetitive caress lulled her to sleep. With short sweeping motions, he traced her brow, then her jawline. She'd become so dear to him in a ridiculously short amount of time. He couldn't imagine what he would've done if the stabbing had been fatal. Without her, life would be forever bleak and lonely.

The tiny mewl she emitted, followed by an unconscious rub of her cheek on his palm, caused Zack's heart to stutter in his chest. He was a goner. Had been from day one.

His phone's vibration signaled him to check his messages.

Bucky.

Zack shot off a quick response letting him know to come by anytime, then he settled into the too-small chair in the corner.

With nothing left to do, he idly watched Erica, noting every microscopic detail. Other than pale skin and shadows under her eyes, she looked relatively healthy. Her auburn hair was still thick and curly, spread around her head, framing her face. Even without makeup on, she was one of the loveliest women he'd ever encountered. Her long, dark lashes rested against porcelain cheeks. With her coloring, she should've been covered by freckles. Yet her skin was flawless.

With each minute that ticked by, Zack's resolve to protect her grew. Whatever the cost, he'd pay it. Finding the fire-starting, side-stabbing lunatic was paramount. Everything else he'd dump in Mason's or Dane's lap for the foreseeable future. Though it killed him to do it, leaving Jacob with his grandparents was probably the wiser course of action for safety's sake.

Zack knew he couldn't go another moment without confessing his feelings. It didn't matter she wasn't awake.

"I love you, Erica."

"I love you, too."

His heart stalled, and he thumped his fist against his breastbone in an instinctive gesture. He hadn't expected her to hear him, much less respond. Unadulterated joy swelled and swirled within his chest, then spread out and filled him to bursting. Everything would be all right. He'd make sure of it.

"Bucky's on the way, babe. Are you up for a visit?"

"Mm-hmm, that's fine."

Her large, brown eyes fluttered open, and she struggled to focus. When she did meet his gaze, the softness and love shining back at him was humbling. Unexpected moisture built behind his lids, and he blinked rapidly in an attempt to master his wayward feelings. The last time he'd cried was the day he'd first held his son.

Love did that. It fed into a deeper sentimentality, bringing forth a gentler side. Some would call it weak. Not Zack. He was stronger with Jacob and Erica. Whole.

"We're going to find the person responsible for this," he promised.

Her shaky, placating smile was a fist to the solar plexus. He sucked in a breath.

She didn't believe him.

"We *are*," he stressed, and the desperate desire for her to have faith in him was strong.

"Can you make it *before* she succeeds in ending my life?" Erica asked with no little humor.

"She? What makes you say she?"

"I'm not sure. It's an impression I had as my attacker ran away. The way they moved, the slightness of frame, struck me as feminine."

"Okay, at least it gives us another thing to go on. Not much, but it's definitely better than nothing," he said.

Who was he trying to convince, her or him? It remained to be seen. They both wanted the assurance this delusional perp would be caught. Neither of them felt comfortable with her assailant still on the loose, and Zack changed the subject.

"I'm assuming your car is still at your place? Do you want me to have Shonda and Mason get it?"

"That works. The keys should be in my purse, although I don't know where it ended up. Maybe with one of my neighbors?" She shrugged and winced, pressing a hand to her side.

Wishing he could shoulder Erica's pain for her, Zack clasped her hand and kissed her knuckles. "Actually, it's in the locked cabinet by the door. I was told they'll give you the key when you're lucid."

"Zack?"

He didn't like the way she spoke his name, all solemn, one octave away from forbidding. Her features were decidedly hard, and he recognized what stubborn determination looked like on her.

"Hm?"

"I don't think I should go home with you. I want to move into a hotel."

"No."

"No?" She squinted in her ire, and he guessed fighting the morphine required all the concentration she had. "You can't tell me no. What am I? Your hostage?"

"No, I am not leaving you, in your weakened condition, to stay at a hotel unguarded. It's not happening."

Her jaw set. "I'm not putting you and Jacob in danger any longer. I'm moving out."

"Erica, you need to listen to what I'm saying. You are not strong enough at the moment. Not only that, but I am sending Jacob to live with his grandparents until this is over," he said firmly.

"Zack, no! It isn't fair to him. If I leave, you'll both be safer."

"Who's to say? Maybe the next step for this fucking psycho is to remove Jacob from my life. Babe, you can't anticipate what is going through his or her mind," he said, standing to pace. "Maybe if we had any idea who was behind this, we might be better equipped to deal. But anyone could potentially walk through your door disguised as hotel staff and slit your throat as you lie there, recovering."

"Way to be gruesome."

He paused at the foot of the bed, eyes beseeching. "Please. *Please* don't go off on your own. I would go insane, worrying if you were all right."

Erica's face scrunched up, and her unshed tears shimmered. "I only want you and Jacob to be safe. I wouldn't be able to bear it if anything happened to either of you because of me."

"It *isn't* because of you. It's because of a random wackadoo's obsession. Try to remember *none* of this is your fault. *None of it.*"

Taking care not to bump her wound, Zack gathered her close and rubbed large circles on her back.

"We'll catch them," he reiterated. "I swear it."

CHAPTER

SEVENTEEN

In the end, Erica complied, but only because Zack pulled out the heavy artillery: her parents and Shonda. He'd been determined she would stay with him instead of fending for herself at a hotel, and he wasn't opposed to using her loved ones to sway her, much to Erica's annoyance.

The expertly applied emotional blackmail was the reason she found herself comfortably ensconced in his bed, being waited on hand and foot. She wasn't angry, though. His concern was endearing.

Yet, Erica didn't realize how much she valued her independence until she was forced to play the invalid. Restricted movements were detestable, and two days in the hospital, added to another two at home, served to make her cranky and peckish.

Throwing back the covers, she swung her legs off the bed and gingerly straightened up. Deep breaths helped keep the bulk of her pain-induced nausea at bay. She called herself twenty kinds of wimp. Other people bounced back a whole lot quicker from incidents like these. Why couldn't she? If she'd led a better lifestyle, would she have physical endurance?

The door immediately swung open, and Zack urged her back to bed. Erica suspected there was a hidden nanny cam. Tomorrow, she'd find it. Today, she'd give in to his demands and lie down. The five steps she'd taken toward the door were exercise enough for one day. Had her perspiration given her a nice glow? Wasn't that how personal trainers preferred to think of sweating?

"Am I glowing?" she demanded.

"Uh, no?"

"Wrong answer," she growled as she shuffled toward the bed.

"Okaaayyy."

In fairness, he couldn't be blamed for his confusion. Erica was half mad from all this nonsense. To expect him to understand the workings of her inner brain would be stretching it. "Never mind."

"Feeling confined?"

His sympathy struck a nerve, and she blinked to dispel the sudden onslaught of weepiness.

Fuck.

She'd blame it on hormones and be done with it. And thinking of hormones... A quick computation confirmed she was rapidly transitioning into PMS mode.

Damn, and double damn!

If he survived the experience, Zack might never want to see her again. Her mood swings weren't pretty. A few brave exes had thrown around the term "cray-cray."

"Save yourself," she blurted.

Zack paused in the process of tucking her in. "Excuse me?"

"Seriously, run for the hills. Save yourself. I'll pay for your hotel. You aren't going to want to be around for the next five or six days. At least until Aunt Flow visits."

"Babe, you aren't making any sense."

"Oh, and so it starts!"

"*What* starts?" He threw his hands up and glared at her in exasperation. "What the hell are you talking about?"

Her sniffles alerted him to the problem he likely had no idea was brewing. As his strong arms drew her close, Erica didn't fight the embrace and allowed herself to be comforted. He ran his fingers lightly down her back, from neck to hips, and back again along her spine. The touch was feathery and the perfect pressure to derail her self-pity train. Her brain jumped tracks and happily chugged its way toward Sex-with-Zack-ville.

Not that *that* was happening anytime soon.

Annnddddd she was back to weepy, with a side of grumpy thrown in.

"Want to tell me what's going on in that beautiful, busy head of yours?" he asked, following it with a tender kiss on her temple.

"No." His snorted laugh drew a watery smile from her. "I'm sorry, Zack. I'm an ugly PMS-er."

It took a few beats for him to register what she'd said, or at least to decipher what "PMS-er" meant.

"Ah. It's okay. We all have our cross to bear."

He startled a laugh from her, and Erica buried her hot face against his delicious, fresh-from-the-shower-smelling throat.

"Thank you, but I'm not kidding. You should make yourself scarce for a few days until the worst of it's over."

"It's a testament to your love that you warned me, babe." He touched his nose to hers. "It's a testament to *mine* that I plan to stick around."

"Sure, you say that now. Talk to me again on day six. We'll see if you're singing a different tune. I'm certain you'll never view me in the same light again."

She felt his rumbling laugh as he hugged her tight.

"Don't say I didn't warn you," she muttered.

"Fair enough," he said agreeably. "I know you're all settled in, but do you want to come out and join the rest of the group? Charlie and Judith brought Jacob over for brunch."

Aghast, she gave him an incredulous look. "I need a shower before I can see people."

The tell-tale squinting of his eyes and the pursing of his lips said he was weighing his next words very carefully. He probably bit his tongue to hold back the truth of how disgusting she smelled from her profuse sweating. He sure as shit hadn't been quick to agree she glowed.

"How about a sponge bath?" he offered with a wicked gleam.

"I'm bloated, and I stink. Do you really think *now* is the time to be all amorous?" Erica shot him a fierce glare.

Her attempt to pull away was met with a brief resistance and then freedom. Zack rose and strode to the adjoining bathroom. She strained to hear what he was doing, and eventually, the sound of running water filled the interminable silence.

Zack was drawing a bath.

For her!

Of all the arrogant—okay, maybe it was a sweet-AF gesture.

He returned, scooped her up without a by-your-leave, and carried her to the tub. His physical endurance was another pro in the workout column. The man wasn't even straining or out of breath by the time they reached the bathroom!

"Um, you know I can't get my incision wet for another week, right?" she said.

"I'm not filling it, and you can sit on the edge for your sponge bath."

"I already told you I don't want your help." Panic besieged her. He couldn't see her naked *and* PMS-ing. The bloat would turn him off sex for life.

"Erica, you're being ridiculous. I love you. Have a little faith in me, okay?"

He'd guessed her fears, making her feel even smaller and more insecure. It felt as if her soul was shriveling to the size of a sunflower seed. The shelled kind.

"Send my mom in, please."

"Fine." Zack flung down the washcloth and spun to leave, pausing at the door to say, "Oh, and for the record, I've seen you naked. *Twice.* And I'm still here. Imagine that."

Her misery and self-pitying tears followed on the heels of his sarcasm. She couldn't have dammed the dike for all the wooden shoes in Holland. And where that analogy had come from, she didn't know, but maybe her next book would be about a lonely middle-aged woman, who was a miserable cow incapable of inspiring love. She'd live in a cottage overlooking tulip fields, pining for the one man who'd been unable to tolerate her over-the-top hormonal tangents. An autobiography of sorts.

Using the long sleeve of her shirt, she wiped her running nose.

Her mother entered, took one good look at her non-glowing face, and offered a sympathetic hug.

Erica wept harder.

"Mom, how did you raise such a complete moron?" she asked, harsh with herself but probably not severe enough.

"I didn't. I raised a bright, talented, and lovely young woman. One who, for whatever reason, doesn't seem to have any self-worth. I don't know why." Honesty shone from her mom's bright hazel eyes. "He's a keeper, Erica. I think you should cut him a break. Don't push him away because you believe he's too good for you."

"That's not what I'm doing!"

"Aren't you?" There was a soft understanding in her mother's look. "There isn't some small part of you that believes if he can love you, screw-up you assume you are, then there must be something wrong with him?"

Erica sat, stunned by the assessment.

"Don't look all betrayed, toots. I'm giving it to you straight. I'm tired of watching you throw your life away on immature assholes." Mary Sutton's hard words were in direct conflict with her gentle touch as she helped Erica disrobe. "A smart, funny, and sexy-as-hell man is catering to your every whim, and you insist on applying the brakes. He loves you, sweetheart. It's evident in everything he does or says. Don't be an idiot."

"You've never called me an idiot before," Erica mumbled sourly.

"You've never acted like one before. Besides, I didn't call you one. I said don't *be* one," her mother corrected. "You have a genius IQ. Use it."

There was nothing like tough love to snap a person out of their self-absorbed state.

Erica conceded the point. "You're right."

"I know I'm right. Where do you think you got your smarts from, anyway?"

They laughed at their long-standing joke.

"Thanks, Mom."

"You're welcome. We all need a reality check on occasion," she said. "Want me to send Mr. Bow-Chicka-Wow-Wow back in here to scrub your back?"

Apparently, a person was never too old to be embarrassed by their parent's sex jokes.

"Okay, you're not allowed to think of him that way, or I won't be able to."

Mary's chuckle was naughty as sin, and Erica grinned. God, she loved her mom. There was no one like her.

Fifteen minutes later, she was presentable.

"Will you have Zack come help me now?"

"Sure thing," Mom said with a wink.

Erica literally felt him enter the room. His physical presence was a force all its own. She fancied he would've made a perfect Jedi if such things were real. Zack easily compelled people and made them want to respond to him without a single word dropping from his lips.

Speaking of lips...

His weren't smiling.

Very unlike him, and she owed him a huge apology for being an ass. Any more of this behavior, and he would think she was as mentally challenged as the crackpot who'd stabbed her and lit her house on fire.

Clearing her throat, Erica offered her almost inaudible words of apology. "I'm sorry."

"Excuse me? I couldn't hear you."

He damn well could!

For fuck's sake, he was only four feet away.

"I'm sorry," she repeated, louder and angrier. The latter was a direct result of the gloating smirk forming on his face.

"For?"

"*Really?* You can't just accept the apology? You have to be a dick about it?"

"Ah, there's the woman I fell in love with. Welcome back, babe."

"Up yours!"

"You're hangry. Let's go get you fed before you rip out our guests' throats, shall we?"

"Bite me," she grumbled and slipped her arms around his neck as he lifted her up into his arms. He nipped her shoulder, and she yelped her surprise.

"What the—?"

"Merely complying with your every wish, my darling snookums," Zack replied, cutting off her half-spoken question.

"Jerk."

His hearty laughter triggered her giggle.

CHAPTER

EIGHTEEN

Standing outside, with a direct view of Erica through the sliding doors, Zack observed her interactions with his family. Brunch had turned into an all-day event, with his brothers, mother, and Shonda joining the crowd already assembled for the late-morning meal.

Jacob had velcroed himself to Erica's side. The only times he moved were to retrieve a drink, food, or napkin for his new idol. She welcomed each return with a grateful smile.

Regret stole in. Had Zack done his son a disservice by not seeking to settle down before Erica? To see Jacob emerging from his shell and responding to her caring touch or to a loving smile was proof a relationship with her was right. He only wished he'd recognized his son's need earlier.

"I thought I smelled something burning." Mason's comment startled him from his musing.

With a jolt, Zack inspected the meat on the grill. Nothing seemed to be... ah, yes. He was a bit slow on the uptake. His sarcastic turd of a sibling was taking a poke at his distraction. "Nice, asshat."

"Someone has it bad," Mason taunted with a mocking grin and a flare of his eyes. He slapped Zack on the back, nearly knocking him into the open flame.

"Shit, man! Have a care."

"If you weren't mooning over your good-looking redhead—"

The comeback was left unfinished, prodding Zack to look up from flipping the burgers onto a platter.

Shonda, tote bag in hand, was preparing to leave. Mason's irritable scowl would've been humorous if Zack didn't know his brother lived in his own personal hell ever since the "casual fuck" fiasco. The number Melanie had done on him years before didn't help his cause. Anger boiled his insides whenever Zack thought about the cheating skank. For Mason, it was doubtlessly worse.

"You should apologize," he advised.

"The hell I will."

"Mason, don't be a bigger dick than you already are. You obviously have chemistry with the woman. Why not see where it leads?"

"Fuck off. Did I ask you?"

Backing off would've been the prudent thing to do, but Zack was tired of sitting on the sidelines and watching his brother's constant parade of loveless conquests. Tired of seeing the misery on Mason's face when he thought no one was looking. It had been fourteen heartbreaking years, and it was past time for him to move on.

"The fuck I will. You're being stubborn." Zack grabbed the dish of burgers from his hand. "Go ask her to stay for dinner. No one is saying you have to marry the woman. Get your feet wet again by dating a nice girl. And she *is* nice."

He left Mason with his jaw hanging and moved inside to the warmth of the house. He detoured to the kitchen for a beer first.

Time to see about his pretty redhead.

Whistling, he sauntered off in her direction.

Yeah, there was something to be said for love, and he was

ecstatic to have fallen in it. Never more so than when Erica glanced at him and lit up with her own inner joy as their gazes connected. Understanding passed between them. A lift of his beer and a nod of her head was the silent acknowledgment of what they shared.

Her attention veered back to her father, who was recalling a story about her childhood exploits. Erica rolled her eyes but joined in the merriment around her.

Her laughter pulled Zack into her orbit, and he was content to circle her sun.

A vibration from his pocket distracted him. Smiling at Pete Sutton's outrageous story, Zack pulled out his phone and read the message.

"Enjoying your party? It will be your whore's last."

His heart stopped.

"Zack? What is it?"

Erica's concerned voice resumed his heart's beat and sent it into overdrive. His jaw locked, and he couldn't speak. Her stalker's threat freeze blasted his core, making it impossible to act.

"Hey, man? What's going on?" Mason pried the phone from his stiff fingers and read the message for himself. *"Holy—! What the actual fuck!"*

All at once, everyone surged to their feet to see for themselves what had Zack paralyzed and fixated on Erica.

Mason swore a listener's ears pink.

The answering chorus of voices all sang a different refrain.

"Oh dear God!"

"What the hell!"

"This person needs to be stopped!"

"Daddy, is Erica going to be all right?"

Rooted to the spot, Zack couldn't assure Jacob that she would be. The stupid heart muscle in his chest hammered at such an ungodly speed that he doubted his most strenuous cardio routines had ever achieved its like. Only when Erica struggled to stand did he react, surging forward to wrap her in a smothering hug. The need to touch her, to assure himself she was alive and well, took precedence.

"Zack, you're hurting me."

Her small grunt forced him to loosen his grip.

"I have to hold you right now, babe. I..."

What more was there to say? Her touch was proof of life.

The hoarse voice, the pounding heart, the sweat running down his back—all a result of his terror—made him physically ill. He carefully set her from him and hustled to the trashcan in time to lose his cookies.

A cool washcloth settled on the back of his neck as he rested his forehead against the cool granite counter.

"Breathe, darling."

For his mother, he tried—inhaling deeply and slowly exhaling. Again and again, he repeated the action, striving for self-mastery in uncontrollable circumstances. On the tail end of his fear came white-hot rage. What was he doing here, acting like a pussy, when a lunatic was out there with eyes on their house? How else did they know about the impromptu party?

He shoved away from the counter and ran for the door. On the off chance they were outside, he intended to put an end to these attacks. *No matter what it took.*

"No!" Erica shouted, correctly guessing his intent. "Somebody stop him."

Spinning back, he threw up a hand to halt his brothers in their tracks. "Don't touch me. I'm ending this."

"Whoever it is doing this is probably long gone, bro." Dane's was the voice of reason. Always calm. Always logical. Annoying with his cool common sense.

"I don't want you going out there, Zachary," Connie stated in the non-negotiable way of mothers everywhere.

"You don't understand! None of you do!" He swore and drove

his fist through the wall closest to him. The painful impact was nothing compared to what he'd feel should something happen to Erica. *"Goddammit!"*

"Zack, look at me." Erica's soft, soothing tone magically brought his frantic pacing to an end. "Currently, she's transfixed on me. But I'm worried if you confront her, going on the assumption I'm right and it *is* a female, she might snap. In her mind, she thinks you're hers, but if you deny her, it puts a target on *your* back as well as mine."

"What do you propose we do? I'm done with waiting for the cops to find a fucking clue." He resumed pacing. "What the hell are they even doing? Sitting on their asses, eating donuts? Because they sure as shit aren't working to find out who it is."

"Please."

One utterance, spoken low and infused with worry, was enough to hobble him. Enough to shake off the raw rage making him behave like a rabid beast to those he loved.

"Who has my phone? Give it to me, please," he demanded, palm up, fingers gesturing in a quick back-and-forth motion that indicated his impatience.

Mason slapped the device into his hand. "Don't do anything stupid."

"Fuck off," Zack growled and dialed Bucky to ream him out and demand results. "I don't want excuses, Buck. Find them, or I will. I can promise you, if I do, it won't be pretty."

CHAPTER

NINETEEN

"I want to be alone, Erica."

Zack's forearm rested on the window casing, and one fisted hand sat deep in the pocket of his jeans. Tension lined his hunched shoulders.

"I can't leave you to wallow. This issue concerns us both, Zack. Please don't shut me out."

"Look, I did as you asked. I'm letting the cops handle it. Don't expect me to like it."

Three days ago, she'd basically unmanned him in front of a roomful of people. Made him feel useless to help resolve the problem. He'd been frosty and distant ever since with no chance of thawing.

A large part of her was grateful her parents returned home yesterday. She didn't want her mother to believe she'd made another poor choice.

His annoyed sigh drew her notice. "I'll be out to make dinner in a bit."

"That's not why I'm here, Zack. You don't need to take care of me or cook for me. I can manage for myself," she snapped.

His derisive snort infuriated her. This whole fiasco was getting to her, too. Did he really think it only involved him?

"You know what? Fuck it. I'm outta here." She threw up her hands, prepared to exit.

"What the hell does that mean?" he demanded.

"Exactly what I said. I'm leaving. You didn't ask for this nightmare, but neither did I," she said. "You've been a bear with a sore paw, growling at anyone and everyone. Well, I've had it."

Disbelief flashed across his face, quickly followed by cold fury. "Wow, you're one to talk. I've dealt with you swearing at me over coffee, pizza, and exercise. I've opened my home to your ungrateful ass. What have I gotten for it but a headache and my kid shuffled off to his grandparents?"

His hostile retort stole her breath. It was reminiscent of how she'd been addressed by ex-lovers. What was it about her that brought out the worst in others?

"So much for love, huh?" she whispered achingly. "I'll be out of your hair within the hour."

"Erica, wait!" His shout followed her out of his office.

She hurried away, not ready for a knock-down-drag-out fight. Not ready to ruin the sweeter memories lingering on the fringes of her mind.

The disdain on his face had been the worst. She wondered how long he'd felt the way he did. Jesus, only a week ago, he was professing his love.

It had all been too much, too soon. Experience had taught her to go slow, but no! She had jumped without a parachute or a thought of consequences should the ground rush up to meet her. And it always did. *Always*.

Well, she was freefalling this time, too. Their whirlwind romance was over.

Rushing into the main bedroom, she slammed and locked the door. Then she leaned against it, fully expecting tears to accompany her ragged breaths. They never made an appearance. She was too numb. Bonus. Hysterics never solved anything anyway.

Zack rattled the knob, then pounded on the door in time with her galloping pulse. "Open up, Erica."

"You wanted to be alone, so go be alone. I'm packing."

"Open the door, or I'll break it down," he threatened.

"Go screw yourself," she shouted, hitting the wood to emphasize her anger.

"You'd better back away because I'm getting ready to kick it open."

"Don't you dare!"

"Then open the fucking door!"

She hurriedly unlocked and whipped it back, allowing him access. "There. Happy, asshole?"

He towered above her, over six feet of seething male. It shouldn't have made her hot, but the tightening, tingly sensation in her nether region assured her it did.

"I forbid you to leave this house." His arrogance grated on her frayed nerves.

"What?"

"You heard me."

"Are you out of your goddamned mind? If you think you can come in here and order me about, you'd best think again. I can promise you, I'll do the total opposite."

Toe-to-toe, nose to nose, they stood, unblinking. Their breathing erratic.

Zack was the first to break. He raked a hand through his hair and scrubbed his scalp, hard.

"Please... please, don't leave," he said, moderating his tone. "I don't want you to go."

"You don't get to be ugly to me and then pull an about-face." She poked his chest. "Not you! You're supposed to be the nice one."

He captured her hand and placed it over his thudding heart. "I'm sorry. You have to know I didn't mean *any* of it."

Now Erica's damned tears started. Vulnerable and hurting, she yanked her hand back. She pivoted away, ready to stalk out before she embarrassed herself for the millionth time since this dreadful New Year started.

"Babe."

His torment couldn't be denied. The tortured sound, more than anything, caused her to pause and reevaluate her decision to leave. She had a choice: Swallow her pride or cling tight to it and discard what they were building toward. The loneliness of her career choice and self-imposed isolation loomed large. But fear of being alone couldn't be the only reason she stayed. Mutual respect was necessary, or she would be miserable and feel trapped in short order.

Unable to propel her feet forward, she remained motionless.

Zack seized advantage of her hesitation. His arms encircled her from behind, and he tenderly eased her backward against his rock-hard frame, curling protectively around her.

"I don't know how to make you believe me, Erica. Believe I want you to stay. Aside from Jacob, you're the absolute best thing in my life." He sighed, his chest expanding into her back. "I'm frustrated with Bucky and the rest of the PD. This is taking way too long. That crazy bitch is out there and could decide to strike at any time."

Her throat was thick with all the overcharged feelings she was experiencing—love, regret, anger, fear, and a whole host of others —and it paralyzed her vocal cords.

He buried his nose in her hair and inhaled deeply. "I lashed out at the one person who didn't deserve it. *You.*"

"Do you really think I'm ungrateful?" she managed to ask past the lump in her throat.

"God, no! Far from it. You've thanked me nonstop from the night your house burned down. And you've been an angel to my kid. He loves you as much, if not more, than I do."

"Then why? What made you say that?"

She wiggled around until they were face-to-face. His eyes would tell the truth, and she needed them to attest to his candor.

"You said you were leaving. It kills me to believe you'd walk out because I'm a surly ass. Growing up with two brothers, my first instinct was to lash out. But I hurt you, and it was a dick move."

"It doesn't change my decision to go."

He dropped his arms, closed his eyes, and hung his head. A muscle ticked in the side of his jaw.

"So I've ruined everything with my temper." His voice was lifeless.

"No!" she insisted.

His eyes flew open, and hope flickered within their depths.

"You ruined nothing, Zack. I swear. But when I leave, you and Jacob can go back to normal. Maybe down the road, the psycho from hell will have moved on, and if you're willing, we can try again and see where this leads."

"Why leave at all?"

"I can't derail your life anymore. It's destroying me," Erica replied achingly. "It's harming your relationship with your son and brothers. They shouldn't have to run the business without you."

He stepped forward and clasped her face between his palms. After judging to see if she was receptive, he kissed her. When he lifted his head, he bent his knees and leveled his gaze with hers.

"It will destroy *me* knowing you're out there, by yourself and vulnerable. There's no guarantee this person won't come after you even if you go. He or she is twisted, and you can't anticipate their next move."

"I don't know what to do," she confessed.

"Stay."

With a mourning sigh for the death of her determination and willpower, she nodded her agreement.

His relieved grin was a balm to her wounded soul, and she laughed when he scooped her up and carried her to the bed. As they lay there on their sides, he traced her lips with the pad of his thumb.

"Thank you, babe."

Erica closed her lids against the building moisture. Gah! When was she going to stop crying? It was difficult when his tenderness plucked her heartstrings.

"I love you, Erica. I always have." His voice was thick with feeling. "Can you believe I remember the first time I saw you?"

Her eyes flew wide and locked with his. Staunch devotion shone in their blue depths

"You were such a dainty, prissy thing. Your sunshine-yellow dress had a thick green ribbon at the waist, and it was tied in a perfect bow in the back. You were an untouchable princess. Your hair was curlier, down to your shoulders, and the sides were clipped up with sunflower barrettes. The color was different. Lighter. More orange than this deeper auburn." He toyed with a strand as he recalled their initial meeting. "You stood at the front of our class, being introduced by Mrs. Clark, and your shyness endeared you to me. My heart literally skipped a beat when you picked the seat in front of me."

"You're making that up," she accused.

"No. I swear I'm not. I'll never understand why, or even how it happened so quickly, but I've loved you from the first moment I saw you."

"But you were mean to me! That was my favorite dress, and you hit me with a clump of mud."

His laughter was a deeper, more robust echo of the child he was twenty-plus years ago. "I wanted your attention. Also, I wanted to ruin your untouchable air."

"Well, you owe me a new dress. The way I remember it, my mother couldn't get the stain out."

"We'll go the first day you're up to shopping." He held up two fingers. "Scout's honor."

"You were never a Boy Scout," she accused, unfurling another of his fingers. "This represents a *true* Scout's pledge."

"Busted."

They dissolved into laughter.

"Want to know something?" Erica asked. When he nodded, she said, "I almost cried when I sat down and couldn't find a pencil in my backpack. Then you leaned forward and handed me yours. I fell for you the second you did." She nuzzled his jaw. "That feeling never went away."

"Really?"

"Really. Although I had second thoughts after you dirtied my dress on the playground," she told him. "I remember going home and sobbing. My mother said things would change and you'd be nicer in another nine or ten years."

"And I was, wasn't I?" he stated smugly.

"Not that I recall," she said to take him down a peg.

"I asked you to prom," he reminded her.

"Yeah, we both know I thought it was a joke. What does *that* tell you?"

"You have a suspicious mind? Must be why you write romantic *suspense*."

"Pfft."

"I can tell I'll be making this up to you for life. Want to start with pizza for dinner tonight?"

"Hell, yes! Should we invite Jacob?"

"Actually, I want to spend tonight with you. Just us," he added, giving her a sweet-as-honey kiss before shifting to exit the bed. "An apology, if you'll accept it."

Erica nodded. "How about we forgive each other?"

"Deal. I'll call it in. Be right back."

She fluffed the pillows and rested her back against the headboard. Tentatively, she probed her wound, testing the healing process. Not that she was a doctor, but the sensitivity level would give her a good indication of when she'd be able to get busy seducing Zack.

They were well past her body-image issues, and he was right. Having seen her naked multiple times, through no fault of her own, he hadn't run screaming in the other direction. For whatever reason, he found her attractive and loved her. She wasn't looking *that* gift horse in the mouth.

Footsteps heralded his return. A shiver of awareness ran through her when he stopped inside the doorway.

"Why do you look guilty?" He tilted his head, and the corners of his mouth turned up, flashing those delightful dimples.

"Guilty? I don't know what you're talking about," she demurred.

He studied her, a questioning frown tugging at his brow. "You're definitely up to something."

"How long before the pizza arrives?"

"Why?"

Instead of answering, Erica studied him in turn. He had a beautifully casual grace. Even now, dressed in a t-shirt and jeans with his hands stuffed in his pockets, leaning one shoulder against the door molding, he exuded sex appeal. It occurred to her she had yet to see him naked.

"Get undressed," she ordered.

Shock wiped the adorable arrogance from his face, and he slowly straightened. "What?"

"You heard me. Get naked."

CHAPTER

TWENTY

Erica's low, throaty demand drained the blood from Zack's brain and sent it straight to his dick. It didn't pass go or collect two hundred dollars. If she gave him a hard-on with a few well-spoken words, what might she do when they were both doing the horizontal mambo?

There was her injury to consider, too. Although the goalpost was in sight, a play for the touchdown was currently out of the question.

With all that in mind, Zack was curious about what she planned to do.

His insatiable curiosity needed answers, and he peeled off his shirt, inch by slow inch, as he strolled closer, examining her wonderstruck expression for a sign. His fingers were on the snap of his jeans when she breathlessly commanded him to stop. Her eyes were laser-focused on his abs and flitted to the happy trail below his belly button. With a wicked grin, Zack ran his palm along the path her gaze had traveled, leading to his groin.

As his dick thickened, he could feel the teeth of the zipper press into his skin. Ignoring Erica's command, he drew down the tab,

138

tooth by fucking tooth, until his penis sprang free of its confinement. And thank Christ because he couldn't take the pressure of his snug jeans.

Erica's indrawn breath caused him to grow exponentially.

Zack released his trousers, letting them slip to the floor, then stepped free, nude and completely aroused. "What's the plan, babe?"

"For me to give you a blow job," she replied in a rushed breath.

Holy fucking hell!

The idea of her pouty, red mouth sucking him dry sent his cock into fully engorged mode. He'd never expected her response, but his penis celebrated her intent. A pearly bead found its way to the surface as exquisite visions of what was about to happen chased each other through his mind.

Then he didn't have to fantasize another moment.

Erica crawled toward him. With one wicked glance from under her dark lashes, she went to work, focusing entirely on her objective.

When her hot, wet mouth welcomed him, he moaned and entwined his fingers in her hair. She lightly stroked the area behind his balls, as she gripped the base of him in her other fist.

Her bobbing head and moans—as if the act of pleasuring him aroused her, too—was titillating. In zero time at all, his entire body tightened, his hips surged forward, and he ejaculated into the back of her throat.

"Jesus, God! That was... was... *Fuck!* Erica!"

Okay, officially, his brain went by way of his seed, as did any verbal skills.

She settled back against the pillow and sent him a smug, knowing smirk.

Zack inhaled sharply, feeling every bit as disconcerted as when she'd first made her suggestive comment.

She was Aphrodite in her element.

A sultry sex goddess come to life.

Had she been draped in a white Grecian gown, with asp bracelets encircling her bare biceps, he would've believed it whole-heartedly.

"I've never shot off so fast in my life. Not even when I was a scrawny teenager dreaming of scoring with you after prom."

His confession caused her eyes to sparkle, and she laughed her delight. Had there ever been a more beautiful sight? Not one he recalled.

"Ready for me to reciprocate?"

She sobered and gulped.

"Get naked, babe."

Her shirt was off a helluva lot faster than his own had. Next, she shimmied out of her shorts and silky underwear.

She was perfection. Soft, supple, and with all the proper curves.

Zack took his time, memorizing and thanking Christ for every exposed inch of her creamy skin. He hadn't been aware of holding his breath until he grew lightheaded from the lack of air.

"Extraordinary," he murmured.

Incredibly enough, a second surge of blood rushed to his depleted member. Another one for the record books. He experienced a full erection with a less-than-five-minute recovery time.

Down boy, he told himself.

Erica wasn't ready for full-on intercourse. Driving mindlessly into her the way he preferred would cause her untold pain. There would be time for sexual calisthenics when she was healed. After the stitches were out and she was one hundred percent, it was game on.

Trailing the tips of his fingers up her shapely calves to her knees, he gently parted her thighs, never breaking eye contact. Trepidation was written on her lovely visage, and his soul ached at the sight. That she doubted her desirability for one goddamned second was a crying shame.

"You are the most beautiful woman I've ever had the good

fortune to meet," he said. "It's taking everything I possess not to drag you down and pound into you until you scream your pleasure, babe."

Her sharp inhale and longing gaze pleased him, and he grinned. "Too much?"

She shook her head, eyes wide.

"Good. When you're able, you can bet I plan to make the Kama Sutra look like foreplay."

"Ohdeargod!"

"I'll sample every part of your delectable body. Feed on every sigh you make. Revel in every pleasure-filled cry falling from your lips. You'll beg by the time I'm done. Then, and only then, will you realize how much I want you. How much you mean to me. Do you understand, Erica?" he asked huskily. "Can you truly appreciate how much I desire you?"

A single jerky nod was all she afforded him.

"Good." With that, he dipped down and tasted her.

He followed up with a soft blowing of air as he teased apart her folds. Filling her opening, he ran the tips of his fingers along the top wall of her vagina, applying pressure. He withdrew with excruciating slowness before entering her again. As he made love to her using only his hand and tongue, Zack enjoyed every second. When she crested, Erica's hips bucked upward, as if she intended to grind her pelvis into his face. He laughed as he held her in place, careful of her healing wound.

The satisfaction he felt in bringing her to completion was no small thing. He felt like he'd achieved the impossible by clearing her ever-active mind. And she was embracing the moment, allowing herself to simply feel. To experience pleasure with no strings or agendas. To know what it was like to have someone who loved her worship her so thoroughly with his mouth.

Raining light, lingering kisses along her inner thigh, Zack caressed the back of her knees, waiting for her to calm before he dove in to taste her for round two. The doorbell rang as the last of her cries died away.

"Damn," he expelled on a sigh. "I think it's the first time Tony's has ever been early with a delivery."

"And it may be the first time I don't give a shit about pizza," she replied with a dazed look.

Zack did his best not to preen. "Be right back."

He tugged on his jeans and went to pay for their food. And sure, there may have been a cocky strut to his stride. On the return trip, he swiped an old towel from the hall closet. He tossed it to Erica as he approached and waited until she doubled it to protect the comforter, then he chose a spot across from her and set the box between them.

They sat cross-legged, eating their pizza directly from the cardboard container like they might've done if they'd hooked up as teenagers. Zack toyed with confessing that he received a clear glimpse of her beautifully landscaped girl grotto whenever she lifted the slice for a bite but quickly dismissed it.

The view was too enjoyable. Plus, if he said something, She was certain to cover up and spoil his fun.

"How many calories are burned during an orgasm?" she asked.

He choked on a pepperoni. She smothered her laugh—barely— as he hacked up a lung.

Zack glared between coughs.

"What?" Her look was decidedly innocent. The twinkle in her eye belied her guiltless act.

"You almost killed me with your ridiculous question. Have you no remorse, woman?"

"None whatsoever," she retorted, gracing him with a smug smile. "Pass me another slice of cheese, will ya? If I reach for it, I'll ruin your view, perv."

"Busted." He laughed, having never experienced such a perfect moment.

Zack hadn't expected his worrisome morning to turn into a

beautiful evening, but he was grateful Erica had decided to stay. There wouldn't have been a moment's peace if she had left as she threatened to. The harrowing thoughts would've kept him up nights, and his days would've been spent in sheer misery.

"I love you, Erica."

For an instant, she appeared startled. As she regained her composure, her face reflected glowing contentment and a love to match his. The light of adoration in her eyes made him feel ten feet tall and bulletproof.

He sobered.

He might need to be before it was all said and done. One way or another, her attacker needed to be stopped. His entire world hung in the balance.

CHAPTER

TWENTY-ONE

The weeks that followed were golden, ideal even, with the one small exception of the texted threats hanging over their heads. In the back of Zack's mind, he feared another attack against Erica. Every mysterious bump in the night had him on edge. More than once, he'd woken in a cold sweat, heart hammering. He'd rush to find her and assure himself she was safe.

He didn't know how Erica remained so calm and unruffled. Whenever he sought her out, he would find her absorbed in her current project or deep-diving into research, oblivious to her surroundings. Unfortunately for him, he couldn't go through life so blithely. Since his brothers were taking care of the excess business workload, Zack had a lot of free time on his hands. The inaction was maddening, and in multiple instances, he found himself grinding his teeth in frustration. Before everything was over, he'd have flat molars.

Bucky and his cohorts at the PD had come up with nothing. The routine patrols on the block were staggered so as not to be obvious, and they'd been kind enough to increase the frequency.

But Erica's stalker was lying low and biding their time. No one believed they'd given up, though.

"She's not going to do anything while you are on high alert, Zack." Erica's sleepy voice traveled through the darkness to where he stood, peering out the blinds to survey the street and adjoining yards.

She was right, and yet sleep was an elusive bitch. An irrational sense of urgency was crowding his mind, making him restless and squirrelly.

"I wish they'd figure out who the fuck is behind this," he said, surly and out of sorts.

"It's going to be okay."

Zack weighed telling her about the random packages being left on the doorstep. How, with all the eyes on their home, did it happen? It wasn't a surprise when the CSI results showed no fingerprints or DNA. The perp clearly knew what he—or she—was doing when it came to avoiding detection.

The contents of those boxes had nearly broken him. One was the barbecued remains of a small animal—innards intact. Another had been a doll, bearing an uncanny likeness to Erica, mouth open in horror, legs charred, and red marks on its chest and back. He assumed they represented stab wounds.

Whoever the fucker was, they had stepped up their terror game. The latest gift of horrors had a note attached.

"SOON!"

Everything within Zack screamed at him to bundle up Erica and Jacob and then skip the country. Australia was nice this time of year. Surely, that damned crackpot wouldn't follow them halfway around the world, right?

"Zack, come back to bed."

The closeness of Erica's voice startled him. Lost in thought, he failed to hear her come up behind him.

Shit.

He had to get his mind back in the game. If she snuck up without trying, what could an intentionally stealthy person do?

"I can't sleep, babe," he replied, keeping watch.

She laughed, then kissed his bare shoulder. "Who said anything about sleep?"

His attention was fully engaged, and standing as close as they were, he saw the satisfied curl of her lips. Naughty Erica had come out to play. Zack fucking loved when her confident goddess emerged.

"Oh, well, in that case." He grabbed her wrist and hauled her back to bed. They fell hard among laughter and kisses. Right when he would've assumed the dominant position, she shoved him flat on his back and straddled his hips.

"Mmm, nope. I got this," she purred.

Leaning in, she grazed her teeth across first one of his nipples, then the other. Desire was never far from the surface when they were together. Her aggressiveness in bed made him burn hotter and faster than ever.

She impaled herself on his hardness.

"*Godddddammmmnn!*" he groaned in pleasure, as she took the lead and rocked her hips against him.

Her tightness worked its magic, and he was ready to lose himself in the wondrous feel of her. When she clenched her muscles and increased pressure, she took him to heaven. He held her hips as he surged up, pumping into her and bringing her with him.

She collapsed on top of him and found a home on the cradle of his arms.

"Where did that come from? I'm not complaining, but damn, woman!"

He drew the blanket over her shoulders.

She laughed, shifted to kiss him, and snuggled the top of her head under his chin. "I don't know. I think it was the moonlight glinting off those unreal abs of yours. I got all kinds of hot and bothered."

"Remind me to install a moonroof—soon!"

Her giggle warmed the part of him still chilled from the danger surrounding her.

"Try to sleep, Zack. I'm going to write for a bit. I'll check the locks and alarm."

He patted her ass and rolled over to welcome oblivion. A few hours wouldn't hurt if she was staying awake.

Perched on the edge of the bed, Erica stroked Zack's hair as he drifted off. Her heart was full to damned near bursting. No one had ever loved her as much.

Her worry about the entire situation included his lack of sleep and constant vigilance. He was relentless in his desire to keep her safe. But she had no intentions of sharing her fears with him. His stress level was unhealthy, and the dark circles under his eyes attested to his restlessness.

If the police didn't find the person creating their living hell soon, Erica would be forced to leave. Zack and Jacob deserved a normal life, and it wasn't possible with all this chaos happening. It wasn't fair to Zack's son to be displaced for her sake.

On the business front, Mason and Dane had been taking on the lion's share of the workload for the better part of a month. They deserved a break, too.

The dissected rodents were supposed to be kept secret from her. However, she maintained one or two trusty contacts at the department, who helped her with police procedure research for her books. They'd been forthcoming with information when she'd asked.

After slipping on a t-shirt and yoga pants, Erica went in search of McFatty. She found him highlighted by a shaft of moonlight. Perched on the back of an armchair, he stared unblinkingly out the bay window. His tail was puffed and twitching like he'd seen a bird or squirrel.

Neither was probable this late at night. A threat was close. Long ago, she'd learned to trust his instincts.

Dropping to the floor, she army crawled to the window. With slow precision, she inched up to peek over the rim of the sill. Across the road, in the driver's seat of a four-door sedan, a person toyed with an object, causing light to flicker on and off. A lighter, if Erica wasn't mistaken. It flared a few times, then stopped altogether. The watcher slid down as a patrol car passed.

As the cruiser's spotlight swept Zack's house window, Erica ducked out of sight. She didn't want to make it obvious anyone was awake in the house. She counted to twenty and peered over the ledge again. The watcher's agitated routine had resumed.

Heart thudding, Erica eased onto the floor and crawled past the front window. When she was clear, she jumped up and booked it to the bedroom, intending to retrieve her phone. In her nervousness, she fumbled it, and the thud was overly loud in the silence.

"What the fu—!" Zack covered his heart as he rested back against the headboard and exhaled loudly. "Christ, Erica. You scared the shit out of me."

"Zack, I need you to listen to me very carefully," she said.

He came alert in an instant.

"What's going on?" he asked. His tone held a dangerous quality, and she feared for the person in the car if he ever got ahold of them.

"Don't do anything rash." When he whipped the covers back, Erica held up a hand. "Promise me."

"Erica, start talking."

"Not before you promise," she insisted.

"Fine."

"That's not a promise."

"It's all you're getting. Talk," he commanded.

She struggled with indecision. Zack was the type to charge into battle without any thought to self-preservation, and fear for him seized her vocal cords.

"Erica!" He gripped her shoulders. "What the hell is going on?"

"I think our stalker is across the street."

"Jesus H—!"

She stilled his hand as he reached to turn on the lamp. "No! We can't alert her we're up."

In the moonlit room, the fervency shining from his eyes terrified her. Even when he was angry enough to break the door down during their argument, he'd never reached the level of fury he currently displayed.

"When last I looked, she was in her car, flicking a cigarette lighter."

Zack paused in the middle of pulling on his jeans, one leg in, one leg out. An expression akin to confusion clouded his features.

"Flicking a lighter?" He made a gesture with his hand. "Like this."

"Exactly like that! How did you know?"

"She's still alive!"

Propelled into action, Zack was dressed in record time and cramming his feet into sneakers without socks, barely stopping long enough to tie the laces. "I don't know how, but she's still alive."

"Who?" Erica struggled to keep up with the conversation.

"Christie."

The shock sent her jaw plunging to her chest.

"Jacob's mother?" she asked.

He nodded briskly. "This is what I want you to do. Call nine-one-one and get an officer out here, stat! Then I want you to find anything you can use as a weapon and close yourself in the master bathroom. There's a lock on the door. Make sure to engage it."

Her heart tripped. "Why? Where are you going?"

His lips flattened.

"No! Nope. Not gonna happen." She emphatically shook her head. "Not out there, you're not!"

"She won't hurt me," Zack assured her.

She grabbed his arm in a death grip. "You don't know that. Hell, you can't even be sure it's her."

"It is. This all makes sense now."

"Please don't go. If it *is* Christie, she's unstable," Erica cried. Hysteria rose in her voice. Cringy, yes, but the thought of Zack injured or killed by that whack job had sent her into a panic.

"Babe." He wrapped a gentle hand around her neck and drew her close. "She's always been obsessed with becoming my wife. The chances of her hurting me and destroying her main goal are slim. *You*, however, are a different story."

"Don't go. Please." Erica hated to beg, but what was pride when his life might be forfeit?

"I'm going. This needs to end." He tilted her chin up. "Call the police and then barricade yourself in the bathroom. Stay on the line with them. No matter what you hear, you don't unlock that door until I come for you or they're knocking. You got it?"

"Zack. *Please.*"

"Tell me you understand and intend to follow the plan."

"Yes," she whispered, resigned. Stubborn-ass man!

"Good." Zack gave her a hard kiss and strode to the alarm keypad by the back door. "Reactivate this after I go."

"Shouldn't you take your phone or a weapon?" A weapon would be good. Adrenaline, mixed with copious amounts of anxiety, coursed through Erica, and she trembled.

"Don't forget to lock the door, set the alarm, and call the police."

She snorted. "As if I could!"

He cracked a smile, but it instantly vanished. "I'll wait one minute before I head across the street. That should give you enough time to hide."

Her head jerked up and down in reluctant agreement. She scarcely had any control over her body at this stage.

"Erica." Zack's deep, calm voice penetrated her numb mind. "Give me your phone, babe." As soon as she complied, he typed in her code and dialed 911. "This is Zack Sharp, 116 Eastside Lane. I need an officer to investigate a suspicious person in front of my house. We suspect it's the stalker who attacked my girlfriend and burnt her home down. Officer Bucky Whitmore knows this case. Here's my girlfriend, Erica."

He handed her the phone and ran out the door. Tapping the glass once, he pointed to the alarm with a hard look. She waved him off with a scowl.

TWENTY-TWO

Once the door was locked and the alarm set, Erica ignored Zack's instructions to hide herself in the bathroom. Instead, she grabbed a large knife and crept to the front window, careful to stay out of view. Sure enough, Christie was still in the vehicle across the road.

"Ma'am? Ma'am, are you there? Where did Mr. Sharp go?" The dispatcher's crisp, no-nonsense questions flooded the line.

"Yes, I'm here," Erica replied absently. "He went to confront her."

"Who is she? Do you know the woman he went to see?"

"No, I don't. But he thinks it's his ex-girlfriend. Is someone on the way? I'm not comfortable with him out there alone. She's crazy."

The dispatcher's voice turned suspicious. "I thought you just said you didn't know who she was."

"That's right, but he thinks she was the one responsible for setting my house on fire and stabbing me a few weeks ago. Can you hurry the officer, please? One drove by less than five minutes ago."

Erica listened as the operator radioed a second officer and sent him to their location. Through the phone connection, she heard Bucky's voice come across the com. "Tell Zack not to confront anyone!"

As Erica crouched in front of the bay window, she saw a Zach-sized shadow creep toward the opposite side of the road. The car's occupant must've spotted him, too, and the engine roared to life. Tires squealed as the vehicle pulled away from the curb, and Zack dove for the sidewalk and safety as the fender narrowly missed him.

"She's getting away! Hurry!" Erica screamed into the phone. "Light-colored four-door car. I can't see the plate, but she's heading north."

"Ma'am, please stay calm. We have an officer in the vicinity."

"Hurry!"

She punched in the alarm code on the foyer keypad and jerked the door open in time to see Zack tear across the front lawn. He was ten yards from her, when two law enforcement officers pulled up, blue lights blinding and eardrum-shattering sirens wailing. One jumped out of the squad car and pointed his service Glock at Zack.

"Don't move! Hands where I can see them!"

"No! Wait! Tell the officer he lives here," Erica yelled at the dispatcher. "They've got guns pointed at Zack!"

"Goddamned Barney-Fife motherfuckers," Zack snapped. "She's getting *away!*"

"I said, don't move!"

The command froze him in place, hands in the air. Helplessness and frustration were distinguishable on his face, followed by disgust.

"Ma'am, go back in the house and shut the door," one of the cops instructed.

"No, you don't understand. He lives here," she argued. Her forward momentum sent the other officer's trigger-happy hand to his holster.

"Do *not* take another step," he commanded.

"Listen..."

"Erica," Zack said, urgency in his low tone. *"Stop moving!"*

She halted mid-step, eyes locked with his. The nod he gave her was barely discernible, but he was reassuring her everything would be straightened out in due time.

"Both of you, down on your knees, hands behind your head."

"You're being extreme," Erica replied. When they refused to let up, she growled. "Where did you get your badge? A crackerjack box?"

"Lady, are you looking to be tased?" The officer's voice was pissy, and there was no room for negotiation. He *was* the law.

Zack snorted his amusement.

"Really?" she hissed at him.

"I'm not telling you again, ma'am. If you don't get down on the ground, I *will* tase you."

"You dare, and I'll—"

She'd ventured close to Zack, and without preamble, he reached up to jerk her down beside him. "She's kneeling. Don't be hasty, Officer."

"I swear to God, when Bucky gets here, I'm going to punch him in the ball sack," Erica promised, on the verge of homicide.

"Ma'am, you realize it's against the law to strike an officer. It's called—"

"She knows," Zack said in a clipped tone with a glare for her. "Be quiet," he mouthed silently.

"You could man up, ya know," she retorted.

"Seriously? You want *me* to get shot? For what? Because you can't shut up?" he asked incredulously.

"I should've told them *you* were the perp. Maybe they'd have shot you in the ass."

Bucky's laughter rang out from behind them. "This is priceless. When you two aren't sucking face, you're fighting like cats and dogs."

Erica surged to her feet and charged, only to be restrained by Zack. Officer Itchy Trigger Finger went for his gun again, but Bucky was quick to put his hand up, forestalling him. The jerk didn't try to hide his amusement as he said, "She's fine. Zack won't let her hurt me. Y'all can go write your report."

"How about they look for the crazy bitch stalking us? Huh?" Erica snarled. "Think they can actually search out criminals instead of frightening law-abiding citizens?"

Another snort escaped Zack. "I think you frightened them worse."

"Shut it," she snapped, poking him in the abs and making him wince.

"Officer Tidwell here is a rookie and quick to react," Bucky said by way of an apology.

"Well, he should have reacted and gone after Christie." Erica was pissed off to her core. Once again, Christie was in the wind, and they had to live their lives in fear of when she'd strike next.

"Christie?" Bucky's surprise and concern were apparent in the way he spoke the question. That she'd supposedly died in the hospital fire was well known. "What's this about Christie? We *are* talking about Christie Bauer, right?"

Erica searched for the cell phone she'd dropped during the commotion. Surprisingly, the dispatcher was lingering on the other end of the line. As the operator lectured her on how *not* to greet a law enforcement officer, Erica disconnected and glanced around at the neighbors gathering in front of their homes.

Charlie was headed in their direction, and Erica didn't want to be part of the discussion involving the man's not-dead daughter. She stormed into the house, swept up her laptop from the counter, and headed to the guest room. Her novel wouldn't write itself, and this clusterfuck had put her in the mood to write a murder scene.

CHAPTER

TWENTY-THREE

The manhunt for Christie was in full swing, and as the hours passed, Zack pondered how one person escaped detection in such a small town as theirs. If he didn't know any better, he'd swear she had an in at the PD.

Over the last day and a half, threats continued to blow up his phone and set his teeth on edge. He'd floated the idea of blocking the number, but Erica had talked him out of it. Her reasoning was that when Christie was harassing, she wasn't attacking. Twisted logic, but accurate. Regardless, he'd breathe better when she was in custody.

Valentine's Day had arrived, and they were determined not to sit around, playing victims. They'd agreed on a shared romantic dinner and dancing. It was their first official date of sorts, and Zack couldn't believe how nervous he was about the whole affair.

As he waited for Erica to dress and put the finishing touches on her makeup, Zack entered their room for a pair of socks. He stumbled when he saw Erica in nothing but a bra and matching lacy panties. Mouth dry and dick setting up shop under the tent in his slacks, he backed from the room. He wanted to sweep her up, deposit her on the bed, then screw her brains out until sunrise.

But he wouldn't.

Considering everything she'd been through, she deserved a special evening. If that meant keeping it in his pants a while longer, he would. After wiping his damp hands on his pant legs, Zack paced the living room and conjured generic, non-sexual thoughts. But if she didn't finish dressing and leave the bedroom soon, his control was bound to snap.

As if on cue, Erica joined him.

The air whooshed from his lungs, and her shy smile scrambled his brain cells to the wind. The way she peered at him from under her thick sweep of lashes was reminiscent of the days when she'd tutor him. She would peek at him when she thought he wasn't paying attention. The funny part? He was *always* paying attention. There was really no choice. Everything about her drew him in. The way she tilted her head in question, her bashful half grin, and her rocking body were temptation personified. As was her lack of vanity. Her inability to see how lovely and giving a soul she possessed, was nothing short of wondrous.

"Okay, screw going out. Let's stay home and have incredible monkey sex all over the house," he suggested.

Her happy laugh pleased him, making his heart fuller.

"Is that a yes?"

"No. I'm starving," she replied with a beatific smile. "Where are you taking me? You haven't said."

"It's a surprise. I *will* say we're going to the city." Zack held out a hand and pulled her close when she placed hers in his. Avoiding her gloss-covered lips, he kissed her temple. "All set?"

"Absolutely, but did you call Jacob to wish him a good night? Should we stop there first?"

Her consideration was another of her endearing qualities.

"Thank you for being kind to Jacob. It means the world to me to know you care enough to put him first."

"I adore him. I only wish he wasn't being kicked out of his own home because of…"

Zack knew exactly why she trailed off. Neither of them wanted to address Christie today.

"I already called him, babe. He said he wants to come home, and I've talked to Charlie and Judith. They both agree he should. We can't continue to live in limbo. God knows when Christie will step up her game."

"How did they take the news she's alive?"

"They were rightfully upset. I mean, can you imagine believing your daughter died in a fire only to learn she faked the whole thing?"

"No." Sadness flashed across Erica's face. As fast as it had appeared, it was gone. In its place was resoluteness. "Zack—"

"No," he stated firmly.

"You don't even know what I intended to say."

"I do, and the answer is no."

"You don't, and I'd like to get a word in edgewise."

"So talk," he invited, challenge in every line of his body.

"Before you rudely interrupted me, I'd planned to say I should stay with my parents in Florida."

"We've been through this before. It's a tired record, Erica. I have no intention of letting you out of my sight until this threat is neutralized. After that, if you are hell-bent on leaving me, we'll readdress the issue."

Erica huffed out a breath. He trailed after her as she marched into the kitchen and flung her purse on the counter. Hands on hips, she stared him down. Her stance was full-on combative, and seeing her in a lather amped up his juices. His inner horn dog welcomed the idea of angry sex. Giving an internal eye roll, he wondered what type of sex he wouldn't want with her.

"Let's not do this tonight, babe," he wheedled. "Why can't the argument wait until morning?"

"Why does it have to be an argument? How about you understand I'm an adult capable of making my own decisions?" she asked.

That she wasn't screaming, that she'd remained semi-calm and presented the questions in a reasonable manner, worried him. Clearly, she'd given this serious thought.

Searching for any excuse, he pounced upon the first his brain came up with. "We have reservations."

Her raised brows and wide-eyed stare told him the lame excuse wouldn't work.

Sighing, he sunk onto a bar stool. "All I want is to spend time with you without any outside influences. To eat a great meal in a romantic setting and hold you in my arms while we dance afterward would make me ecstatic. If this is all you're permitting us, can we have this one perfect night?"

She closed her eyes. "Yes."

"Thank you," he said, his voice thick and husky with gratitude.

Zack gathered her close and cradled her face in his hands, admiring her tear-bright chocolate eyes, with their thick lashes, the arched brows no longer lifted in challenge, her straight—if slightly long—nose, her high cheekbones, and her perfectly pouty pink lips begging to be kissed. And kiss them, he did. Slow and soft, before deep and seeking. What he sought, he didn't know. Maybe he wanted to sear into her mind how much he desired and loved her. Maybe he wanted her to remember this shared earth-shattering desire when she was hundreds of miles away. Or maybe it was to persuade her not to leave at all because she loved him, too.

Fighting the impulse to lead her to the bedroom, he pulled back and ran a thumb over her kiss-swollen mouth. Her lipgloss needed to be reapplied, and she wouldn't thank him for the mess he'd made of it, but damn, it made her sexier. She resembled a tumbled sex kitten fresh from the sheets. The kind who left nail and bite marks on his flesh.

"I love you, Erica," he said without any agenda, speaking only because it needed to be uttered. It was imperative she knew how much he cared.

The moisture in her eyes built again, spilling over to trail down her cheek. She pursed her lips as if to speak, but no words formed over her convulsive swallowing. He knew she was speechless from past experience. He'd been there when strong emotion hit her.

She loved him, too. There was no doubt in his mind.

"It's okay, babe. Go touch up your makeup, then we'll head out."

CHAPTER

TWENTY-FOUR

Zack pulled out all the stops for dinner, and Erica couldn't recall a time when she'd been so spoiled. The meal was incredible and like nothing she'd tasted. From the appetizer to the dessert, she consumed each bite with relish and a moan, much to Zack's amusement.

"Okay, I have to admit, this was a great idea," Erica said slipping her arm through his. As they strolled along the river walkway, she admired the dancing moonlight on the water's surface. "I love this area of downtown."

Even though they were bundled up against the cold, damp night, magic swirled in the air, touching on them. Other couples wandered hand in hand and lent to the overall romantic atmosphere.

Erica tugged Zack to a stop to behold the stars in the vast night sky. Ah, the mysteries they held. Was it written they would get their happy ending? Or were the planets aligned in Christie's favor? Life and relationships shouldn't be so hard.

"You seem serious suddenly. What's going on, babe?"

The rich tone of Zack's voice startled her out of her musings.

"It's nothing."

"Should I be a guy and act like I'm taking your comment at face value, all the while secretly trying to avoid the landmine waiting for me?" he asked dryly. He rested an elbow on the railing, and the breeze tossed his inky locks over one brow, giving him a carefree piratical vibe.

Unable to help herself, she laughed. "Could you be any more perfect?"

"Most definitely. But I'm glad you think I am."

Erica pressed her mouth to his. As she shifted away, he wrapped an arm around her waist and held her against him. She delighted in the warmth and safety his embrace provided. With her ear pressed against his heart, she couldn't be more content.

"I love you, Zack. I wasn't able to say it earlier, but I didn't want another second to pass without you knowing the truth in my heart."

"I *do* know. It's in everything you do, Erica. The way—holy shit!" Without warning, he tackled her to the ground.

Stunned breathless, lost to what was happening, she lay there. Adrenaline kicked in, causing her heart to thrum loudly in her ears. She barely registered the resounding pops, uncertain what they were or from where they were originating.

"Are you all right? Erica! Tell me you're all right!" Zack's agitation increased as she remained silent and tried to form a coherent thought. *"Babe!"*

In place of words, she gripped his jaw and nodded.

"Jesus! That was close. Stay here," he ordered, prepared to spring into action. "Call 911."

She snagged his sleeve and refused to let go. "You are *not* going to do what I think you're planning."

"She's getting away," he cried. "It's our chance to capture her."

"Did she or didn't she just take a shot at us?"

"She did."

"So your plan is to chase after a psycho *who has a gun?*"

"Dammit, Erica! She's get—"

"Yeah, yeah, yeah," she snapped. "I know. Well, let her. Tomorrow, we *all* move to Florida."

He plunked down next to her and pulled out his cell to call the police. Dispatch informed him officers were already on their way from another report.

His impotent rage simmered between them. Sitting this close, it was impossible not to feel his furious energy. It was a living, breathing entity. His inability to look at her, the staring off into the darkness in the direction Christie had fled, and the beating of his fist on his thigh were all signs of his heightened emotions. Half of her brain screamed at her to remain silent, but the not-so-smart side decided to speak up.

"How did she know we were here?"

"What?"

"I watched you on the drive, Zack. You took every precaution. Multiple turns, running the yellow lights, pulling off at a different exit. Hell, if I didn't know any better, I would've said you had spy training."

His brows collided. "That's a damn good question. Only her parents knew we were going to dinner. I never said where."

"Have you ever brought her here?"

"No. The restaurant opened right before Christmas. The reservation list is months out." He scratched his jaw, thoughtful.

"A guess on her part, then," Erica concluded.

"No, I don't see how. The open table fell into my lap. Bucky booked it some time ago, and he offered it to me two nights ago, after his date fell through," he told her. "He suggested I take you out as a surprise. Said it might help you forget about what's been happening lately."

Erica's mind raced, trying to make the puzzle pieces fit. "Zack, I want you to think back carefully. Did Bucky and Christie ever know each other? Were they friends?"

His hand tightened over hers, close to crushing her fingers.

"What are you saying?"

"There have been one too many coincidences. Humor me."

"Yeah. I think they may have been friends. I seemed to recall her saying something to that effect once."

"How deep did their friendship go? How did he take her 'death'?"

"Hard," he answered, voice grim. "He literally broke down, sobbing, at the service." He slapped a hand against his forehead. "Ah, Christ! How the hell did I miss it?"

"You see the connection, too? It's not my writer brain seeing a plot where none exists?"

"That he happened to be working every time she's attacked? That in a town where the response time should be mere minutes, it's taken officers ten or more to arrive after a call? That he seems too fucking jolly after he shows up? And he does show up, doesn't he? Every time."

"She has to have assistance. I can't determine how she's pulling all this off by herself," she said. Her teeth worried her lip as she thought back. "You said something about the night my house burned down. Christie hacked your tires before heading to my house. Do you think she had enough time?"

"What do you mean?"

"You said the hooded person struck you as bigger than Christie should've been and that they 'ran' away. Not that they jumped in a car and drove."

"Right, but I also spent time filing a police report."

"True. Where was Bucky? Was he at *that* particular incident?"

"What are you accusing me of, Erica?" Bucky's biting voice drifted out of the darkness, giving her an awful fright.

Zack jumped to his feet and gave him a rough shove. "You're the only one who knew where we'd be tonight, Buck. Why don't you start talking? Where are the other uniforms, huh? How did you know we would be in this *exact* location? For that matter, why are you even here?"

"A call on the scanner. I happened to be in town shopping because I had the night off. Jesus, Zack," Bucky exclaimed and rubbed the spot Zach had thumped. "You know me better than that."

"Do I?" Zack's growled response woke the fine hairs on Erica's neck. She almost felt sorry for Bucky.

"We've been friends since school. I would *never* do anything to harm you or Erica. Never!"

"Then why did you meltdown at Christie's funeral the way you did?"

"Jacob. I was thinking about what your poor kid would go through without a mom. He didn't know her well, but she was still his mother." Bucky's expression screamed offended. "My mom died when I was eight, remember?"

Unless Bucky had majored in performing art, he was being truthful. Erica couldn't see any deception on his face. She should know. Having dealt with liars and cheats for years, she was adept at spotting dishonesty.

"He's not lying, Zack."

"*Fuck!*"

Together, she and Bucky waited quietly as Zack paced off his residual anger. After what felt like a century or more, the police joined them, once again late to the party. Zack explained seeing a hooded figure pointing a gun in their direction. Of how he threw Erica to the ground, anticipating she'd been the target, and why. A report was filled out, and they were encouraged to return to the safety of their home.

"I'd like to know what's so fucking safe about my home. Please, feel free to explain it to me," Zack demanded. He nodded his head in her direction. "Erica's was burned to the ground, and even with countless routine patrols, that psycho sits outside my house, stalking us." On the receiving end of their sympathetic looks, he threw up his hands. Once again, no one was rushing to apprehend Christie.

"We live in a goddamned one-horse town where nothing happens, and still, our police force can't find one small woman carving up cars, slicing tires, stabbing residents, and setting houses ablaze," Zack ranted. "For fuck's sake!"

"Sir, have you been drinking tonight?"

"What?"

"Oh, shit," Bucky muttered. Stepping forward to stop World War III from commencing, he gave everyone a conciliatory smile. "Zack's not drunk, guys. You can check the facts of his case with Stonebrooke PD."

Either Zack had been thoroughly shocked by the question, or an aneurism had burst in his brain from head-pounding fury. It scared Erica to witness his immobile stance. She sidled up to him and clasped his hand. "Let's go. Bucky can finish up here."

Worry had her tugging him toward the parking lot. She'd never seen his eyes so bone-chillingly cold, and his face appeared chiseled from granite.

"Baby, please," she whispered, stroking his arm. "Let's just go."

His head inched around, like an automated robot, jerky in its motion. Zack glanced down, acting surprised to see her next to him. His brows drew together as he focused on where she plucked at his coat sleeve. With a twist of his arm, he dislodged her and stomped off.

"Bucky, please come by the house tomorrow if you have time," Erica said. "We need to talk."

"Will do. You'd better hurry."

She whirled back around to find Zack. He paused about thirty feet away to turn, threw up his hands, and bellowed his frustration to the heavens. People paused to watch the scene unfold.

Erica, too, stood transfixed.

Zack appeared immortal. The earthly elements were building around them, and the wind whipped his coat, causing it to flap behind him. Rain drizzled, and the stars had long since gone to bed, having been obscured by the storm clouds. Yet there he was, water streamed down his flinty face. Black hair and dark clothing were barely discernible against the night sky that acted as a backdrop. Brilliant blue eyes reflected lightning as it flared. Fists were clenched and raised up, as if in challenge.

His unbelievable beauty robbed her of breath.

Without warning, he strode in her direction, swept her off her feet, and hugged her. Locked within his embrace as tightly as she was, her ability to inhale was restricted. His arms were steel bands around her rib cage, securing her in place.

She didn't care.

All she wanted was to drink the rain from his lips and to send a huge "fuck you" to their audience. A sixth sense said *she* would be watching. Perhaps Zack sensed it, too. Maybe it was why he so blatantly ravished her mouth right there on the sidewalk. He also didn't seem to care if anyone noticed his impressive erection pressing against her abdomen. Going a step farther, he gripped her thigh and dragged it around his waist, creating groin-to-groin contact.

Erica felt lightheaded and crazy hot for him at the same time. If Zack wanted to throw her down and have sex then and there, she would've been powerless to stop it. Passion swept her along in his wake, blocking out consequence and reason.

Nature raged around them. The drizzle became a downpour, and thunder shook the ground beneath them. The earth's fury made itself known with echoing rumbles. The resounding noise brought them back to themselves long enough to realize humping in a public park would end with them in a jail cell for indecent exposure. It was neither the time nor place for what they truly needed: an affirmation of love and life.

Still, they remained unmoving, gazes locked, seriously overheated. Erica was surprised steam didn't rise from their tangled forms. A slow, wicked smile curled his mouth. A matching one transformed hers. He released her and waited as she kicked off her heels. Together, they raced for the hotel on the far side of the park.

CHAPTER
TWENTY-FIVE

Erica had no recollection of how they'd checked in and made it to their room. She briefly recalled the elevator ride, but only the instances of his seeking mouth on hers and his hands caressing her everywhere. His naughty grin was clear as a blue summer sky, though. Who cared if she couldn't remember getting there?

What did matter was Zack tore at her clothing as she did his. Coat, shoes, tie, pants, socks, and then he was as gloriously naked as she. His chest heaved as his eyes made a slow descent of her body, and when he licked his lips, gaze locked on the junction of her thighs, she gulped.

Another grin, this more sensuous and devilish than the last, lit his face. "Guess what I had delivered to this room earlier."

How did he know they were coming here? How far in advance had he planned it, and how had he kept it a secret for so long? She shook her head, unable to imagine or care about anything but him inside her.

"Lemon-filled donuts," he said, answering his own question. "Two dozen of them."

Her body shuddered in appreciation, and she was pretty sure she came at his suggestive tone, but she couldn't be positive. Momentary insanity ruled, and a throaty growl escaped her as she launched herself in his general direction. Zack, God bless him, anticipated her move, catching her midair. The momentum carried them backward and tumbling onto the bed, where they bounced. Hard.

Tomorrow she might be in traction, but tonight, she couldn't care less.

His mouth fastened on her nipple, suckling the sensitive, puckered tip. Taking his sweet time, he cupped her breasts and turned his head to lavish her other one with similar thoroughness. His lips left a blazing trail as he explored her body. Her fingers felt their way along his back, shoulders, and neck. Eventually, she burrowed them into his thick mane of dark hair, holding him to her as he worked his tantalizing magic. Tongue, teeth, or lips—it didn't matter. He utilized them all in addition to his talented hands, making her beg for release as he brought her to the brink, only to deny her the pleasure she sought and begin his sensual torture again.

There was a recklessness to their lovemaking. A desperation she'd not felt before. Only Zack could make her sob his name at key moments. Make her believe in herself as she never had before. Convince her she possessed the skills to satisfy him and keep him that way for years to come. And she loved him for it. Loved his ability to make her eagerly anticipate the race to the finish line, knowing she would, without fail, be the first one to experience the euphoria of great sex.

Like now. She cried out his name as her body trembled in the throes of an orgasm. There was no time to recover her breath before the cool gel of lemon filling hit her tightly beaded nipple.

Dear God!

He was going to kill her. Of a certainty, her heart couldn't maintain its fierce rate. But what a way to go!

The raspy texture of his tongue was in direct contrast to the silky line of goo he'd created. A new, deeper thrill shook her as he drew her breast into his mouth and swirled the tip of his tongue around the tip. The sight of his dark head bent over her was in line with the endless fantasies she'd had of them together over the years. From her first understanding of intercourse, her young imagination pictured Zack as her partner—whether she was with another or not. What didn't she adore about making love with him? About Zack himself? Now, her two favorite things in the world, donuts and him, came together in one supercharged night. If she had a camera handy, she would've memorialized the moment for posterity. Also, to reminisce whenever she needed inspiration for her novels.

"You're thinking. I can feel it," he murmured. Amusement sparkled in his electric eyes when he lifted his head to survey his lemony design.

"I understand why people make sex tapes," she said, running a finger across her breast and scooping up curd to smear on his muscled chest.

He laughed and lay on her, squishing the mess between their bodies. "You want to make a sex tape? Hell, yes! I'm in."

"Perv."

"You know it."

Erica slid her hand down his front, enclosed him in her sticky fist, and stroked with agonizing slowness. "Ya know, it's occurred to me that I haven't sampled my dessert. Maybe I—"

He placed a finger to her mouth, silencing her. "Say no more!" Flopping on his back, he spread his arms wide like a human sacrifice. "I'm all yours, and we have all night."

Leaning in, she nuzzled the throbbing vein in his neck. "But right now, I want to suck you until you scream."

He released a strangled sound.

Erica laughed. The power was heady. Zack was beyond receptive to dirty talk, and it added another fun facet to their play.

Smearing the filling along his torso and penis, she went to work. She experienced a sense of pride as he peaked, released a guttural cry, and shouted her name. No longer would she feel like a failure in the bedroom. With Zack, she'd proved to herself she had what it takes to satisfy a partner.

"Let's hit the shower." He pulled her to her feet. And when she tried to stand on shaky legs, he lifted her in a fireman's hold, and she giggled as he carried her to the bathroom. "I feel this is very reminiscent of the first night we reconnected. You, unable to stand after your workout. Me, seeing you naked in the bathroom and wanting to bend you over the rim of the tub."

She beamed up at him.

"You have a siren's smile," he told her lovingly. The look in his eyes was dazed, and her heart beat faster.

"Before you arrived, I was in my tub, dreaming of all the ways I would maim you if I had to do one more spin on that fucking bike."

His belly laugh echoed off the tiled surround. "I don't doubt it."

They entered the shower to remove the worst of the mess. Zack adjusted the water a smidgeon north of warm and crowded the two of them into the stall. As they stood under the waterfall shower head, he lathered Erica's hair and thoroughly soaped her body, all her nerve endings came alive and responded. Every caress was magical, and she was convinced he was a sorcerer.

"You should be a professional masseur," she said with a long, drawn-out moan. "You missed your calling."

"I'd go broke because I only want to offer my services to you."

"You say the sweetest things."

He chuckled. "Yeah? How about this? I don't want to use a condom tonight, babe. I want to feel you as I enter you, again and again and again."

She faced him on his first "again," stretching to wrap her arms around his neck. Their kiss held less urgency than the ones shared earlier, though their need hadn't diminished. Zack acted as if he could drink the passion from her lips and never tire of it. She sure as hell wouldn't.

"Yes," she said in answer to skin-on-skin, already aware they were both disease-free.

Bending his knees, he lifted her, his arms secured under her bottom. Her belly was pressed to his chest and her breasts were at his eye level. His grin widened in approval when her nipples hardened as they transitioned from hot water to cool air. "Have I told you how much I love your tits, babe?"

"I'm beginning to believe that's why you keep me around," she quipped with a laugh.

"Well, they're definitely on the top-ten list."

"Hush, and take me."

"Gladly," he growled, pausing only long enough to deliver a love bite to her breast before pressing her back against the wall. His powerful thighs supported her weight and spread her legs to accommodate his hips. He sank into her, and his shuddering sigh next to her ear was matched by her own delicious response.

Easing out, he paused overly long.

"Look at me, Erica."

Opening her eyes, she met his. They blazed with a fierce love, and she caught her breath, fearful of being burned to a cinder by the heat they held.

He thrust upward with one powerful motion. His fullness was exquisite and next-level. Her pleasure built, and he wrung cry after cry from her lips with each smooth stroke. She bucked in the final throws, bringing him with her, careening over the cliff to fulfillment. Over and over again, he plunged, deepening each movement until they were both beasts, seeking what the other's body promised.

The water temperature changed from steaming to lukewarm, and it was their only warning to vacate before the icy blast doused them. Laughing and screeching, they dove out of the stall. Erica wrapped herself in a hotel waffle robe and wound a towel as a turban for her dripping hair. On her way back to bed, she snagged a donut.

When they were semi-dry and laid out on the king-sized mattress, Zack scooted to sit between her thighs. Giving her a wicked look of intent, he hooked her knees over his shoulders.

"Dude! I'll never walk again," she warned.

"Is that a 'no'?"

The challenge in his eyes brought out her competitive spirit. "All I'm saying is that I need sustenance." She bit into her donut and tossed the rest onto the nightstand. "Carry on!"

Chuckling and sporting a self-satisfied, sexy-as-fuck smirk, he gripped her ass and met her eager gaze. "Hold on, babe. It's gonna be a bumpy ride."

———

"THOSE NEED TO LAST THE NIGHT," he cautioned, sometime after midnight.

"Pfft. Yeah, well, so does my energy. For that matter, yours too, since you seem to be doing all the work. You'd better have two."

Zack grabbed one for himself. His eyes widened after the first bite.

"*Holy-shit-thasss-freakin-good!*" His words ran together, muffled by the doughy goodness.

Erica snorted in glee. Yep, through her, Zack was learning how incredible junk food could be.

"Welcome to the Dark Side."

They lay cuddled together, an old black-and-white film playing on low, as his fingers created lazy patterns over her back. She rested under his arm, head over his heart. If there had been no threat to her, the moment would've been as perfect as it got.

The question needed to be asked, though, and Erica voiced it. "Do you think they'll catch her anytime soon?"

She felt his heavy sigh before he answered. "I don't know."

"I'm honestly not sure how much more of this I can stand. Every time I leave the house, she does her damnedest to murder me."

His fingers paused in their motion as he contemplated her upturned face.

"She won't succeed," he promised.

"You can't know that." Erica closed her eyes and shook her head. "What if Christie had hit *you* tonight? Jacob would be without a parent. We can't continue to risk it, Zack," she said in a low, sad voice. "It's selfish of us. We need to put him first."

Zack's lips tightened, and he dropped his head back to stare at the ceiling. "It's not an issue, Erica. They'll find her."

She knew he wanted to believe it. Hell, *she* wanted to believe it. But there were no guarantees Christie would be captured or that she wouldn't mortally wound one—or both—of them in the process. Dreading what was necessary, she sat up and toyed with the bunched sheet.

"I'm leaving, Zack."

Tension-filled silence greeted her statement.

"You aren't going to say anything?" she asked, her voice hardly above a whisper.

"What do you want me to say? We've played all this out before," he rasped. "Too many fucking times to count. If you're determined to go, then go. I can't stop you. I won't."

One tear, two, and then a shit-ton more trailed down her pale cheek. "I'm sorry."

"For what? Being a coward?" he snapped.

"*What?* How is that fair?" How could he not see reason? Not acknowledge hers was the best way forward? "She's slashed tires, carved a warning in my car, burned down my goddamned house, stabbed me, and now—*now*—has shot at us."

She met his disillusioned gaze, and her heart ached at the sight of his building anger.

"Zack, *please*. I'm tired of waking up wondering if it's the day my life is ending."

"Yeah, whatever." He shoved off the bed and stalked to the window.

"Whatever? Are you kidding me right now?" she demanded. "How does any of what I've gone through warrant your scorn?"

He spun to face her, stunning in all his naked glory and righteous rage. "Because you won't *fight*! You're letting a crazy woman dictate our lives."

"I'm not as strong as you. And I'm tired of strife," she said. Her exhaustion was more than simply being physically worn out. Mental and emotional fatigue played into it, too. "If we were dealing with someone sane, if this was a court battle over custody or some everyday situation with a bitchy ex, I couldn't be pried away with a crowbar. But it's not." Joining him, Erica placed one hand alongside his jaw. "Please understand. I'm putting everyone in danger by staying. I have a horrible feeling about this. It grows stronger every stinking minute of every day. Like if I don't leave soon, it'll mean my life or yours."

"If you leave, I can't protect you," he said. The hint of desperation in his voice was troubling. "Don't you get it?"

She didn't know how to break it to him that he hadn't been able to protect her to date, and she said nothing.

TWENTY-SIX

Zack recognized the exact second Erica firmed her resolve to leave. A chill settled in his bones and the muscles in his body tensed to the point of pain. The thought of her out there, without him to watch over her, was making him physically ill. His stomach was a pool of toxic acid, burning the lining, and his gut clenched in reaction. He'd fallen so fast and hard for her, he might never recover if she left him.

"Go to sleep, Erica," he said, weary to the bone. "You don't have to make arrangements tonight."

"I'm sorry."

He fucking hated the regret in her voice, and seeing her eyes shimmer with tears was like a corrosive agent to his soul. It stung, and there was no relief from the suffering. He wasn't immune to her pain, but he was dealing with his own hurt. With nothing left to say, no argument to persuade her, he gave a curt nod. Picking up his pants from a nearby chair, he started to dress, for once feeling vulnerable in her presence without clothes on. Each article of clothing was another layer of armor.

"I'll book another room for tonight."

She gaped. "Zack, that's stupid. Why not stay with me?"

He met her wounded gaze, knowing he'd stare into her soulful eyes for forever, if possible. A plea filled his mouth, begging to be spoken. He told himself it was no use swallowing his pride and pleading. She wouldn't be swayed—not this time. And if he remained, he *would* end up pleading with her before the night was over. What would be the point? The outcome would be the same, and he'd embarrass himself.

He spun on his heel, prepared to exit the suite.

"You can have the room. I'll take a cab back to your house and pack," she said stiffly.

"You're not going back there by yourself, dammit," he snapped. "Do you have a fucking death wish?"

"Well, I'm not staying here with you acting like you are," she fired back.

"Fine, get dressed. We'll go check out."

"Fine!" she yelled.

"Fine!" he snapped.

"For the record, you're being a *dick.*"

"I got your dick," he said nastily.

"Oh, that's right. *Do* resort to being a vulgar *ass.*"

She was like a duck on a carnival shooting game. Going in one direction, jerking to a stop, and heading back in another. Periodically bending to pick up her bra, a shoe, or some such, all the while flinging the sheet, comforter, and pillows out of her way. She spent an inordinate amount of time hunting for a particular item. He suspected it was her thong, tucked safely away in his jacket pocket. He was of the mind to let her continue her search because he wanted to be petty—and also because he had no intention of relinquishing his souvenir from tonight.

While he waited, he picked up the second box of unopened donuts. With regret in his heart, he tossed them in the trash. Her scandalized gasp preceded her red-faced outrage.

"You don't throw perfectly good donuts in the trash, you idiot! What the hell's the matter with you?"

Her fury reminded him of the morning when she couldn't find any coffee in his kitchen. Self-preservation screamed at him to run for it, to save himself, but he was reckless and spoiling for a fight.

"They were for one reason only, and that clearly went to hell," he stated coldly. With a sneer, he lifted the trashcan. "Should I dig them out for you? Maybe you can snuggle up with them when you're lonely at night. Oh wait, isn't that why you joined my gym in the first place?"

She paled but held her ground. "Dig them out for yourself, and I'll tell you where you can shove them!"

Erica was stunning in her rage, and he almost dropped to his knees to beg her forgiveness. The devil on his shoulder reminded him she wanted to go, even after the incredible night they'd shared, and it killed him.

"Are you ready yet? I don't want to keep you from running away," he sneered.

Her eyes turned glass hard. "When you look back, remember *you* were the one who made a beautiful thing ugly, okay?"

Suddenly, he found it hard to breathe. He experienced tightness in his chest, and his mind went blank but for the pain he was feeling. Maybe it was a heart failure. Wouldn't it be better than the alternative of heartbreak? He imagined they felt the same.

"Weren't you checking out?" she reminded him with a pointed look toward the door.

If he stayed, he'd strangle her... or offer to give up everything he owned—his career, home, and relationships—and follow her to Florida. He wrenched open the door and hurried down the hall, eager to be away, if only to breathe and get his head on straight. It took ten minutes to hunt up the nighttime clerk and another eight to settle the bill. When he returned, it was to find Erica gone.

Zack wanted to bellow the rage brought on by his fear for her. If she was safe, he was going to kill her!

Erica was fit to be tied. Who the hell did he think he was? Man, had she misjudged him! Fuming in the back of the car she'd hired, she replayed their argument. It took a solid ten minutes to calm down and realize whatever landmarks she recognized were leading away from the direction they should be traveling.

Leaning forward, prepared to inform the female driver of her mistake, she caught sight of a compact handgun in the front seat. Ripping her gaze away from the weapon took a concerted effort, and she raised her eyes to the rearview mirror and met those of the female driver. Hatred shone in the cold stare.

The color and make of the car sank into her sleep-deprived brain.

A cream-colored sedan!

The exact one parked across the street from Zack's house a few weeks back.

Shock held Erica paralyzed.

Sake's alive! She was a moron, and no better than one of those too-stupid-to-live characters in a novel or movie. She'd allowed her fight with Zack to distract her, and she played right into Christie's lethal hands. Why hadn't she listened to the persistent inner voice screaming danger was imminent? As angry as she'd been, she should never have left the hotel without informing Zack or checking the car at the curb was the one she'd hired. But really, how many Toyotas could possibly be loitering in front of a hotel entrance?

Eyeballing the speedometer, Erica mentally calculated her odds of jumping. Not a brilliant idea. If the fall didn't kill her, it might damn well break her neck. A better course of action consisted of biding her time and trying to escape at the first opening. Suppressing the urge to bang her forehead on the seat back, she closed her eyes. She'd be lucky if she survived this fatal faux pas.

As the miles passed, so did her chance of survival. Her only hope was to attack Christie as soon as she slowed to turn. She might not expect Erica to spring into action since she'd been the model abductee.

It wasn't long before they were weaving into a subdivision, and the car slowed to a reasonable speed. Going for broke, Erica dove toward Christie and wrapped an arm around her neck. Anticipating a move for the gun, she grabbed her right wrist. The brakes squealed under the applied pressure, and Christie lifted her hands from the steering wheel, producing a taser from nowhere.

There was a joke in there somewhere, but other than to give taser-threatening Officer Tidwell a laugh when he discovered her extra-crispy body, Erica didn't know what it was. She scrambled backward, but the prongs connected before she got far. Before her body regained function, the car skidded to a halt, and Christie was administering a drug to Erica's system.

The sharp prick was over in a second, and it only took another one or two for the sedative to take effect. How the hell did the raging psycho from hell obtain tranquilizers? If Erica survived, she planned to write a strongly worded letter to her government representatives about the drug crisis in America.

"Fucking bitch!" she slurred. The insult sounded better in her head.

Her consciousness began to fade, and her last thought was of Zack. She should've stayed and made the most of their night together. Likely, they'd never have another.

CHAPTER

TWENTY-SEVEN

Zack checked his messages for the millionth time since Erica left the hotel. The screen showed the last six he sent to her.

> Why the hell did you leave without telling me? Do you have a screw loose?

> Look, I get that you're mad. I'm sorry. Just tell me where you went and that you're okay.

> Erica, please don't give me the silent treatment. I only want to know you're all right.

> Babe, please, tell me you're safe.

> God, I'm losing my mind over here. Where are you?

> If you get this, I love you. I'm worried out of my mind. Call me.

Within an hour of Erica's disappearance, Zack was beside himself. As mad as she'd been, there was no way she wouldn't assure him of her safety. Even if it was to say, "Go fuck yourself."

By two hours, he was in a full-blown panic. By three, he was ready to commit murder. His house was crammed full of people: the police, his brothers, and Shonda. Sometime during the night, Charlie and Judith had brought Jacob home as the commotion exploded on their block.

If one more person asked Zack the same sonofabitching thing, he was going to jail for assault. The wary looks from Bucky and Mason assured him they recognized he was at his wits' end, and thankfully they did their best to field questions while Zack paced.

"Why are any of you still here? You have everything I know! Fucking find her already!" he yelled. His hands gripped his hair, and he was ready to rip the studs from the walls in his frustration. The inactivity was killing him.

Bucky charged forward and slapped a hand on Zack's chest, shoving him back a step. "You need to calm the. Fuck. Down! Everyone here is doing the best they can. They're working overtime to help." He inhaled deeply and gave Zack a look of reprimand. "You should know, we don't typically get involved unless a person has been missing at least twenty-four hours. But we've all made the exception for Erica because we know the circumstances, and we want to bring her home safely."

Jolted by the aggressive gesture and authoritative tone Bucky adopted, Zack acceded to the order. He'd underestimated his long-time friend. Forgotten he was more than a jovial buddy who liked burgers and beer.

Zack searched the faces of the officers in the room, seeing compassion on some and anger on others. No one liked to be told how to do their job. He should have remembered that. As a boss, he knew about tact, but his had gone by way of his patience. His only excuse was temporary insanity. The worry had turned his mind to mush and pushed him past the point of reason. He now resided in Mentalville. How long he would stay there was anyone's guess. If Erica wasn't found soon, he would find himself in the same situation as Christie had when she was committed.

He was deeply ashamed of his behavior and said as much.

"I'm sorry," he said as calmly and contritely as possible. One by one, he stepped up to each of the officers and shook their hand. "I really do appreciate what you are doing. I'm..."

To a person, they all nodded when he trailed off to clear his throat. Their softening expressions told him he was forgiven for his lapse and they understood the stress he was under.

"We'll find her, sir," Officer Tidwell promised, clasping Zack's shoulder and giving a gentle shake.

The unmistakable feeling of suffocation came over him, and he hurriedly nodded. "Thanks. If you'll excuse me..."

He raced to his room and gave in to the threatening panic attack. It impacted him like a wrecking ball to a building. His anxiety grew until it felt as if he were buried under thousands of pounds of rubble, and he struggled to move or draw a breath.

Shonda followed and dropped down next to him on the floor. Compassion was reflected in her troubled eyes, and she rubbed small, comforting circles on his back.

"Breathe," she urged.

"I-I... ca-can't..."

"You can, or you wouldn't be speaking right now."

Able to acknowledge the logic, he attempted to regulate his breathing. Without thinking of how it would seem, he clamped a hand on her knee, seeking stability in a spinning room.

Mason joined them, lurking in the doorway and glowering at the offending limb.

"The only reason I'm not breaking your hand is because you're hurting," his brother said, shifting closer. "After this, it's another matter."

His brother's territorial bullshit was what Zack needed to rein it in and center himself. He suspected Mason threatened for that exact purpose.

"Thanks, dickhead," he muttered.

"You're welcome, asshat."

He relinquished his spot to his brother, absently noting how Mason's shoulder brushed Shonda's and how he did nothing to add distance despite his claim of indifference. Knowing him, he didn't want to feel the attraction. But Shonda was a tractor beam, and he was caught in her gravitational pull.

Zack's thoughts drifted back to Erica and to how she'd find the situation between his brother and her friend amusing. Worry amped him up and created a restlessness. He paced the room, hoping to dispel his agitation.

"Dad?" Jacob's timid inquiry cut through his turmoil.

"Hey, lil man."

Jacob rubbed the last of the sleep from his eyes. "Is it true? Is Erica missing? Was it my mom who hurt her?"

"Who told you that?" Zack folded his son in a bear hug, casting an anxious glance at Dane, who'd trailed after him.

A negative head shake from Dane said he wasn't the one to spill the beans.

"I heard Grandpa yelling at Grandma."

Zack pulled back to view Jacob's face. "Why was he yelling?"

"He said it was all Grandma's fault. That she cud-cod..."

"Coddled?"

"Yeah, coddled her too much. That maybe if she hadn't hid the fact my mom hadn't died in the fire, this would never have happened."

Hearing the retelling of Charlie and Judith's argument was like an MMA kick to the forehead—staggering. Christie's mother had known all along! She'd probably been the one helping to conceal her daughter's whereabouts. Erica had called it when she said Christie needed assistance. The real concern was how far Judith had gone to shield her daughter, and whether she would continue.

"Son, I need you to stay here until I come for you. I need to talk to your grandparents. Can you do that?"

Jacob nodded his agreement.

"I'll stay with him," Shonda said.

"Thanks."

Mason jumped up to follow Zack out.

As he stood in front of Charlie, flanked on both sides by his brothers, he demanded answers.

"Are you telling me you knew all along Christie was alive and that she was behind the early attacks?" The menace in his tone couldn't be mistaken for anything other than promised retribution should Erica be hurt at Christie's hand. He'd see the Bauer's pay if they were involved, as he suspected.

Judith cringed but rallied to thrust her chin in the air and stare down her nose at him. Her disdainful expression said he was the dirt beneath her feet.

Charlie stepped to one side, no longer willing to protect his wife's folly. "Ask *her*. I only found out tonight."

She refused to answer.

"Judith, for God's sake, a woman's life is at risk!" he shouted.

"Then she shouldn't have thrown herself at Zack," she spat. The venom behind her words startled their group.

Zack leaned forward until his nose was inches from hers.

"Listen to me *very* carefully. I know you love Jacob, so I'm only saying this once. If you want to continue to be a part of his life, you *will* tell me everything." His icy tone could flash freeze ocean water. "You're lucky I am not turning you over to the police as an accessory to the crimes she's already committed."

Judith remained mute, fierce hatred burning in her eyes.

"You blame me," Zack surmised aloud.

How had he been so oblivious? She held him responsible for all her daughter had gone through, and he couldn't believe he'd never seen it before. How the hell had she hidden her loathing for as long as she did?

"Why, Judith? What did I do?"

"You didn't love her!" she screamed. "All she dreamed about was being your wife and a mother to Jacob. You rejected her and took her son away."

"No, Jude. You're remembering it wrong," Charlie said, aghast, clearly disturbed by his wife's tangent.

Zack cut him off. "You're right, Judith. I never loved her. Not the way she deserved to be." He held up his hand when a smug smile curled her lips. "But I *did* care for her—in the beginning, before she played me. It was her games and disregard for anyone else's feelings that turned me off. That, and the fact she tried to *drown my son!*"

Instant rage transformed her features to grotesque, and Judith lunged, hands extended like claws.

Charlie caught her before she could strike. His shocked gaze met Zack's. "You have to believe I had no idea, son. Please."

The sincerity in the older man's gray eyes cut through his disillusionment. He knew Charlie well enough to understand he would be beating himself up over their situation for a very long time.

"I still need to know where she might've taken Erica, Charlie. Is there anywhere you can think of?"

"I'm afraid not. But if I had to guess, maybe where you first met or some significant date you had with her in the past?"

"You'll never find her. Your whore is as good as dead." Judith cackled.

A chill ran down Zack's spine. He knew, beyond a shadow of a doubt, Christie's mother had not only helped her daughter in her diabolical schemes, but had also fueled the flames into an inferno. Was she ultimately responsible for Christie going off the deep end all those years ago? Or did madness run in their line?

"I'll find her. Never doubt it," he assured her in a hard voice.

When Bucky positioned himself to arrest Judith, Zack blinked in surprise, somewhat stunned everyone was still there. He'd been focused on her, and he forgot anyone else was in the room but the three of them.

"I'm sorry. I have to take her in, Cap," Bucky told Charlie. "She's an accessory to multiple crimes."

"Of course," Charlie said, looking as if he'd aged a decade in the last five minutes.

Judith spewed vitriol as they cuffed her. "You spineless bastard! Do you know what it was like being married to you all these years? You are a pathetic excuse for a man. You cozied up to the one person who treated our daughter like she was worthless garbage to be tossed away."

As Zack watched in silent horror, he felt terrible for Charlie. The man had been like a father to him after his own had taken off. Too many times to count, he'd been lenient with the Sharp boys, in his position as police captain. The three Sharp brothers had been hooligans, but they were never cruel and never intended actual harm. Charlie understood that. It was probably why he'd been inclined to let them off with a warning more often than not.

After Judith was hauled away, still spouting hate, Charlie turned to him, apology in every line of his body.

"You don't have to say it, Charlie. None of this was your fault," Zack said.

"None of it was yours, either. It was hers. Or rather, theirs. I'm ashamed I didn't see it before. Some police captain, huh?"

"They're your family, and you love them. It's easy to be blind to their faults or overlook them. You never want it to be as bad as it is," he said. "But I never intentionally set out to hurt Christie. I need you to believe that."

Charlie offered up a sad smile and placed a comforting hand on Zack's shoulder. "I do, son. I do. Should I take Jacob back with me?"

"No." As hurt flashed in Charlie's tired eyes, Zack saw where what he said might be misconstrued. "I want him here, where I can see him. I know you would never let anything happen to him, but I need to have him close tonight. You're welcome to the spare room."

"No point in that. I'm just a few doors down, and you have my number. Don't hesitate to call me if I can be of service."

Sorrow for Charlie filled Zack's heart. The man had lost everything, and yet, there he stood, proud and offering to help. Zack was humbled and grateful to have this influence in his and Jacob's lives.

"You got it," he told Charlie with a tight hug.

"I'll be praying for Erica."

"Thank you." When the older man would have stepped away, Zack called him back. "Charlie? You're the father I always wished I had."

Tears filled his shadowed eyes. "Thank you, son. I love you."

"I love you, too."

"Grandpa!" Jacob came charging out. "Don't forget tomorrow night is our school play. You said you'd go with us."

Zack met his eyes over his son's head. "I'd be grateful if you would take him. Until I find Erica…"

Charlie squatted at eye level with Jacob. "You betcha, sport. I wouldn't miss it for the world."

"Off to bed, Jacob," Zack said.

"But I want to be here when Erica comes home."

His heart stuttered. Jacob, too, considered her a part of their family.

"It may be a while, lil man, but I promise to wake you as soon as I have any news."

"But, Dad!"

"Come on, fry guy," Dane said. He scooped his nephew up and tossed him over his shoulder with ease. "Let's go."

CHAPTER

TWENTY-EIGHT

As consciousness returned, Erica remained as still as possible. What she really wanted to do was jump up and pound in the face of the dumb bitch who'd drugged her. Her bound hands and feet made it impossible, though. She experienced a split second of panic when she couldn't open her eyes. The scratchy material against her lids registered with her foggy brain.

Blindfolded.

Erica's other senses assumed the workload of processing her surroundings. She was cold, but there was no breeze to indicate she was outdoors. Basement, warehouse, or garage, she deduced. Mustiness and a burnt-wood smell added to the ambiance of the horror house she'd built in her mind's eye.

Gasoline. The unmistakable strong stench indicated a container of it was close by. Tucking her head minutely, she took a whiff of her clothing. She wasn't wet and couldn't smell anything but the remnants of the rainstorm and lovemaking. Christie had practiced remarkable restraint in not dousing her and lighting her on fire, for which Erica was extremely grateful.

"I know you're awake."

Erica stayed silent and unmoving.

"You might as well talk now, while you can. Soon, you won't be saying anything ever again," Christie said with a raucous laugh.

Ignoring the not-so-subtle threat, Erica remained quiet and was rewarded with a vicious kick to her ribs.

"Jesusfuckingchrist!"

The pain was as savage as the woman who'd administered it.

"I thought that would get your attention." Christie's was the smug tone of someone who had the upper hand. If Erica managed to turn the tables, she'd be rabid and ruthless.

"Is that what you want? Attention?" Erica gagged and gritted her teeth to stem off the vomit tickling the back of her throat. Any serious physical discomfort—like busted ribs or stab wounds—had that effect on her. "Well, I'd say you got it with the keying of my car. You didn't have to go to extremes, ya know."

Clicking started.

Flare. Snap.

Flare. Snap.

The sharp sound echoed around them. The continual action finally sank in, and Erica went cold inside.

Christie was playing with her lighter.

With one wrong move, the entire place would ignite. Although Erica would delight in cussing out the Looney Tunes bitch, discretion was the better part of valor. Taking digs at the nutter might provoke the woman into severe measures.

As if abduction and burning down houses weren't enough!

"Did it hurt?" Christie asked.

"What?"

"When I stabbed you?"

"What the fuck do you think? It felt like a damn walk in the park?"

A second kick to her abused ribs wrenched a cry from her.

"Mind your tone, whore!"

If she got up—no, *when* she got up—Erica was going to rip that twat's face off. Admittedly, being hog-tied as she was made it difficult, but her chance would come.

Dear God, please, please, let her chance come.

To die this way would be tragic. To die without ever having another chance to tell Zack she loved him was unthinkable.

How would he feel knowing his last words to her were in anger? Would he understand the pressure had been caused by their stress and throw away his regrets? Or would he beat himself up for the rest of his life for those impulsive, hurt-filled words, never quite knowing she was well aware he hadn't meant them?

And he hadn't. She wanted to live through this nightmare to tell him she'd stay with him forever if he'd have her.

"What's your plan, Christie?"

Why the hell had she asked that? Maybe because knowing was better than not? Doubtful. Either way, if that batshit-crazy hag waited too long before doing her in, the interim would be a living hell. No way would she treat Erica humanely. It begged the question: was a quick death preferable to a drawn-out one with dwindling hope riding shotgun?

"You'll find out soon enough."

It was odd how casual and warm her nemesis' tone turned out to be. Surely, she should have a screechy voice and a high-pitched giggle like a dastardly cartoon character, right? Yet she sounded normal and borderline sweet. Her dulcet tones annoyed Erica. Hell, her own vocal cords probably emitted a much more irritating sound. There was no justice to Christie being a skinny blonde with perfect breasts. Erica intended to derive great pleasure in maiming her after she got loose.

As the hours dragged on, Erica grew progressively colder. Her teeth chattered, and her clenched jaw ached from the effort to stop the clashing. Nothing had been said for the longest time, and beyond her fear of being with the hair-brained harridan, was her worry about being left to die alone, tied up and freezing to death.

"Chr-Christie," she called out. "Are you st-still here?"

"What do you want?" Christie sounded surly and tired.

Erica hoped she was frozen to the core, too. It would serve her insane ass right.

"I'm c-cold. Can I g-get a blanket? Please?" It galled to have to ask her for anything, but beggars couldn't be choosers.

"No."

"Are there n-not enough to go a-around, or are you b-being spiteful?" Erica tried to keep any judgment out of her voice. Tried to sound more curious than pissy. Hell, the conversation might help warm them both if Christie was so inclined.

"I only have the one," the woman grudgingly admitted.

"Oh. Ok-kay. Thanks," Erica said. "C-can I ask y-you a question?" She took the silence as agreement. "Why Z-Zack? Why are y-you so f-focused on him?"

The lighter lid began its continuous cycle of opening and closing.

When no answer was forthcoming, Erica continued. "I m-mean, how c-can you love s-someone who refuses t-to return your aff-affection?"

There was a whoosh of air movement before she felt a sharp slap. Fury reared its nasty head, and she bit back an angry retort. The burning in her cheek provided a little heat at least. Maybe she could provoke Christie into finishing her off here and now. An Erica bonfire was better than this fucking arctic night.

"He loves *me*! Soon, I'll prove it." Christie's spittle landed on her face.

She shuddered. Spit was plain gross. What if she got rabies? People could absolutely contract the disease from animals, but could they be infected by another person? She added it to her list of things to do if she survived: google human-to-human rabies.

"You w-want to know the iron-ny in all of this?" Erica asked, not expecting an affirmative answer. "I w-was leaving for F-Florida when you p-picked me up. Isn't th-that hilarious?"

"You're lying."

"I'm n-not. Why d-do you think I was c-calling a ride? I told Zack t-tonight I was d-done with the attempts on my l-life," she said. "That's w-what I find so f-funny about all of th-this."

"I saw you kissing him!"

Christie grabbed a fistful of Erica's hair and viciously shook her before letting go. Agony ricocheted through her as her abused skull was slammed on the ground. Was this what it felt like to crack open her head? This instant migraine?

Fuuucccccckkkk!

The bare concrete floor undoubtedly aided in a concussion. Then and there, Erica decided to snatch the she-devil bald before ripping her apart. She gave her bonds a test, wishing she'd suddenly develop superhuman strength. They held tight. Goddamned heavy-duty tie wraps.

Wasn't there a trick to breaking them? She'd viewed a video where someone showed the steps to escape, but recalling it was too difficult with her throbbing head and numb mind.

"The kiss was Zack's doing," Erica said through gritted teeth. "But really, who wouldn't give it up to someone resembling an underwear model when he makes a move on them?" she added, unable to shut up.

Dear God, why couldn't she shut the hell up?

On a positive note, her teeth weren't chattering. She was either too fired up or pissed off to worry about the cold anymore. Perhaps the warmth was from the memory of Zack's steamy kiss. It didn't matter. Not convulsing from the dropping temperature was a bonus.

Christie's palm connected again.

Erica should've expected the second strike, but really, couldn't the woman develop a sense of humor and agree with her, for a change?

"If I carve up your face, he won't find you so attractive, will he?" Christie snarled.

A sharp object connected with the side of Erica's cheek, and she swallowed hard.

"Probably no one would," she agreed, careful not to move her mouth more than necessary, cautious of the pointy tip. "But you don't have to go that far. I promise, if you release me, I am on the first plane out of this hellhole."

"You had your chance to leave. I tried to warn you, but you wouldn't listen," Christie said, pressing the weapon deeper. Her skin parted under the knife's pressure.

Blood trickled into her mouth as the stinging pain started. The urge to scream made holding still an effort in concentration and discipline. Admittedly Erica had very little of both. But if she struggled, the sadistic bitch would gleefully cut her open. She'd forgotten how much a knife hurt when it pierced the flesh. Which was ridiculous when she thought about it because she'd been stabbed fairly recently.

Another thing to research: were there more nerve endings in the face? She felt she should know.

"Please," she whispered. "Don't do this."

The pressure eased, but the stinging didn't stop. Face on fire, Erica was hot and cold all at once.

"Christie, I don't know what your plan is, but in another few hours, it won't matter. Hypothermia will set in. Can't you feel the temperature dropping? It's getting down in the thirties tonight. We'll both freeze."

Why she was trying to reason with a crazy person?

Perhaps it was her optimistic nature. Who knew she even had one? All she *did* know was that she wanted to live, if for no other reason than to pulverize Christie. Being an author, she was positive she could come up with a creative and justified payback.

Once again, the lighter clicked open and closed.

The fucking repetitive sound was getting on Erica's last nerve.

Her willpower, ever lacking, was thinning, and she held on to her temper by a thread.

"Lay there and be quiet," Christie ordered.

Erica did as she was told and heard the rapid clicks of a camera shutter. Part of the plan must be to taunt Zack with images of her bound and bleeding. Her heart wept for him. To receive those pictures and be helpless to find her would drive him mad.

CHAPTER
TWENTY-NINE

A chime indicated an incoming text.

The image of Erica, hogtied and blindfolded, high-lighted a gash on her cheek and blood streaked down her pale face. No message accompanied the picture.

Was she dead?

Other than the one mark, he didn't see any stab wounds.

"Bucky!" he croaked.

Dane and Bucky were first to their feet. Mason, half-asleep on the sectional, was delayed by Shonda's form draped across him.

His brothers swore in unison, but Bucky kept his thoughts to himself as he studied the picture. After another nerve-wracking minute, he asked Zack to send the entire message to him, which he immediately forwarded to someone else.

"I've sent it to the lead detective," Bucky told them. "If I had to guess, I'd say Erica's being held in a garage. See here? It's a speckled floor coating."

Zack examined what was visible in the image background. "You're right! Check out the back wall. I can't be positive, but doesn't it look pretty dark? Like it's scorched?"

Thrusting his phone at Dane, he ran to the dining room and swept open Erica's laptop. After keying in her passcode, he searched for the insurance photos.

"Here! Right here. It's the same coating on the floor. That's Erica's garage!" Excitement curled in his belly, sending his pulse into overdrive. Zack shoved the laptop into Bucky's hands and ran for his keys and coat.

"Wait!" Bucky morphed into commanding officer mode. "You can't rush there. Christie might have a weapon and hurt Erica if she feels threatened."

The warning stopped Zack mid-motion. Dammit! The endless inactivity had made him reckless, but Bucky was correct.

"Right. What's our next step?" he asked. "And don't say we wait, because I can't." It chapped his ass to be idle when Erica was in danger. His body's very fiber screamed at him to go rescue his woman.

"Why would Christie send this?" Dane asked. He rubbed the back of his neck as he held up the phone. "She had to know you might recognize the place."

"Maybe she didn't think that far ahead. Maybe she just wanted to torment me so badly she didn't consider it," Zack suggested.

"I'm not buying that." Mason shook his head. "She's been extremely careful not to get caught up until now."

They were right. Zack dragged his hands down his face, halting to steeple them over the lower half. Erica liked to joke it was his "thinking pose" whenever he was struggling with a problem. His soul ached, remembering her teasing. She'd only been gone five and a half hours, but it felt like forever. Like he'd lost a vital part of himself along with his mind.

"What do we do?" Asking grated. He was better at taking action than waiting.

"*You* do nothing. Let us handle it," Bucky said. A protest formed on Zack's lips, but his friend continued, speaking over him. "I'm serious about this, man. We're trained for these situations. You're not. If you charge over half-cocked, you'll get Erica killed."

"Dammit, Buck! I'm dying here." Zack groaned and slapped a hand against the wall, jolting Shonda awake.

"Do you want me to arrest you for obstruction and throw you in a cell to cool off?"

"Are you getting me back for suspecting you earlier?" he asked, more than half serious.

"Partly." His friend smiled before his expression turned solemn again. "I want to bring Erica home to you. Let me do that."

It cost him everything to agree, but he did. Itchy with inaction, he said, "I'm going to check on Jacob."

Zack opened his son's door to an empty room. It wasn't unusual for Jacob to hit the head in the middle of the night, but the light was off in the adjoining bathroom. A double-check revealed it to be empty, too.

"Jacob?"

Nothing.

Zack hustled to his bedroom, finding no sign of his son. He tore through the house, hollering for Jacob. His brothers followed suit, as Bucky ran outside to check the grounds.

"*What the fuck?!*" Zack shouted. "How the hell does an eight-year-old boy disappear with a half-dozen cops surrounding the house and five adults inside?"

"Stay calm," one of his brothers commanded. He couldn't say which one since he was mindless and mid-meltdown.

"Would he have gone to Charlie's?" Mason asked.

Zack dialed Jacob's grandfather. After a series of rings, he disconnected the call and ran for Charlie's house. Along the way, he tried the number a second time, and for a third as he pounded on Charlie's door.

When no one answered, Dane twisted the knob, and when it turned under the pressure, he shoved it open. Mere feet from the entryway, Charlie lay in a pool of his own blood. For one heart-stopping moment, they froze.

"You got this?" Zack asked, pushing through his shock. At Dane's nod, he hauled ass toward the bedrooms. "Call an ambulance," he hollered over his shoulder to Mason.

Dane had dropped to his knees and was searching for a pulse. With no time to waste, Zack ran from room to room, ready to tear the fucking walls down to find Jacob. But he was nowhere to be found.

His brothers glanced up as he returned.

"Jacob?" Mason asked.

"He's not here." Fear uncoiled in him like a snake, striking at his heart and mind. "That unbalanced bitch has my son," he whispered. "She has them both."

"We'll get them back," Dane promised him.

Zack lacked his confidence.

"I'm sorry, Zack. Someone had been there, but when we got to Erica's house, they were already gone."

It wasn't hard to tell Bucky had a difficult time delivering *that* bit of bad news. His friend was sweating profusely and looked like he'd rather face a guillotine than confess they let Christie slip through their fingers.

Trying his best to remain calm, Zack asked, "Anything on Jacob?"

"No. Again, I'm sorry."

This time, there were no false promises. The situation had turned dire. During questioning, all they'd gotten from Judith was an evil laugh and a giant "fuck you." Now, they all sat, gathered at the hospital awaiting any news about Charlie's condition. The initial CT scan had shown bleeding on his brain, and surgical intervention was mandatory. If he made it through the operation, it would be a wait-and-see game until he woke up.

Dr. Montgomery didn't offer false hope. He merely informed them brain injuries were tricky and the best they could do was remain positive.

Shonda had offered to remain at the house with a plainclothes officer in case Jacob miraculously made his way home. But Zack and his brothers, who all viewed Charlie as a father figure, felt the need to be here for him, whatever the outcome.

Their mother had joined them and now occupied a visitors' chair as if she had a stake in Charlie's recovery. He'd never seen her look so haggard.

"Mom?" His inquiry pulled her out of her inner reflection. "What's going on? I thought you barely knew Charlie. I mean, except for greeting him with coffee and muffins every time he brought one of us home, you never acted as if... *Oh!*"

Wry humor twisted her mouth. "We were childhood sweethearts."

"You never said anything," he said, sounding accusatory to his own ears. Giving her a sickly smile, he shrugged. "Sorry."

"Do you tell me about all your romantic interludes?"

"Um, no. It would be disturbing, don't you think?"

She lifted a brow, waiting for him to get her point.

"Oh. Yeah. Okay," he searched for something to say. The idea of his mother getting it on with anyone was destroying his brain cells at a rapid rate. He needed brain bleach.

"Besides, it wasn't like that. We only dated a few times in high school," she said. Her face twisted into a mask of dislike. "I really thought we had something until Judith played the pregnancy card."

"But Christie is younger than us," he said, confused.

"Precisely. Later, Judith claimed she suffered a miscarriage, and perhaps she did, but Charlie had made a commitment and planned to see it through. By then I was dating your father." His mother paused to take a deep breath and exhale. Shaking her head, she continued, "The truth finally came out during her pregnancy with Christie. When I think of her lies, I want to smash her face in."

"When did you become violent?" he asked with an incredulous laugh.

"When she and her lying clone set out to hurt you," his mother replied fiercely.

"Is Charlie the reason you and Dad never worked out?"

"No... maybe... I don't know. I loved your father and tried to be a good wife, but he was too busy hiding his other family who had no idea we existed, either."

"I'm sorry." Hurting for her, Zack clasped her hand.

"For what? That I have crappy luck with men? It's not your fault," she said. Leaning in, she kissed his cheek. "But it's sweet of you to say."

Dane and Mason stepped through the door with breakfast for everyone and two cups of coffee for Zack. He couldn't remember when he'd last slept, and the fatigue was limiting. His thoughts circled back to Erica and Jacob.

Where the hell were they?

His phone dinged, and he scanned the meeting reminder.

"Did either of you check in at *Workout World*?"

While business was the last thing he cared about, it was a necessity and paid the bills. It gave him something to concentrate on other than the horrific shit show running through his mind.

"I did," Dane replied. "Lacey has everything handled. We really should offer her a managerial position."

Zack considered it as he sipped his coffee. "Yeah, it works for me. Todd might have a meltdown if we offer her the position first, though. He's been with us the longest."

"But she's got better business sense and people skills. We can always make him the manager of the Sagefield branch. It wouldn't be a bad idea to separate them, anyway," Mason said. When Zack sent him a questioning look, he shrugged. "Todd can't keep his eyes off her when they're scheduled together. I'm worried we'll have a sexual harassment suit on our hands before long."

"That's fucking great. We should get rid of him all together. Dane?"

"I can't say I love the guy, but he's a good enough worker when she's not around. I've kept an eye on him, and his focus is strictly on Lacey. He doesn't appear to be a creeper in general," Dane replied around a mouthful of food.

"Do we need to worry about her safety?"

His brother's expression tightened. "No. He's asked her out, but he respected her refusal and the fact she's engaged."

"And there's no harassment going on? She's not upset by his attention?"

"No, but I made note of it in both their personnel files. I don't expect anything to come of it, but I wanted to be sure any hint of sexual harassment was squashed." Dane shrugged and went back to eating.

Zack considered their options. "Okay. Can one of you handle Lacey's promotion paperwork and speak to Todd about his options? As a condition of his continued employment, he needs to behave around Lacey." He scowled. "She shouldn't have to feel uncomfortable. Tell him he's lucky he's a good employee in every other way and that we've never had a hint of complaint."

Mason lifted his plastic utensil to volunteer. Zack glanced at Dane, who agreed with a silent nod.

"It's settled, then."

"You should try to eat something, bro," Dane said as he shoved a food container closer.

The congealing contents turned Zack's stomach. "Yeah, I'm not sure I can."

"When did you eat last?" Connie asked.

"I had a donut about eight hours ago," he admitted.

Mason paused, spork halted mid-shovel. "A *donut*? Since when do *you* eat donuts?"

"Fuck off, asshat."

"Dickhead."

At the reprimand from their mother, they exchanged grins. They sobered almost immediately, recalling their situation.

Zack's phone chirped.

> "I have them both. You really should be more careful about letting your whore and our son wander the streets."

"That fucking bitch!" he swore and flung his phone. Dane, in a move to do pro athletes everywhere proud, snatched the device out of the air before it smashed against the wall.

"Zack!" his mother gasped.

"Not now, Mom," Mason warned with a shake of his head. "What did she say this time, Zack?"

"She has Jacob." Zack's throat felt thick with fear.

"Why the hell can't they use the GPS on her phone?" Dane asked.

"According to Bucky, she sends a text and turns it off immediately afterward."

"Can't they tell which tower the phone pinged from?" Connie asked.

"Mom, we're a small town. All carriers use the same tower here. It won't pinpoint her location." Mason grimaced. "You have to stop watching so many crime dramas."

"Okay, but I'm certain I read they can track phones even if they're off."

"Again with the crime shows," Mason said, earning a glare. "Seriously, I don't know. Maybe she's removing the battery or the SIM card?"

"Erica would know," Zack said absently. "It's something she would've researched for her novels."

"She writes the best books." Connie smiled dreamily. "I've read every one. Some of those sex scenes? Wow!"

"Mom!" Three male voices groaned in unison.

"Oh, I forgot. All mothers are saints," she said drily.

"That's right. And don't forget again," Mason growled. "Can I scrub this conversation from my mind? I need brain bleach."

Zack snorted. "I was thinking the same thing not ten minutes ago."

"Back to the subject at hand. You should report the text to Bucky, Zack," Dane said, handing him the phone. "Maybe there's something the PD can do. Now that a child is involved, they might bring in the FBI."

"I don't think she'll hurt him. At least not yet. She isn't through baiting me," Zack replied. "But Erica..."

CHAPTER
THIRTY

Erica had no idea where she was. Sometime during the night, Christie had hauled her off the frigid cement floor and shoved her into the trunk. The only bright side had come when her legs were freed. It was impossible to escape with crippling pins and needles, but the relief she felt by straightening her legs for the first time in hours was immense. Her new prison was warmer, and there was carpeting to cushion her from the bare flooring. She didn't want to experience gratitude for her captor for anything, but she was thrilled to be out of the damp evening air.

While Christie was gone, doing God knew what, Erica had tried to work her bonds loose, to no avail. She'd felt behind her, hoping to find something, anything, sharp enough to saw through the tie wraps. Nothing. She'd screamed her frustration. All she'd gotten for it was a raw throat and aching shoulders. She'd give half her next book earnings for water and a lozenge.

Hours after she'd left, Christie returned with another prisoner in tow.

Crying began in the next room. A sick sixth sense said it was Jacob. Who else could it be? How the hell Christie had managed to nab him was beyond her deductive reasoning. It was difficult to believe Zack would let his son out of his sight, but perhaps Charlie and Judith had something to do with it. If Zack hadn't known they were involved, he'd still believe them trustworthy.

There had been plenty of time to think over the last eight hours. The only people who'd possibly help Christie in all this were her parents. No other sane person would cover up the fact she hadn't died in the hospital fire. The body count would've been off. All patients and staff would've been accounted for. But if that was the case, how had there not been a statewide manhunt for an escaped patient?

The only reasonable explanation was Christie had been checked out sometime in the days prior. The only ones able to were her mother, father, and doctor.

Considering Christie's penchant for fire starting, it didn't take a genius to guess she had something to do with the blaze that had destroyed the hospital. Gruesome scenarios for the future danced through Erica's weary mind. Christie had transported the container of gasoline to the new place. She had arson on the brain.

Was it possible the whacko planned to set this house on fire with Jacob and her in two separate rooms? Would Christie force Zack to choose who lived or died? Or did she plan to burn them alive, leaving him helpless to save them? If so, she didn't know him very well. There was no way he wouldn't risk his life to rescue them.

"Hello?" she called out. "Christie? Psycho?"

The sniffling stopped.

"Erica?"

She fought back tears. It made her sick to know Jacob's fate was now tied with her own. If she'd never appeared on the scene, would Christie have ever stooped to victimizing her own child?

"I'm here, sweetie," she rasped, voice hoarse from her earlier rage.

"Are you okay?" His voice sounded shaky as if he were struggling to be brave.

Her heart melted. There he was, a young kid scared out of his mind, asking about *her* welfare at a time when he should be concerned with his own. Erica's tears flowed freely, and it took all her acting ability to speak normally.

"Y-yes. I'm okay. How about you? Are you hurt?"

"Not really. My mom smacked me when I tried to help Grandpa. It doesn't hurt anymore."

"She definitely likes to hit. Do you know where she is now? I didn't hear her leave."

"She left after she tied me up," he said. "Erica? I have to pee real bad."

"Hold it as long as you can, sweetie. But if you can't, that's okay, too." She didn't want him to feel shame. Her own bladder was full to rupturing. It was doubtful she would last, either. It would be humiliating to be rescued in wet pants, and that mortifying image was the only thing keeping her from christening the carpet.

"Dad was worried about you. He yelled at Grandma. Then the cops took her to jail."

So, Judith *had* been involved.

His earlier comment registered.

"You tried to help your grandfather? What happened?" she asked sharply.

"I couldn't sleep because I was worried about you. But Dad said I had to go to bed. Grandpa sent me a text. He wanted me to come keep him company because he couldn't sleep, either," he said. "But my mom was there and Grandpa was on the ground. He was bleeding."

Erica felt helpless as he caught back a sob. What she wouldn't give to comfort him! To hug and tell him everything would be okay. Jacob was a smart kid, though. He'd know she was lying.

"I think my Grandpa's dead. I think my mom killed him."

"Maybe he was just knocked out." She strove for positivity, but he wasn't buying it.

"He wasn't moving, Erica. I think it was really her who texted me."

"I think you're right. She's sneaky. But your dad will make sure Charlie gets help. I know it. When he finds you missing, he'll check with your grandfather first."

"You think so? Maybe he isn't dead? Maybe Dad helped him?"

"I'm sure of it," she lied, sending up a silent prayer it had happened just like that.

"Erica?"

"Yeah?"

"I'm glad you're okay."

"I'm glad you're okay, too. We'll get out of here. I've been working on some ideas." All of which included cutting through these damn wraps. As of yet, she'd failed, but she refused to go out this way.

"Like what?"

Leave it to a kid to ask a million questions.

"It's a surprise." Lame, even to her.

"Um, Erica?"

"Yeah?"

"You don't have a plan, do you?"

She snorted a laugh. He was Zack's kid, all right! She should've remembered how freaking smart he was. "A tentative one. Like I said, I'm working on it."

"Okay." He sounded skeptical.

"Jacob?"

"Yeah?"

"Everything *will* be okay. We're going to look back on this as a strange adventure one day." She hoped he believed her.

"Okay," he said, weepy again.

She feared her words had the opposite effect. Instead of reassuring him, she'd probably convinced him they were going to die.

"I mean it, sweetie. Your dad won't let anything happen to you. Between him and the police, they'll find us soon. I'm sure of it."

"I don't know. He called them Barney's Wife motherfuckers."

Erica sniggered.

"Fife," she choked out. "Barney Fife."

"What's a Barney-Fife Motherfucker?"

Erica fought to contain her laughter. It didn't say much for her state of mind that she was reduced to hysteria. Hers triggered Jacob's. Listening to him giggle warmed her heart, providing a sense of rightness in all this insanity.

"Barney Fife was a silly cop from a TV show when your grand-parents were young," she managed to say a short while later. "He was always accidentally causing problems for Sheriff Andy in the town of Mayberry."

"Ah."

"Ah? Why ah?"

"He said Stonebrooke was as backward as Fucking Mayberry."

Erica lost it and laughed again. "Hey, sweetie? Um, you might not want to repeat any of that to anyone else, okay?"

"Okay," he said cheerfully.

"Are you somewhat comfortable, Jacob?"

"I guess."

"Can you close your eyes and try to sleep? It might help if you're rested later when we're rescued. Okay?"

"Okay."

A few minutes passed, and she missed the conversation.

"Erica?"

"Yeah?"

"I love you," his wobbly voice said.

It hurt her to hear he was back to being scared.

"I love you, too, sweet boy. How about when we return home, you teach me how to play video games?"

His tone was filled with hope. "Really?"

"Really. It's past time I learned to kick your dad's butt, don't you think? I'll never surpass your skill, but I can probably whoop *him*."

He giggled. Then he proceeded to tell her all about his favorite elements of play. She inserted the proper responses here and there to keep him preoccupied. She'd much rather he concentrate on a video game than on being a hostage.

Eventually, his voice grew sleepy, and he wished her good night.

"Good night, sweetie."

Then Erica was alone. Periodically she dozed, but she'd snap back awake, listening and planning for the right time to escape.

The slamming of a car door created knots in her stomach. So much for executing one of her many ridiculous escape plans before Christie returned!

Sunlight peeked through the bottom of her blindfold. Somewhere along the way she'd lost track of time.

"Hello, whore," Christie said by way of greeting.

"Hello, psycho. I see you've kidnapped an innocent child. How very enterprising of you," Erica replied, careful to keep her tone light and pleasant. "Did you not think about bringing the FBI down on your head, genius?"

The fist to the side of her head wasn't as light or as pleasant. Jesus, she really needed to curb her tongue. But she was hangry, and her inner demon was settling in for a spell. How long had it been since she had a carb? Her body might go into shock soon. It wasn't used to deprivation.

"Didn't your mother teach you it isn't nice to strike out at the other kids on the playground?" Erica taunted. "Oh, that's right. She encouraged your fucking nutso behavior."

She took great delight in imagining how beet red the other woman's face must be in her rage. A vicious kick to her ribs bent her double, or as far double as her bound wrists would allow, and she lost the vision bringing her such pleasure.

"Shut the fuck up!"

Because she'd surpassed pissed off and was heading into Incredible Hulk territory, Erica refused to be ordered about. "Go fuck yourself!"

Admittedly, her comeback lost its effectiveness through pain-filled panted breaths, but her point came across well enough.

Another blow landed in the vicinity of the first.

"Godfuckingdammityoucrazyassbitch!"

"Erica? Erica?" Jacob's frightened cry brought her back from the edge.

She summoned every ounce of control and made her voice as normal as possible. "I'm okay, Jacob. Just having a bit of a dis..."—she paused to catch her breath—"disagreement with your mother. It's all good."

"Don't you talk to him, or I'll slit your flabby throat," Christie threatened, low and fierce.

"Flabby? Who are you calling flabby, you—" A blade met the skin protecting her carotid artery.

"Not another word," Christie warned.

How was she supposed to respond to that? If she agreed, she'd get her throat slit for speaking, but if she said nothing, it might provoke Christie into stabbing her anyway, believing she was being obstinate. After what felt like the longest standoff in history, the knife was withdrawn.

Although it was removed from alongside her neck, Erica held her breath for an additional ten seconds in case her nemesis decided to plunge the blade to the hilt. When a brutal stabbing no longer seemed imminent, she breathed an abbreviated sigh of relief. She was fairly certain her ribs were cracked, and inhaling was uncomfortable.

Maybe Christie would burst a blood vessel or suffer a paralyzing seizure, continuing until help arrived. No such luck. *She* was the one who had hulked out. One more thing to Google: had there ever been a second Hulk, and if so, was there an epic battle? Who won? The good guy or the nemesis?

"Erica?" Jacob's concerned shout carried to her.

"Shut up, you little brat!" Christie yelled.

"No! I want my dad!"

Hearing Christie stomp away, presumably in Jacob's direction, Erica taunted her, hoping to draw her wrath.

"Hey, psycho! Did you bring me any food, or was your grand plan to starve me to death? Order a damn pizza or something, will ya?"

Christie laughed. Not maniacally, but more like actual amusement as if Erica had tickled her funny bone. "I'll say one thing for you, whore. You've got balls of steel. I'll miss our interactions after you're gone."

"Yeah, me not so much. By the way, the kid probably has to go to the bathroom."

When the slap came, there wasn't as much force behind it, and Erica was eternally grateful. Losing teeth was a stupid thing to worry about at this juncture, but the vain part of her didn't want to have a gaping smile. If she lived, of course. Surely, they wouldn't have an open casket for a battered woman, would they? Doubtless, her skin was bruised black and blue. The undertaker would have to slather on the foundation to cover the marks. A caked make-up look was never attractive, dead *or* alive.

Yes, her thoughts were maudlin, but an author's brain never slept. She retreated into her mind to plot out the next section of her current novel. One where she killed a crazy stalker bent on destroying her life.

THIRTY-ONE

Bucky had changed into civilian clothes after his shift ended and arrived back at the hospital to sit with Zack's family. The show of support humbled him. Less than twenty-four hours ago, he'd been ready to accuse the man of being Christie's accomplice. Bucky was due an apology.

The wait for news on either front was interminable. Zack met with another officer and provided details about the additional texts he'd received. They agreed to call off the policeman sitting with Shonda at his house. Knowing Christie held Jacob hostage, there was no point in anyone staying there.

Mason had encouraged Shonda to head home to rest, but she refused and claimed rank as Erica's best friend. She, too, took up residence in the hospital waiting room.

An Amber Alert was issued and sent to all media outlets. The idea was to saturate the news stations with images of Jacob, Christie, and Erica in hopes someone might've seen something. Erica wasn't as easy to move as a child without raising a ruckus, and, to that end, she was expendable. Zack hoped like hell she would keep her head and not antagonize Christie in any way.

Uniformed officers roamed the hospital corridor as an added measure. Bucky had surmised Zack would be her next target. He'd also placed a call to the FBI, who intended to send an agent from the local bureau.

As they waited for the agent to arrive, Zack created a list of all the places he and Christie had visited together and the various dates. Going a step further, he cataloged all of Christie's likes or dislikes, figuring they might play into her hiding spot in some small way.

During their relationship, he'd humored her every whim, contributing to her obsession. It was no wonder why she was convinced she owned him.

"Fuck it. I need coffee," he muttered, heading for the nearest exit. The walls were closing in, and claustrophobia had a stranglehold on him. Inactivity had never been his friend, and the longer it went on, the more squirrelly he got.

"I'll go with you and help carry the drinks back," Dane offered.

"No!" Zack snapped. Seeing the shocked faces of those around him, he held up a hand in apology. "Can I have a few minutes to myself? Please?"

"Sure. I'm sorry. I wasn't thinking."

"Thanks, man."

As he wandered the halls, he idly wondered if Dane, the most mild-mannered Sharp, had ever lost his cool. He couldn't remember a single time his youngest brother had ever gotten in trouble for starting a fight or letting fly his temper. How was it possible when Mason was so hotheaded and he, himself, was prone to erupt when pushed too far?

His phone pinged. Another missive from Christie. Catching a glimpse of Erica, injured and bound on the floor, Zack couldn't bring himself to look at it. How long would this shit continue? Bearing witness to Erica's and Jacob's suffering while unable to save them was breaking him. Christie's intent, no doubt. If he could stand not being the first to know, he'd hand over his cell to one of his brothers to screen the messages.

He dropped his head back and inhaled deeply. His longing for stimulants and fresh air was strong. The antiseptic odor had infiltrated his nostrils and given him a raging headache, and his mission was to find caffeine and pain relievers. In that order!

A curvy blonde at the coffee kiosk did her best to flirt with him as he placed his order. Three months ago, he might've flirted right back and taken her up on what amounted to a blatant offer. But today, in comparison to Erica, she seemed extremely young and lacking. If that didn't tell him he was too far gone, nothing would. He should send Mason back and gauge his reaction to the hottie. Odds were his brother was in the same boat over Shonda.

"Anything else?" she asked suggestively.

As she leaned over the counter, displaying her double D's, Zack purposefully shifted his gaze to the donuts under the clear dome. What were the chances any had lemon filling? He peered through the glass and noticed a raspberry jam. Any flavor would make him feel closer to Erica. It was ridiculous to believe she could feel his love via a donut, but he would embrace any connection, however small. "I'll take the raspberry unless you have lemon."

Her disappointment was displayed in her exaggerated lip pursing. Without acknowledging the practiced pout, he accepted his change, dumped it into a tip jar, and strode away. As he loitered outside, he sipped his coffee, ate his donut, and considered his game plan. He needed to find a way to let Christie know he was ready to enter the playing field.

Winner takes all.

CHRISTIE BAUER LOUNGED in the corner, watching Erica alternate between struggling to stay awake and working her bonds.

Spider and the fly.

She smiled.

Would Erica's writer brain figure out the plot of this little story? The chick was smart and actually quite funny at times. When Christie forgot to hate her, she quite liked her. Earlier, while she was out getting supplies, she'd swiped Erica's latest novel from the local library. Maybe she would have her sign it before she killed her. Wouldn't that be a fun trophy?

Eighteen hours had passed since she picked Erica up. During that time, her plan had been put in motion. Snatching Jacob from under Zack's nose had been orgasmic. The continued euphoria was the only thing keeping her from ending the little brat's life.

Christie experienced a pang of remorse for striking her father down. Seeing him bleeding, so motionless and vulnerable for once in his life, had given her pause. What if he died? Phone calls to the hospital had produced no information. Privacy laws made it diffi-cult, and the receptionist would only give information to the family. And of course, she couldn't admit who she was.

Thoughts of her father dying made her itchy and moody. Her parents were the only two people to have ever cared about her. Well, at least until her father *hadn't*. It all went to hell when he committed her six years ago. Christie had spent her entire incar-ceration trying to convince her father to sign the release forms, and when he continued to refuse, she relied on her mother to help.

A sound from the neighboring bedroom made her sit upright.

Crying.

Ugh, the stupid boy!

Nothing had changed in the years since they were separated. One day, when he was two years old, she had to run errands, and she'd tied him up at home for his own safety. It wasn't as if she was gone long. The store was located five minutes from the condo. But all he did was wail and wail when she returned, crying until he puked. The constant caterwauling was rage-inducing. Why wouldn't he stop? He was dry and fed.

"Why wouldn't he stop?"

She hadn't been aware of screaming the question until she saw Erica's head whipped her way. The stupid bitch acted as if Jacob was *her* son—always trying to insert herself, trying to protect him.

"Christie? How about that pizza? Surely you have to be hungry by now," Erica said in another attempt at distraction.

As if she was an idiot! As if she couldn't see through the whore's game!

"Shut up, or I'll cut your fucking tongue out. You and the brat are making me nuts."

Erica's snorted disbelief nearly upset her. To soothe herself, Christie clicked open her lighter and envisioned Erica screaming and writhing in pain as flames licked up her legs.

Not long now.

The next stage was fast approaching. Once Zack let his guard down and lost the law enforcement tail, the final step of her revenge would be complete. She intended to gleefully watch him shrivel and die in slow degrees as first his lover, then his child burned. Keeping him around to wallow in his misery for a few extra days might feed her need for justice. But he'd die, too.

Continually informing Erica that Zack loved *her* was provoking the other woman. Oh, to see her face when she recognized the ploy for what it was! And she would, but too late to stop Christie's plan. It was almost sad to lose such a clever adversary, but she couldn't be left to live.

Christie glanced at her watch.

Time to text Zack again.

Positioning the light to enhance the bruises and blood on Erica's face, she switched the filter to black and white to begin her photoshoot. For added drama, Christie punched her ribcage, capturing Erica's open-mouthed screams.

As her hostage struggled to breathe, Christie blissfully scrolled through the camera roll, adjusting exposure and shadows, creating macabre masterpieces. She smiled. The next round would be Jacob's photo shoot. A picture of him suffering would really scramble Zack's brain, and he'd throw all caution to the winds. The moment he reacted, she'd have him.

She sent the file and was disconcerted when a return text popped up.

"Enough! Tell me what you want."

Well, good for him. Zack must've prepared it ahead of time. Christie hadn't had a chance to power down the phone, but the accidental delay brought more than she hoped for.

"Lose the cops. We'll talk. I'll call in 1 hr. Don't cross me."

After she hit send, she shut down the phone, removing the SIM card and battery.

THIRTY-TWO

Slack-jawed, Zack gaped at the screen. He couldn't believe Christie had responded. In one hour, he'd be a step closer to bringing them home. Exhaustion was weighing him down, and the repeated refrain through his mind was, *"What if you can only save one?"*

No contest. He'd pick Jacob, but his soul would shrivel and die. Forgiveness would never come if he failed to rescue Erica.

"You're awfully quiet," Shonda noted.

Her shrewd look said she knew what was up. Guilt kicked in. She'd never forget he was the one ultimately responsible for Erica's death, should it come to that. By extension, he'd ruin any relationship Shonda and Mason might have. *If* his dumbass brother didn't do it all on his own first.

Crikey, he was pessimistic, and he blamed lack of sleep. He was a cranky fuck if he didn't get a minimum of seven hours per night during normal times.

Shonda's voice dropped to scarcely above a whisper as she asked, "What are you planning?"

"Nothing."

Her eyes narrowed in suspicion.

Yeah, he wasn't the best actor.

"You *are*, and I want in," she insisted in a harsh whisper, darting a quick look at Mason.

A check over his shoulder assured him Mason didn't like their closeness. As scowls went, his brother's was grade A. Zack's faux grin turned real when Mason rolled his eyes and presented his back. Let him think the conversation involved him. Maybe he wouldn't interfere when the time came for Zack to go after Christie.

"Nicely done," Shonda murmured. Her eyes held an appreciative twinkle.

"Years of practice."

"Your brother's an easy mark. Now spill."

"You aren't letting this go, are you?"

Tone steely, she said, "Not on your life."

She was beautiful. More so than Erica by society's standards. He attributed it to her exotic features. One would assume a blonde-haired, green-eyed woman would look like the all-American girl next door, but her olive complexion and high cheekbones hinted at Asian ancestry. Standing around five-ten without heels, Shonda was the perfect height for Mason, who had resumed staring them down from his side of the room.

"What's he so angry about?"

"He probably thinks I'm going to seduce you to the dark side like I did Dane," she replied dryly, but her comment contained an underlying hurt.

"You and Dane? What did I miss?"

"Earlier, your mother sent Mason for coffee. When he didn't promptly return, she asked me to find him." Shonda's shrug was far too casual. Clearly, she'd been upset by what she'd found but was desperately trying to hide it.

He was bothered to see he'd misjudged Mason. Disappointed

his brother hadn't ignored the blonde barista's come-on, Zack grimaced. If Shonda caught his brother flirting, it had to suck.

"Your mother employed the brilliant idea of having Dane steal a kiss if you can believe it." Shonda rolled her eyes. "Mason broke his nose."

Zack sputtered a laugh.

"It's not funny!" she exclaimed.

He laughed harder as Mason surged to his feet, flipped them off, then stormed out the door.

Shonda bit her lip to suppress her own amusement. "Okay, so maybe it's a little funny."

"I wondered where they were. Thought maybe they went for dinner."

"No, your mom drove Dane home after all the nurses gushed over him. She said she wanted to take a nap, but she'd return with food for everyone."

"So you've been trapped here, subject to the silent treatment for the better part of the day with my idiot brother and me. Poor baby," Zack said with sympathy.

"Okay, enough stalling. He's gone so you can tell me what's going on. And don't you dare say nothing. I want to help."

He popped up to pace. "I can't involve you in this, Shonda. Christie is clinically insane. It's impossible to know what's going on in that messed-up head of hers."

"I'm involving myself. Erica's the only real family I have left. We're sisters of a sort," she insisted.

Giving her comment due consideration, he nodded. Although he couldn't drag her into the active part of his plan, maybe he'd run ideas by her. Get another person's take on what to do. Wordlessly, he unlocked his cell, pulled up Christie's texts, and handed it over.

Her hand flew to her mouth, and moisture flooded her eyes as she scrolled through the attachments. "Ohmygod! Have you shown these to the police?"

"Not the recent ones. She wants me to meet her. Alone. You can see where she intends to call me."

"Zack, you probably don't know, but I'm a retired real estate agent."

She wore a thoughtful frown, and his hope fluttered to life.

"Tell me you recognize those rooms."

"I believe I do. It's this fireplace, here." She pointed as she zoomed in on one of the images. "It's unique to that particular house. I remember taking a potential buyer on a tour of the place. I can't be positive, but I think the house is part of an unfinished subdivision over in Stapleton. It's mostly abandoned now. The city condemned the third stage of the project a few years back. Rightly so since the contractor was a shady bastard."

Zack jumped up and jerked her to her feet with him.

"Where is it?" he demanded, gripping her shoulders.

"Let her go!"

Mason's low-voiced command was animalistic in its implied threat. The hairs on the back of Zack's neck stood at attention as he sensed the danger.

"Jesus, Mason. I'm not hurting her."

"But you are," his brother returned silkily, menace thick in his tone.

Zack gazed into Shonda's face and noticed her compressed lips. He released her. "I'm sorry. I..."

It belatedly occurred to him that he couldn't have caused such discomfort with his heavy-handed grip, and he dragged down the shirt's neckline, exposing her shoulder.

"What the fuck? Who did this?"

She winced and avoided looking in Mason's direction.

Zack lost it. Fury boiled inside him, and he swung to confront his brother.

"You did this?"

"No! Jesus, Zack. Give me some credit." The look Mason sent Shonda was uncharacteristically tender before he remembered himself. "She was mugged last week. Earlier today, I forgot and grabbed her arm."

"I'm sorry, Shonda." Ashamed of his impulsive act, Zack felt heat creep up his neck. There was no excuse for his behavior, regardless of how worried he was for his family. "I didn't know, and I definitely shouldn't have touched you without permission."

"No harm, no foul, but how about you step away from her and let her fix her shirt, Mr. Grabby," Mason groused, joining them.

"Why should it matter to *you*?" Shonda retorted.

She shoved past Mason, prepared to leave.

Zack lunged forward, blocking her path but not touching her. "Shonda, wait! Where's the location of the house?" His desperation made the question sharper than it should've been, but her eyes held understanding.

"I'll need to check my old files for the exact address. Do you want to follow me back to my apartment?"

"No," Mason bellowed, stepping between them and cutting off Zack's reply. "No one is going anywhere until you tell me what the hell is going on."

"Dammit, I don't have time for your jealousy, Mason. Get a clue already," Zack shouted with a hard shove to his brother's chest. The force of the blow drove him into the wall.

Zack knew he'd feel remorse later, but right now, he had to find that abandoned house.

"I wasn't jealous, and I'm not a complete idiot," Mason replied sourly. "I recognize you're planning something. Did you find where Christie's holding Jacob and Erica?"

"We think so."

"Then let's go. I'll drive."

"No. Someone has to stay for Charlie," Zack protested. "We can't leave him with no one."

"The doctor said he wasn't waking anytime soon. I already spoke to Mom, and she's on the way." Mason's large hand on the back of his neck guided him toward the exit. "No more arguments. Let's go."

Mason lost his tan when he saw the condition Erica was in. Although he always presented as the toughest of the three brothers, he possessed a pure marshmallow core when it came to abused women or children. He'd been volunteering for years at a local women's shelter, and he always took it hard if he failed in his mission to help a female or family in need.

"Mason, we can do this," Zack said gently, concerned for his brother's state of mind.

"No, it's okay. *I'm* okay," he stated, grim but determined.

They all selected a set of files to browse and compare to the background of the pictures Christie had sent. As they finished searching the last of Shonda's files, the phone rang.

Unknown number.

Gesturing for them to stay silent, Zack answered.

"Hello, lover," Christie purred.

He struggled mightily to keep the hatred out of his voice. "Christie."

"Are you ready to play a game?"

"I thought we were already playing. You drew us into this farce against our will weeks ago," he retorted.

Mason mouthed, "Don't piss her off."

"Yes, it's been pretty fun." Her brittle laughter grated on his last nerve.

"I want to speak to Jacob."

"Not your little whore? You surprise me, Zack. I mean, I know you sent the kid to live with my parents when your slut moved in," she said nastily. "I assumed she meant more to you."

A pain-filled cry sounded in the background.

Erica.

It had to be. Bile burned his throat, and he fought for control of his stomach's contents.

"Please. Just to see if he's all right," Zack pleaded. Yes, he was giving her the advantage, but he needed to speak to Jacob.

"Sure thing, lover."

Her shoes squeaked on the hardwood, and the sound echoed as she journeyed through the house. It revealed their first clue: her hostages weren't together.

"Jacob, talk to your father," she ordered.

"Dad? Dad?"

Tears flowed from Zack's eyes. He was powerless to stop them. The terror in Jacob's voice was supplanted by budding hope.

"Hey, lil man. You doing all right?"

"Yeah, but I think Erica's hurt. She—"

"Enough!" Christie yelled before coming back on the line. "You've heard him. He's fine. I'll call you in an hour and tell you where to go."

"Christie! Christie, *wait!*"

Dead air.

She'd already disconnected, and Zack barely curbed his impulse to pulverize the phone. Instead, he tossed it on the table and stalked away. If he got his hands on her, he'd kill her. He wanted her dead. For real, this time.

"Zack."

"I need a minute, Mason," he croaked. His anxiety was at an all-time high, and if he didn't get his blood pressure down, he'd likely stroke out.

"Shonda thinks she found the house."

CHAPTER

THIRTY-THREE

"When I couldn't find it in the files, I did a reverse image lookup on my phone. I was right. It's located at 116 Eastside Lane, in the center of Wisteria Estates, over in Stapleton. That's about thirty minutes from our location," Shonda said, adjusting her laptop screen for the men to see.

"You're shitting me! The same address as Zack's? What are the chances of that?" Mason asked.

"Pretty good," she replied with a grimace. "You'd be surprised how many duplicates there are and in a fairly close vicinity, too. It made showing houses a nightmare some days."

"I'm not surprised. To Christie, it would be the ultimate joke." Zack shook his head. She was always three steps ahead of them. At this rate, they'd never catch her. "Any way we can get a floor plan?"

Shonda wasn't optimistic. "This time of day, all the courthouse offices for permits and planning are closed. But let me call a friend and see if she has one from when she used to show the house."

Ten minutes and an email later, they had memorized the online layout of the house.

"Pull up maps on your laptop. Let's see if we can find an aerial view of the landscape and neighboring houses," Zack directed Shonda.

"Smart," Mason muttered.

"I have my moments."

"No house directly behind," Shonda pointed out. "But on either side, there appears to be tall vinyl fencing."

"What if we plan a backyard approach? Think she'll be on the lookout for us?" Mason asked.

Zack put himself in Christie's shoes and tried to determine what he'd do if he were the one holding hostages. "If I had to guess, she'll have Erica in the front room and Jacob in the back of the house."

"What makes you say that?"

"Erica is the bigger threat if she gets loose. Christie would want to have her within sight at all times. It stands to reason, if she's watching out the front for any attack, then she would have Erica tied up there, where she can keep an eye on her." He ran a hand through his hair. "I don't think she would view Jacob as a potential problem. She'd be more inclined to leave him alone for longer periods. In a rear room, he's far enough from the road that if he yelled, he probably wouldn't be heard." He exchanged a look with Shonda. "Erica wouldn't call out and risk Christie hurting Jacob in retaliation. She cares about him too much."

"I agree," Shonda said.

Mason nodded. "Makes sense. Zack, I think we should call the police. A SWAT team might get in there with no casualties."

"They won't show up without fanfare. I don't trust that she won't set the house ablaze the second she sees anyone close," he said raggedly. "I can't take the risk."

They all shared a worried look. Shonda was the first to break the silence. "Okay, here's what we do. I have a handgun in the safe. If you know how to use it, one of you can take it. I'll grab the first-aid kit and wait by the fence line." She touched Zack's arm, and he felt oddly reassured by her all-business tone. "We get Jacob out first. Have him run to me if he's able. If not, shoot me a text, and I'll come for him. That leaves you two to split up and search for Erica."

So far, her plan was sound, and he remained silent, waiting for her to continue. The strangest part was Mason taking the backseat to her command. He wasn't one to sit idle and needed to be in on the action from the start.

"Once I have Jacob, we'll go for the car and phone the police. You'll only have about seven or eight minutes max to save Erica afterward. Also, Mason should have the gun."

"You think *he* is the clearer-headed one of the two of us?" Zack asked, shocked she would think so.

"In this case, he is. Otherwise, I would say you most definitely are."

"Thanks for the show of support," his brother's caustic reply nearly made him laugh. In a different circumstance, it would've.

"Hey, you're the firm believer in people telling it like it is," she said with sourness in her voice and expression.

Zack quickly changed the subject. Their conversation could only deteriorate. "Where did you learn tactical planning?"

"I've helped Erica plot a few novels."

Her cheeky grin was priceless, and Zack hugged her.

"Hey," Mason warned.

"You snooze, you lose, pal."

"Whatever. Let's go. We only have a half-hour remaining, and it might take us that long to get there. If she leaves in the meantime, we're screwed."

Mason wasn't wrong, and his comment made Zack reconsider a call to the police. Instinct shouted against that course of action. He'd learned the hard way to trust his inner voice.

By the time they arrived, only ten minutes of the initial hour remained. Christie was due to call, and Zack hoped to be in position before she did. He and Mason walked stealthily through the wooded lot. The backyard was wider than it was deep, which worked in their favor. The quietness of the abandoned neighborhood was strange, bordering on creepy. This subdivision had a surplus of like-new homes in the middle of a housing shortage, and it felt like a waste.

As Mason turned back for Shonda, the phone rang.

"Christie?"

"Hello, lover."

"Tell me what you want. What can I do to get you to give me Jacob and release Erica?"

"You don't want her back, huh?" she asked. Her demeanor was surlier than it had been earlier, and she sounded more combative. "I guess you won't mind if I kill her, then."

"No!" he shouted, then winced. His yell echoed through the empty lot, and he freaked out inside, fearing she was within hearing distance. If she suspected he was mere feet from the back door, they were screwed.

Fuck!

His brother and Shonda appeared in his peripheral vision, and he held up a hand, halting them.

"What I mean to say is, I don't want anyone to die, Christie. She'd planned to go to Florida. She was leaving me. Wasn't that what you wanted?" he implored, prepared to plead for the lives of those he loved. "Can't you just let her go? What do I have to do for you to release them unharmed?"

"I'll tell you what. Come into the house, Zack."

"What do you mean?"

"Oh, don't for one moment believe I'm not aware you're close, lover. You come inside, and I'll let you pick which one gets to live."

"What are you talking about?"

How had she known?

Mason, unable to hear the conversation, stayed watchful and

detailed Zack's every reaction. His hand was clasping Shonda's, and their fingers were tightly interwoven, locking them together.

"Lie to me, and they both die," Christie said in a chilling manner. Calculated, almost. Her response wasn't heated, and it bothered Zack, though he couldn't understand quite why.

"Come into the clearing. Bring your brother and his friend," she ordered.

He swore savagely as she disconnected. His frustration levels were at an all-time high. How the hell did she manage to continually best them? Was she that smart, or was he predictable?

"She knows we're here," he told them flatly.

"How…" Mason turned in a half circle to study the trees. With a thoughtful frown, he dropped Shonda's hand and retraced his steps. "There it is."

"What?"

"An outdoor cam. Why the hell didn't we consider she'd have security measures in place?"

Maybe workout supplements produced dumbing side effects for jocks. Some rich motherfucker somewhere needed to host a study. Zack worried he was turning into a goddamned meathead, unable to think clearly where Christie was concerned.

"She wants us to step into the backyard. There's no guarantee she won't pull something or shoot us where we stand." Zack sighed heavily. "I can't ask either of you to take that risk."

Before Mason or Shonda responded, an explosion rocked the ground. Debris landed feet from where they were gathered, dumbfounded.

The reality struck.

"*No!*" Zack screamed.

He hauled ass for the house.

"*No! No! No! No! No!*" fell from his lips and accompanied his pulse, pounding in time with his arms and legs. Right as he prepared to run through the flames, Mason tackled him. As they crashed to the hard-packed dirt, his brother's arms cradled Zack's head and kept him safe from impact. Still, he clawed at Mason's steel-like grip and scrambled for purchase.

"Jacob!" he shouted, fighting his brother's hold. "I've got to get to Jacob!"

Mason hollered his name repeatedly, hanging on despite the flying fists. Unwilling to let him endanger himself on a lost cause.

***

Zack waited on the tailgate of the rescue vehicle as paramedics treated his minor cuts and burns. Devastated and brain-dead, he was unable to answer any of the million questions the police put to him. Fortunately, Mason and Shonda were composed and took up the slack.

As he stared at the charred, smoldering mess, he replayed the entire scene. What might he have done differently? What might he have said to convince Christie to release them? What the hell had he missed? Had she always intended to murder them? What-ifs were on a fast-track train, speeding through his chaotic mind.

The body bags were brought out, and he shrugged off the last of the first responders' ministrations to make his way to the gurneys. His driving need to see the destruction his carelessness had wrought hounded him. As he reached for the zipper, Bucky gripped his wrist.

"No, Zack. There's nothing to see. You don't want to remember them like this."

"Any sign of Christie?" he asked hoarsely, throat scratchy from sobs and smoke.

"None yet. But we'll find her. She won't get away with this."

"I've heard that tired fucking tune before." His disdainful words were an arctic blast, matching his now-cold and lifeless soul. What had once been a warm, beating heart now lay as icy shards on the ground. Nothing remained inside but hatred.

"I'm going to kill her," he said flatly, as he stared at Erica's and

Jacob's bagged bodies. "She can't run far or fast enough."

"Zack," Bucky warned.

He raised uncaring eyes to his friend. His main reason for living now was revenge.

"I'll take him home," Dane said as he joined them.

His brother had shown up sometime in the last hour, and Zack assumed Mason or Shonda had called him.

"I can't go back." Zack swallowed hard. "Not tonight."

"Okay. No problem. You can crash at my place."

"I can't..." What? Sleep? Eat? Live?

"Zack, let Dane take you home," Mason suggested. His voice was gravelly from exhaustion. "I'll see to everything here."

Haggard was the only word to describe his brother. Haunted worked, too, he supposed. Mason would blame himself for failing to protect those in need. He always did.

Beside him, Shonda stood, silent and mourning the sister of her heart.

After nodding his agreement, Zack climbed into Dane's black Enclave.

If he could summon up an ounce of concern, he would have felt terrible for how heavy the smoke stench clinging to him was. Had the situation been different and it been his vehicle, he'd have been pissed at how many detailings it would require to remove the stink.

But their situation was the worst-case scenario, and he couldn't drum up an ounce of give-a-shit. He stared unblinking through the front windshield, watching the powwow between his siblings and Bucky. A heated debate ensued, with Mason at its core.

Let them sort it out, Zack's tired mind urged. He couldn't play referee with nothing left in the tank. Fatigue hit. Closing his burning eyes, he rested his head against the seat. How was he supposed to pick up the pieces of his shattered life? How did normal people survive this godforsaken grief and guilt? The rage?

THIRTY-FOUR

Zack slept around the clock for the next thirty-six hours. He woke twice for bathroom breaks and to take a shot of whisky or two before heading back to Dane's guest room. Early on in his misery, he remembered McFatty and farmed out the responsibility onto his younger brother's wide shoulders.

"I'll see to him."

Trusting it would be done, Zack went back to bed.

On the third day, as he lounged against the headboard, staring at the dark television screen atop the dresser, his mother entered.

"Charlie?" he croaked.

"He's going to pull through," Connie said with a bittersweet smile.

"Good. That's good."

Sorrow crowded her beautiful blue eyes, identical to his. "Zack, you need to shower and eat."

"I can't eat anything. Not yet."

"Will you at least shower?"

He ran a hand over his whisker-laden jaw.

"Sure," he agreed but made no move to climb out of bed.

Connie crossed from the doorway and sank down on the mattress's edge. "Judith was released. According to Bucky, the D.A.'s office is attempting to build a case against her. She's made a point of staying away from the hospital, refusing to see Charlie." She shook her head in resignation. "She's so filled with hate. I can't believe she hasn't been here to offer her condolences about Jacob and Erica. She—"

Zack held up a hand, cutting her off. "Mom, please. I couldn't give two shits about Judith right now."

"Zachary!" she gasped.

Sighing with regret, he lifted her hand and pressed her palm to his cheek. He offered a conciliatory smile but it likely resembled a grimace. "Sorry. I can't do this, Mom. Not yet. Please understand."

"Don't ask me to leave you alone. Seeing you hurting like this is killing me," she said raggedly.

"That's not changing anytime soon," he whispered past the grief clogging his throat.

And like she'd done when he was a small child hurting over some unfortunate incident or accident, she hugged him. If she had the ability to ease his suffering and take away his pain, Zack was sure she would. But she couldn't.

For what felt like the millionth time since the explosion, Zack sobbed.

<hr>

THREE HOURS, a shower, and a change of clothes later, Zack joined his family, who were gathered in Dane's dining room. Mason promptly informed him Shonda had left to pick up Erica's parents at the airport.

The idea of facing her mother and father after being directly responsible for her death gnawed at his insides. Zack's last words to her had been in anger because she'd wanted to leave him and avoid the one person bent on destroying her. His self-hatred and anger were all-consuming, and he doubted he'd ever be able to recover. Peace and acceptance were never going to come.

He rested a shoulder against the window frame, watching his family bustle about, setting out various dishes. The mixed scents of the meal flipped his stomach and caused it to rebel.

Would he ever be hungry again?

The closing of car doors sparked his family's curiosity.

"Shonda shouldn't be back yet," Mason stated, a deep frown marring his handsome albeit tired visage.

The doorbell's peal beckoned them down the hall. Dane admitted Bucky and another plainclothes cop, who introduced himself as Detective Fields.

The man had the jaded expression of a long-time veteran. The thumb of his left hand was tucked in the band of his belt, and his right hand rested on the butt of his service weapon.

"Bucky. Detective. What's up?" Zack asked, not really caring one way or the other what their visit was concerning. Unless they'd come to tell him Christie was in the morgue. Then he'd absolutely give a damn. He'd buy them all celebratory drinks while he was at it.

"Zack, we're sorry to disturb you at a time like this, but may we speak with you privately?" Bucky in professional officer mode was disturbing. The absence of a smile didn't fit.

Zack sent a sharp look Mason's way. Although his brother's expression was grim, he merely shrugged.

"Right through here." He led the way to an open sitting area. When all parties were situated, he asked, "What's going on?"

Fields took the lead. "The coroner pulled DNA samples from the bodies recovered on the scene. We'd like to test yours against the boy they found."

"Is that all? A phone call wouldn't have sufficed?" Dane asked.

Heart thudding heavily, Zack leaned forward in his seat. "What aren't you telling us?"

The two officials exchanged a speaking glance.

"Buck," Zack growled.

"The female's DNA came back to a woman reported missing four months ago. We're still waiting on the boy's results."

The implication was slow to register with his tired brain, but when it did, he jumped to his feet.

Erica was still alive!

Jacob might be, too!

Afraid to hope, Zack said, "I can go to the hospital or to the station right now."

Bucky forestalled him with a tight smile. "Actually, that's the reason Byron is here. He's the head of our forensic team, and he brought the swab kit."

"Let me get this straight. You're saying the woman found in the ruins after the explosion was *not* Erica?" Connie asked.

"That's correct, Mrs. Sharp," Bucky confirmed.

"So it is possible, maybe even probable she's still alive?" When he nodded, she asked, "Do you think it's possible my grandson is, too?"

"We're hopeful, Mrs. Sharp."

Connie raised a fist to her mouth, and Zack hugged her.

"It's a good thing, Mom."

"I know. I..." She shook her head, and he understood. No words could express the hope they were feeling. Gripping the material of Zack's Henley, she cried out. "I have to tell Charlie! He'll be—"

"No!" Byron surged to his feet with a wince for his audibly popping joints. Gracing her with a compassionate smile, he said, "We want to keep this under wraps, Mrs. Sharp. At least, for the moment."

"But Charlie is Jacob's grandfather. He has the right to know," she protested.

"Mrs. Sharp, no one but those in this room can know we suspect the bodies belong to anyone other than Ms. Sutton and your grandson. It could hamper our investigation and alert

Christie Bauer we're on to her deception. Do you understand?" he asked, not unkindly.

"Yes, but we can swear Charlie to secrecy," she said, patting Zack's chest and gazing at him for support.

Weighing the risks, he shook his head. "He's right, Mom. We need to keep this under wraps until we locate them. If Christie finds out, she'll hurt them for real."

"What about Erica's parents and Shonda? They'll be here any second."

He cast Bucky and Fields a worried glance. It went without saying; the smaller the circle, the more likely they were to contain the secret.

"I don't think we should tell them, Mom," Mason said.

"Mason! You can't keep something like that from Erica's parents *or* your girlfriend," his mother scolded.

"Shonda's *not* my girlfriend! For Christ's sake, Ma. Stop with that shit already!"

Those were the harsh words Shonda and the Suttons walked in on. Her immediate flash of hurt was uncomfortable to see, but she recovered quickly and composed her features into a cool mask.

Mason's colorful string of curses would make a sinner's ear tips red. He rubbed the spot between his brows in agitation.

"I should go." Shonda hugged Mary and Pete. "Call me when you're ready for me to pick you up."

"Shonda, hold up," Mason barked.

"I'm fine. It's not like I wasn't aware of the score from the start. Take care of your family, Mason," she said crisply before making good her escape.

Swearing viciously, he followed her out.

"Ohhh, he's in big troublllle!" Dane quipped.

Zack shoved him. "Behave."

With one last glance at the others, he explained the situation to the Suttons.

Fields retrieved the DNA samples needed and cautioned them

to maintain a facade of mourning. No one knew if or when Christie might be observing them, and it was important to keep up appearances if they stood a chance of catching her.

THE LAB AGREED to prioritize the results on the child's identification, but in the meantime, Zack had Jacob's dentist forward his records to the detective for a secondary comparison. Within eight hours, they'd concluded the child found in the house wasn't Jacob.

Alone in his room, for the second time that day, Zack sobbed. This time the tears were those of relief. After he mopped up his face and blew his nose, he guzzled the water Dane had left for him. Half suspecting his brother was a ninja, he grinned. He wanted to utilize those skills to catch Christie.

She wouldn't win. She couldn't!

With luck, she'd never see them coming. They only needed to think like her. To consider what might be the next steps in her twisted desire to hurt Zack. And he'd figure them out. He had to because he intended to bring Jacob and Erica home soon, whatever the cost.

That evening as he readied for bed, he replayed the day's events and belatedly remembered McFatty. Death would be a reprieve if Erica discovered he'd forgotten to care for her fur baby. It was past time to return home, anyway. Dane's tolerance had to be close to an end. No one liked an invasion of their private space.

He located Dane in the living room. His brother paused in the act of sipping his drink and glanced up from the flames dancing along the frosted teal stones of his gas fireplace.

"You okay?" Dane asked.

A shudder rippled through Zack. There wouldn't be a time he looked at a fire and wasn't reminded of Christie's pyromaniac ways or of all the damage she'd done due to her sick obsession.

"Not sure. I'm better knowing Jacob and Erica might be alive, but the uncertainty is making me insane."

His brother snorted humorlessly. "Don't be throwing the 'I' word around so readily."

"I hear ya." Zack settled on the edge of a leather armchair. "Dane, I wanted to thank you for the last few days."

Moody blue eyes shifted to meet his, and he was momentarily thrown by the unsettling emotion his brother displayed. Dane was the happy-go-lucky one of their family without a care in the world.

"You don't have to thank me, man. Not for having your back."

Zack shook his head in disagreement. "You're wrong. I totally do. And I need to apologize, too. I've been little more than an animal, but you've never said a negative word." He lifted the glass from Dane's hand and took a hearty slug before handing it back. "Thank you." Sincerity and love hung in those gruffly spoken words.

"You're my brother, and I love you." The solemn reply said it all, and they both absorbed the impact of what it meant. The Sharp men would do *anything* for each other.

"I'm heading home tonight."

"Why not wait until morning?"

"McFatty."

Dane laughed as he always did when anyone mentioned Erica's ornery cat. "Do you suppose he's mean because of the name?"

"He's mean because cats are assholes." Chuckling when his brother toasted him with his glass, he added, "But I'm sure the name didn't help."

"You don't have to rush off," Dane said. "I actually picked up a feeder and a continuous-fountain watering bowl. He should be good until morning."

"What about the litter?"

"Erica set up an automatic scooper. Don't tell her I said so, but those things are awesome."

Zack tossed around the idea of staying and sharing a few drinks with his brother, but eventually he caved to the niggling feeling he'd been experiencing for the better part of the day. "I can't explain it without sounding like a fruit loop, but something's screaming at me to go home. *Immediately.*"

Dane stood and set his glass aside. "Let's go."

"No. I didn't mean you had to go, too. It's probably nothing."

"When has your inner voice *ever* been nothing?" His brother offered a hand and hauled him to his feet. "If Mason had listened to you all those years ago, Melanie might be alive today. You told him something was off that day."

"Yes. The same thing happened when Erica's house burned down. My gut reaction was to compare it to Christie's handiwork. I dismissed it as paranoia."

"Well, you know what Mom would say. 'Although your last name is Sharp, it's McAdams' blood that runs through your veins.'"

Both brothers shared a grin. Their mother, a McAdams by birth, always swore *her* ancestry was what made them great. All throughout their lives, she'd told them about family members who'd possessed a sixth sense or the second sight. Connie constantly asked for Zack's opinion on every major financial decision she made. Ninety-eight percent of the time, his predictions were correct, which lent to her belief that her middle son had received the family gift.

"Well, if anyone was blessed with the sight, it's Josh." Zack sobered as he thought of his cousin who once ran McAdams Pub in town.

Josh's wife and son went missing four months ago. Six days into their disappearance, much to his own detriment, he'd informed the police he believed they were dead. Law enforcement had interrogated him endlessly on the assumption he'd harmed his family. After he was finally released, Josh had stayed in a drunken stupor for about a month. On his first sober night, he'd been hit by a drunk driver while walking home. The near-fatal accident left Josh in a coma. As far as Zack knew, he hadn't woken up. Josh's siblings, Derek and Rosalyn, assumed charge of the family bar.

The truth was a sledgehammer to Zack's head, and he shared a horrified look with Dane.

"*Angela!*" they shouted simultaneously.

Dane reached for his phone, presumably to call Derek.

Zack hit the speed dial for Bucky. "Have you checked the woman's DNA against Josh's missing wife?" he asked without preamble.

"How did you guess it was her?" Bucky's surprise flowed across the line.

He whooshed out a breath he wasn't aware he'd been holding. "Dane and I were discussing the situation. It occurred to us it might be Angela."

The truth brought with it the sad realization that Christie was likely responsible for the disappearance of Josh's wife and child. Had she fixated on *him* at some point, or had she randomly selected Angela and Ryan for a different nefarious purpose?

"So it's her? Angela?" he asked, mouth dry.

"Yeah, Derek and Ros are being informed as we speak," Bucky told him.

Dane's tragic gaze met his as he signed off with Derek and disconnected the call. Zack switched to the speaker option so his brother could listen to his conversation.

"Buck, why did you need my DNA if you knew it was Angela? Why didn't you test the boy's against hers? Wouldn't it have told you if it was Ryan? Not to mention, it would have been an easy matter to get a sample from Josh."

As tired as he was, Zack didn't immediately piece together what the hell was happening or why. The extended silence on the other end of the call was the lightbulb he needed to shed light on the reason. He sucked in a breath.

"You *didn't* know it wasn't Erica and Jacob when you asked for my DNA, did you? You used the sample to see if I was behind their abduction," he said slowly. Instant rage filled him. "You know what? Fuck you, Bucky! Fuck your whole piss-poor department! You've known me my whole goddamn life. Do you really think I'd do something like that? Charbroil my own fucking kid? You were here when Jacob went missing, for fuck's sake!"

"Zack, it came from higher up. I'm sorry. We had to be sure." Bucky's tone was apologetic and yet not really. It was as if he expected him to be okay with the ends justifying the means.

He wasn't.

"Go fuck yourself," Zack snarled. He jabbed the screen to end the call.

Dane plucked the phone from his hand and replaced it with the empty whiskey glass. With a sweep of his hand, he gestured toward the far wall.

Zack hefted it up and hurled it toward the faux brick with all his might. Shattered glass rained down on the carpet.

"Feel better?"

"No! Those fucking bastards!"

Dane plucked another glass off the sideboard and handed it to him. "Have at it."

After his fourth smashed glass, Zack was somewhat calmer.

"Done?" his brother asked, no inflection or judgment in his tone.

"Yeah."

"Good. Those glasses are expensive, and I expect you to replace them. Let's go. You drive, I'll have Mason meet us at your house."

CHAPTER

THIRTY-FIVE

When they were a block away from his home, Zack's nerve endings went haywire. The whole thing was off. The oddest sensation tickled his brain and put him on edge. Bringing his vehicle to a halt one street over from his house, he gestured to the backseat.

"Do me a favor, Dane. Duck down until we're in the garage. If Christie's around, I don't want her to know you're here." After another considerable pause and running possible scenarios through his head, he said, "Text Mason and tell him to come through the side yard, then use his alarm app to disengage the sensor and unlock the back door."

The sick feeling in the pit of his stomach might be nothing and all his tactical planning would be for naught, but he'd rather be prepared.

Thankfully, his brother agreed with him.

"Dane, encourage Mason to clear the air with Shonda. God forbid the worst happens tonight, they shouldn't have any regrets between them."

Of course, his older brother, being the stubborn asshat he was, responded by labeling Zack a meddling dickhead, then added the words, "Fuck off."

"Still think he's coming?" Zack asked dryly, knowing it wasn't a question at all. Mason would be there.

Dane snorted a laugh. "Why did you tell him to make it right? You don't think anything will happen to *him*, do you?"

"I don't. It's just..."

"A feeling," they said in unison.

"When are you going on the fortune-telling circuit?" Dane asked with a wry grin.

"To quote Mason, fuck off," Zack replied without heat. "Okay, let's get a move on. Stay low and quiet." Once they'd pulled into his garage, he reached over the seat back to clutch his brother's hand. He squeezed to convey his deeper feeling. "Thank you, Dane. Thanks for trusting me on this."

"I've always got your back."

"Thanks for that, too. If Christie's in there, I'll try to direct her away from the garage door. It'll be cracked open so the chime shouldn't sound when you come through. Don't let it close, or you'll give yourself away." Zack inhaled and exhaled a steadying breath. "Feel free to bash her skull in from behind, but only after I have a location on Jacob and Erica."

"You do realize it's murder and not self-defense if I were to kill her without her attacking me first, right?"

"I don't care," Zack said coldly, determined to end this.

"If I go to prison, my milkshake will bring all the boys to the yard," Dane quipped.

"Do you even know what that means, you idiot? You'd have to have breasts to have a 'milkshake,' and you only wish you were that hot."

"Wow, look at you, Mr. Pop Culture." Dane chuckled, amusing himself as always. "Maybe I'll get implants. I can charge admission. They'd be worth two packs of smokes on the inside."

"Will you focus and shut the hell up before she hears you?" Zack shook his head.

"You don't even know she's here."

"She's here," he replied grimly. "Her presence feels like a pain in my ass."

Dane went on high alert. "Maybe we should consider notifying the police."

"No. This ends now."

Zack didn't try to muffle any noise from his entrance. There was no point. If Christie were around—and he strongly suspected she was—she would've heard his car and the overhead garage door.

The pounding in his ears drowned everything out. His heart was ready to burst from his chest, rip through his t-shirt, and take flight. Despite a lifetime of physical activity, he'd honestly swear his heart rate resided in the danger zone, having never beat so fast or hard before.

Fear caused that. For Jacob. For Erica. Prior to their entry into his life, he hadn't experienced it, or not at that level. Yet now, their safety was all he thought about.

Zack's hands shook as adrenaline surged through his body, and he dropped the key fob on the hall table, with a glance at the alarm keypad. Deactivated. Yep, they were here. Or at least Christie was.

"Oh Evil Spawn of Satan, I'm home," he sang out as he strode down the hall. He hoped to ease Erica's mind if she was close. A muffled snort assured him she was here, too, and he expelled a sigh of relief. Regardless of the situation, she appreciated his snark.

"In here, lover," Christie called out.

That bitch probably thought he was referring to her, and he was inclined to let her.

The instant Zack joined them in the living room, his heart stopped.

In the center of the room, Erica and Jacob were bound with their hands in front of them, facing one another. Their chairs rested inside separate kiddie pools filled with a light amber-colored liquid. The scent of gasoline permeated the air, and Zack covered his nose as the overwhelming smell hit him.

Good Christ!

Did Christie plan to burn one—or both—alive? How could someone demented to such a degree ever escape detection? Her path of destruction was immense.

Over the expanse of the room, his eyes locked with Erica's. Hers were tired and held a hopeless light. She looked like hell. As if she'd hardly slept in the four and a half days she'd been a prisoner. Her ragged half-breaths were indicative of a severe injury, and there was a gray pallor to any skin that wasn't covered in the multitude of purple-and-green bruises.

Zack studied Jacob for similar signs, but other than fatigue and fear, his son didn't appear to be suffering from abuse.

Christie stepped from behind Jacob. In one hand, she held a flip-lid lighter and, in the other, a compact Beretta. "Nice of you to finally join us, lover. Took you long enough."

Blind fury, like none he'd ever known, gripped him. His body trembled with the need to separate Christie's head from her neck. How fast could he get to her before she riddled his body with bullets? How many shots could he withstand until he reached her and wrapped his hands around her throat?

"You know damned well I thought they were dead from your exploding house stunt," he growled.

Erica gasped.

Apparently, Christie hadn't bothered to share *that* small detail with her victims. It actually surprised him. He'd have thought she would've enjoyed taunting Erica with the knowledge.

"Yes. One of my finer ideas. Similar to the hospital fire," Christie stated proudly.

"Have you had Angela and Ryan all this time?"

Erica frowned, her confusion complete. She'd once told him

Angela was one of her two best friends, and at any minute, she'd put two and two together, realizing who was responsible for their disappearance.

Zack concentrated solely on Christie. If he became distracted, it could cost them all dearly.

"What was I supposed to do?" Christie sneered and waved the gun around. "She showed up with her sniveling boy to clean the house where I was staying. It wasn't like it was planned."

The breezy, uncaring attitude infuriated him. Only a complete psychopath with no limitation went around taking lives and destroying others with no concept or care for the grief she instilled in others.

A darting glance showed silent tears streaming down Erica's face. She'd summed it up.

"How long have they been dead?" he asked, fighting like hell to keep his tone level and relay curiosity while not showing his horror. Ryan was related to him by blood, and the family had adored him. The loss was greater than any the McAdams clan had ever suffered.

"Since the day she found me," Christie said airily. "I don't know. Three? Four months?" Her fingers flicked the lighter lid, beginning a cycle of opening and closing. The habitual movements revealed her agitation. "Why do *you* care? It's not like you were dating her. She was married to that loser who runs the bar."

"That *loser* is my cousin Josh," Zack growled. "And that boy you killed? He was our son's best friend, you bitch!"

"Whatever. Jacob will have other friends—*if* I decide to let him live," she stated dismissively. "That brings us back to now. It's time for you to choose."

Zack crossed his arms, prepared to wait her out.

She merely looked amused by his efforts. Her lack of concern was worrisome. There was a smug confidence in her demeanor that sent a chill down his spine. She had an ace up her sleeve.

What the hell was it?

"I'm not going to choose, Christie. What would be the point?" he asked, as unaffected and casual as he could. Inside, Zack's guts were in knots. Sweat pooled in his pits, and his knees felt shaky.

Dropping his arms, he took a single step forward. "It strikes me that you'll do the opposite of whatever I want. Out of spite or revenge? Regardless, I suspect you intend to kill whoever you think I hold in higher regard."

A mixture of madness and rage burned within the depths of her eyes.

"Am I wrong?" he asked softly, knowing he'd guessed correctly.

"You have ten seconds to pick," she snarled.

The minute shake of Erica's head caught his notice. Resolve lit her gaze as she silently conveyed all the things they couldn't say aloud. Zack was full of regret, too. She straightened as best she could.

"Oh, for god's sake, Christie," Erica snapped. "Just let Jacob go. His only crime is being born to the two of you. Of course, a father will love his son and choose him over a woman he's sleeping with. Why wouldn't he?"

Horror donkey kicked Zack in the chest, and he gasped for air.

What the hell was she doing? Christie wouldn't think twice about hurting her own son. Erica *knew* she'd tried to drown Jacob as a toddler. He wanted to slap a hand over her mouth and make her stop speaking.

As if guessing his thoughts, Erica raised her brows and sent him a challenging glance. Turning back to Christie, she shrugged. "But like you said, Zack sent Jacob to live with your parents. What does that tell you? I'm really the one he wants. It's why he won't say it." Her lip curled in disdain.

Christie's narrowed gaze darted between the two of them.

"He doesn't want Jacob's last memories to be about coming in second," Erica scoffed. She gave Jacob a pitying glance and tsked her tongue. "Sorry, sweetie, but facts are facts. Because you're *her* child, there will always be a part of you that repels your dad."

In an instant, Zack understood Erica's intent.

Her sneering speech was designed to sacrifice herself!

His terror was complete and all centered on her. It was moronic and brave of her to continuously antagonize Christie, leaving her no other option but to retaliate. But Erica failed to consider how unbalanced she truly was. Or if she did weigh it, she'd mistakenly assumed she'd be the only victim. Zack knew better.

"Is this true?" Jacob asked him, silent sobs wracked his body as tears streaked down his dirty face. "You don't love me?"

There was no way he intended to answer. To destroy his son by admitting to a lie, even if it was to save him.

"Let's see, shall we?" Christie called their bluff and put the gun barrel to Jacob's head.

"No!" Zack and Erica screamed in unison.

"Do you think I'm stupid?" Christie shouted into Erica's face.

"Yes?" Erica quipped.

The gun butt was slammed into the side of her temple, and she moved no more. Zack managed three steps before Christie swirled the muzzle back and pointed it at their son's heart.

"Uh, uh, uh," she warned. "Stay right there, lover. Any closer, and I pull this trigger."

Where the fuck were his brothers?

"I'm tired of this," he ground out. "Do what you're going to and end it."

A low groan from Erica suggested she was coming around, and Zack sent a silent thank you to the Powers That Be. Still, he remained attentive to Christie. She wanted all his attention, and she had it. Hopefully, she'd provide him with an opportunity to strike.

"Mason, you might as well come out," she called. She lowered her voice and directed her next dig at Zack. "I know you'd never come here alone. You don't have the balls."

"Actually, I *did* come here by myself." He spoke a fraction louder than normal, trying to seem casual while still relaying the bluff to his brothers.

"Hmmm. Well then, let's see about that. Mother?"

CHAPTER

THIRTY-SIX

The door behind Christie opened, and Mason entered, followed closely by Judith, who had a Glock jammed against his spine. His brother's fury was substantial.

An inappropriate laugh bubbled up, and Zack would've let loose if the situation wasn't so dire and didn't require his undivided attention.

"Dude, you let an old woman get the jump on you?" Apparently, Zack's inner child couldn't resist.

"Fuck off, dickhead."

He flashed a smile to show he held no hard feelings. If they didn't make it, Mason should know he greatly appreciated the effort. He hoped like hell Dane found an opening and was able to tip the scales soon, though. His younger brother hadn't made a move yet, and the inaction was nerve-racking.

"Come out, Dane, or my mother will shoot Mason where he stands," Christie called out.

"He's not here," Mason deadpanned. "That pussy's at home, nursing a broken nose."

"Is that right?" she asked. Skepticism dripped from her voice, and her eyes were diamond-hard. Three heartbeats passed before she whipped the gun around and pulled the trigger.

"Jesusfuckingchrist!" Mason dropped where he stood, pressing his palms flat against his thigh wound and applying pressure. Blood oozed between his fingers, and his complexion paled as he pressed his lips into a tight line.

Please, God, don't let her have hit an artery!

Zack managed three steps before Christie spun around and aimed at him. "I told you not to move," she spat out.

His breath came in short huffs as if he'd finished a 10K instead of moving three feet. The demented whacko intended to take them all out, and he needed to act or all would be lost. With a mental plea to Dane to contact the police, Zack lifted his hands. It's not as if his brother could read minds, but maybe some supernatural force would intervene on their behalf.

He caught movement in his peripheral, and it required every ounce of staying power not to look down the hall. No one should be entering from that direction, and Zack hoped like hell whoever it was had their best interests at heart.

Perhaps Dane had circled around the house? He dismissed the thought. The French doors in Zack's room required a key, and as far as he knew, Mason possessed the only spare.

As the person crept forward, Zack surreptitiously gestured with the universal sign to stop. If Christie or Judith saw his signal, the gig would be up. Yet he hoped to alert the newcomer about the loose board one foot in front of them. The squeak would be a dead giveaway.

Zack's warning miraculously worked. Moving only his index finger, he twitched it to the right and hoped it conveyed the need to shift, thereby avoiding the soft spot.

Again, the cue was received. After another couple of steps, the full shape materialized. Tall and fit, but definitely feminine.

Shonda.

Had to be. No one else knew of their predicament.

Another small shift poised her to strike when the opportunity presented itself. In her hands, she held the gun she'd offered up to Zack and Mason when they went to Stapleton.

Where the hell was Dane? Had Judith found him first? Was his brother, even now, lying in a pool of his own blood?

Shoving aside his maudlin thoughts and the ever-building anxiety, he dared another step forward, careful not to block Shonda's sight line.

"Christie, call this off. Please. I'm begging you." He was the crazy one in trying to get her to see reason, and they were *all* in danger now. "Surely the neighbors heard the gunshot. The police routinely patrol this block, looking for you. They'll be here any minute."

Dane appeared out of the shadows with a shovel raised high above his head, ready to strike.

"Christie, for fuck's sake!" Erica groused. She was facing Dane's direction, and although she wasn't looking at him, of a certainty, she'd seen him, too. "Light the damned match already. I need to sleep."

Red-faced with instantaneous fury, Christie stepped forward and pointed the barrel at Erica's head. Dane struck, and the shovel connected with her wrist, sending the gun skittering across the floor toward Zack.

Right as Judith aimed at Dane, Shonda stepped into the room and squeezed off two rounds. Christie's mother fell next to Mason, who was quick to scramble for her weapon.

As the scene played out, Zack rushed to Jacob and jerked him out of harm's way. With a gentle push, he directed him toward the garage door, then spun back for Erica.

Christie was standing over her, with her thumb positioned to flip open the lighter.

"*No!*" Zack tried like hell to gain purchase on the slick, gas-drenched floor.

Two reports of gunshots sounded, and a look of stunned disbelief crossed her face before she dropped to the floor. Luck was with them, and a whoosh of air extinguished the flame on the way down.

Tentatively, Erica straightened from the chair, shuffled her way to Christie, and kicked her torso.

"I hope you're dead, you fucking piece of shit!"

Whack.

"Rot in hell!"

Whack.

Erica got off two more well-placed kicks before Zack pulled her to him, releasing her just as quickly when she hissed in a breath and paled.

"I think my ribs are broken," she explained between shallow pants. "I forgot for a minute."

In the distance, sirens wailed, and the sound was the sweetest Zack had ever heard. Tenderly, he held Erica's head between his palms and dropped a featherlight kiss on her split lip. "Don't you *ever* go off on your own again, babe. My heart can't take it."

"Yeah, well, I don't think you h-have to worry ab-bout that happening," she retorted, very little fire left in her. And with a suddenness that stole his breath, her skin turned ghastly gray. He dove for her as her eyes lost focus and rolled back in her head.

THIRTY-SEVEN

The overhead light burned brightly as Erica struggled to open her leaden lids. The surrounding machines beeped in an annoying cacophony, and multiple voices could be heard in the distance, but conversations were indistinguishable. As she shifted for comfort, piercing pain radiated through her upper torso. A distinct reminder of the beating she'd taken.

How much time had elapsed? She couldn't remember anything past kicking that twatwaffle, Christie. A sweeping look around the room found it empty. No visitors.

Of course, Zack would be with Jacob, and it was likely Shonda would be with Mason if they had taken the next steps in their relationship. Erica was the odd victim out, but it didn't bother her much. As long as she wasn't in the clutches of an evil schizoid, she had nothing to complain about.

Recalling the last week, she was in awe she survived at all.

Christie, the sadistic comedian she was, had considered it a hoot to "help her along with her diet" by not providing Erica any sustenance besides stingy amounts of water. The goal had been to keep her alive until she could bonfire her ass in front of Zack.

"After all, that's why you went to the gym to begin with, isn't it?" Christie had said in her smug, condescending way, cattily adding, "Well, to drop sixty pounds and to steal *my* boyfriend."

Erica shuddered at the memory. With any luck, Mason's or Shonda's bullets had rid the world of that raging bitch and her evil-incarnate mother.

Grief for Angela and Ryan rose up. They'd been close. But Erica had isolated herself to put the finishing touches on her last novel, and they hadn't spoken with any consistency. Profound regret weighed on her.

The last time they'd bumped into each other was at the grocery store, and they'd promised to schedule a date soon. But their standing monthly girls' night had never happened. Yes, she remembered hearing Angela had disappeared, but like everyone else, Erica had suspected her of skipping town. It wasn't as if she had a reason to believe Angela would ever leave Josh, but one never really knew what went on in someone else's relationship. How heartbreaking her relocation wasn't the case! Never again would Shonda, Angela, and her celebrate their triumphs with wine, pasta, and rom-com movies.

"I'm glad to see you're finally awake."

Zack's husky voice startled her out of her musings. He hovered in the entry as if fearful of his welcome, and his was the most beautiful and welcome face she'd ever seen. Coffee in one hand and a box of donuts in the other, he smiled. "Hi."

"Hi." She brushed a tear away.

His wary blue gaze swept over her. "You okay?"

"Yeah. Just thinking about Angela."

His pain drew his mouth down. "I can't believe Christie was behind her death. How the hell does one person destroy so many lives?"

"It's hard to imagine, isn't it?"

Zack looked down at the donuts, then at her, and shuffled his feet, seemingly unsure what to do.

Erica understood his reticence. She felt the same. Her recklessness had nearly cost them both everything. If he could forgive her —and here, she fervently hoped he would—then she'd spend the rest of her life making it up to him. A plea for forgiveness stuck in her throat, and the silence grew longer.

Grabbing the bull by the balls, she gestured to the box. "So, are you going to stand there all day, or are you handing over the goods?"

"Yeah, sorry. I..." He trailed off and looked awkwardly at his gifts.

Erica strongly suspected he was on the verge of an emotional breakdown, same as her. They'd parted on such an ugly note and then suffered, each believing their terrible fight would be the last memory of the other. Tears burned the back of her lids as she closed her eyes and sighed. The discomfort of her ribs helped her refocus.

"Let me put this another way. Hand over the donuts and no one gets hurt," she growled.

Zack's air of worry dropped the instant he registered her playfulness. After placing his bounty on the table, he wedged in next to her on the bed, careful not to knock into her but still close enough for full-body contact—something they desperately craved.

And because it had to be said, she addressed the life-size elephant in the room. "I'm sorry I left the hotel. This is all my fault."

"No."

"Yes. It is," she whispered, tearful again. "If I hadn't been so stupid, if I just listened to you, this all could have been avoided. I almost cost Jacob his life."

"None of this is your fault, babe," he insisted, twisting to make eye contact. "If it wasn't you, it would've been someone else. She was clinically insane, Erica."

Picking up on the past tense, she asked, "Was?"

"She never made it through surgery."

She caught her breath, afraid to believe.

He nodded, gaze frank.

"Thank you, Baby Jesus!" she gushed.

His mouth kicked up at the corners, and she touched a finger to one of his dimples.

"I should've asked before now. How is Jacob? Please tell me he's okay," she said.

"Surprisingly well," he replied. "I thought he'd have nightmares these last few nights at the very least. But he's been a trouper."

She frowned. "Few nights? How long have I been out?"

"Not counting the day we found you, this is the third full day."

She processed it with a nod. "And Judith?"

"She's all patched up and cooling her heels in a jail cell. She's facing charges of accessory to kidnapping, assault, attempted murder, and murder," he said, toying with her fingertips on the hand closest to him. "I don't think she's going to see the outside of a prison before she dies."

"You sound sad."

"I am, for Jacob's and Charlie's sakes." With a small grimace, he intertwined their fingers. "She always seemed kind to both Jacob and me. Who would've believed all that hatred resided in her heart?"

Erica hadn't had many interactions with Judith, but the woman was off-putting. What must it have been like to have a starchy mother like her? She sent up a silent thank you to the Universe for gifting her the parents she'd been blessed with.

"I'm assuming you informed my parents when I went missing. Are they in town?" she asked. His gulp was overly loud, and worry ricocheted through her. "What? What aren't you telling me?"

"Nothing, babe. Stay calm. They're fine. Everyone's fine. Promise."

"Then why did you sound nervous?"

"Technically, I'm not supposed to be in here with you. They

ordered me to stay away and threatened me with legal action if I didn't adhere to their wishes."

"*What?*"

"They thought you were dead because of me, Erica," he explained gently. "Your father is a bit unstable at the moment."

"That's ridiculous! None of it was your fault," she echoed his earlier denial, gripping his hand tighter. "You're my boyfriend, and I love you. They'll have to deal." When his startled gaze shot to hers, her old insecurities raised their ugly heads. "That is, if you still want me…"

Her uncertainty got the better of her. What if he didn't? What if the donuts and coffee were his way of easing the blow when he told her to hit the road?

Disbelief settled on his face. "Really? You have to ask? I brought you a dozen lemon-filled donuts as an apology. It's the equivalent of roses."

Her tender ribs aborted her laugh. "And if that didn't work?"

"I have the pizza place on standby."

"Good plan." She nodded approvingly.

"I thought so. And I love you, too." His devotion and affection were glaringly obvious.

Just when she couldn't wait another moment to feel his lips on hers, Zack read her need and kissed her. Hesitantly at first. But when she moaned her appreciation, he stepped it up, and he turned demanding. She gave him mad props for his care in not jarring her body.

"*What the hell is going on here?*" Pete's strident tone jerked her away from Zack, and she winced at the abrupt movement.

Fuck!

"I thought I told you to keep away from my daughter?" he blustered, his complexion fuchsia.

"Calm down, Dad," Erica urged. "You're going to have a stroke."

"The whole Sharp family is trouble," her father declared. "I've told you that from day one, but did you listen? *No!*"

"You talked to your dad about our relationship?" Zack asked in an aside, clearly horrified she might've.

"What? No! Are you nuts?" She scowled at her dad. "He's referring to the time you threw dirt on my dress."

"Oh, that." Zack gave her a dimpled grin and addressed Pete. "I promised to buy her a new one, sir."

"Oh, Lord," she muttered. "Now you've stepped in it."

"You think a damned dress will fix what you've done here? That you can take her shopping and all is forgiven?" Pete ranted.

"Dad, stop!" she cried, cradling her angry ribs. "This is none of your business. And besides, he brought me donuts. A dozen!"

Her father's face went from angry to confused to amused in the span of seconds. "Well, if he brought you donuts."

Her mother breezed in, carrying a box from Addie's Bakery, but she stopped short when she saw Zack's offering on the tray table.

"This is the best day ever," Erica crowed, turning her head to accept her mom's kiss on her cheek.

"You're so easy," Zack murmured in her ear once Mary was out of earshot.

"You'll find out how easy when you spring me from this joint." His amused snort made her grin. "Oh, I forgot to ask about Mason. How is he?"

"Complaining." He eased to his feet and tucked the blankets around her. "If he were on life support, Shonda, Dane, and Mom would've conspired to pull the plug."

Erica giggled at his silliness. "That bad, huh?"

"Worse. Your friend is a saint, by the way."

"She really is. She's dealt with my crazy ass for years."

"Let's not use the term crazy anytime soon," suggested Mary, handing Erica a paper plate containing a donut sliced in two. Her mom always applied her social graces, and cutting up pastries to eat fell under the 'good manners' category.

"I'll go and let you spend time with your parents." Zack kissed her and stole a donut half. "I need to make the rounds here at the hospital. Although, really, it's just you and Mason now. They released Charlie yesterday."

"How's he taking all of this?"

"Pretty hard."

It had to be rough to miss what was right under his nose, and Erica sympathized with Charlie's pain. "When you see him again, will you tell him no one blames him?"

The sudden brightness in Zack's eyes made her wonder if she'd misstepped. Did *he* blame Charlie?

"You're one in a million, you know that?" he said with a shake of his dark head.

"Is that a good thing?" she asked, relieved he didn't appear angry.

He leaned in, lips to her ear. "The best. I'll prove it when you come home."

A shiver of anticipation skated through her.

Her father's loud "ahem" broke their stare.

Zack leaned in once more, and in a low, laughing voice, he said, "Awkward."

Erica giggled as he sailed out the door.

Minutes later, Dr. Montgomery arrived, and she smiled her welcome.

"Hey, Doc. What's the verdict? Am I going to live?"

"You are." His frown spiked her anxiety.

"But?"

"Erica, I'd like to speak to you in private, if I may."

"Is something wrong, Doctor?" Panic edged into her mother's voice.

"Not at all, Mrs. Sutton. I just need a few minutes with your daughter." He flashed a reassuring smile. "Nothing to worry about."

"Go on, Mom, Dad. It's fine." Once they were alone, Erica

turned to him. "Okay, Doc. Lay it on me. Is it terminal? How long do I have to live?"

He rolled his eyes, and she knew it wasn't anything serious.

"I wanted to examine you and ask a few questions. Would that be all right?"

"Sure. Mind the ribs, though. They feel like the whole cast of Riverdance did an opening number on them."

After he palpated her stomach and tenderly ran his fingers over her ribs, the doctor drew the blanket up to her waist.

"Erica, is there any chance you might be pregnant?"

"What the hell? Where did that come from?" she asked, shock nearly unhinging her.

"I have to ask. Zack didn't seem to think so when you were brought in, and X-rays were taken," he said. "We always take precautions, but you should know the risks and percentages."

"I don't think..." After a mental calculation, she covered her mouth with her hands to stem the outpouring of profanity. Her last menstrual cycle had been around the time she was stabbed. "It was the antibiotics, wasn't it?"

She stifled a groan as he nodded.

"We gave you some heavy-duty stuff when you were here last. Chances are it interfered with your birth control."

"Oh God! Please tell me it's possible I missed my period because of the trauma of this week. I'm not ready to be a mother."

"Possible, yes. Probable? Unlikely," he said gently. "I didn't order a test when you came in a few days ago because Zack sounded sure. But if you think there's a chance, I'd like to do blood-work and schedule an exam with an OB-GYN."

"Yeah, okay." Right when he would've left, she called him back. "Do you think, if it turns out I am, the baby will be okay, considering everything that's happened?"

"In the event you *are* pregnant, yes." He watched her, his mocha eyes kind. "My understanding is that your ribs took the brunt of the abuse. It's a good sign that you aren't cramping or having a discharge." With a pat on her hand, he smiled. "If your fetus is half as tough as you, it'll be fine."

"Thank you."

"Don't worry, Erica. These things have a way of working out. But promise no more picking fights with escapees from the psych ward, okay?"

His teasing made her feel a great deal better. "No promises, Doc. The looney ones are attracted to me. I'm the flame to their moth."

"That's what I'm afraid of," he responded in a tone drier than dirt. "I'll send a nurse in."

Within a few hours, Dr. Montgomery was back to discuss her results. She sat in stunned silence as he congratulated her on her impending motherhood. Fifteen minutes later, as the Sharp clan descended, she was still staring into space, shell-shocked.

"Erica?"

She wasn't sure how many times Zack had called her name or for how long, but she slowly became aware of the concerned crowd.

"Oh. Sorry. Plotting a story." Offering up a phony smile, she hoped her distraction passed without further comment.

Zack's penetrating look said he didn't believe the shabby excuse, and she couldn't blame him. She wouldn't have fallen for it, either. Thankfully, he didn't immediately call her out, but it wouldn't be long before he did.

Shonda had no problem busting her chops, though. "Was that uber-hot Dr. Trace Montgomery I saw leaving? What did he have to say?"

THIRTY-EIGHT

Zack was surprised Shonda wasn't decimated by Erica's death glare. Had it been life and death, she wouldn't be gabbing in such a blasé manner. For the time being, her secret was safe, but once everyone left, it would be game on. If he had to hold the donuts hostage to get answers, he would.

"He said I'm no longer dehydrated, and tomorrow if I have someone to drive me, I can go home," Erica said with an odd catch to her voice. "Of course, I don't really have a home, do I?"

Her comment was a smack in the face. Weren't they fine a few hours ago? Zack wasn't exactly sure what he'd expected, but it wasn't for her to move out. He'd assumed they would take up where they left off.

"Of course you do, dear. Your home is with Zack," Connie stated firmly. He could've kissed his mom for speaking up.

But Erica's chocolate eyes darkened with worry. What did she have to be afraid of?

"What's wrong?" he mouthed.

Her mouth tightened in a minuscule grimace before she worked up a smile and a shrug. She was faking it, and his stomach knotted because she felt she needed to. But he'd had enough and wanted answers.

"Okay, everyone out." Gasps of every kind greeted his demand —outrage, amusement, and shock at his rudeness. "Out!" he ordered. "Erica and I need five minutes."

Closing the door after the last straggler, Zack returned to her bedside. Her bottom lip was sandwiched between her teeth in her fight to contain her laughter.

Without ceremony, he plucked the plate from her hand, put it on the tray, and rolled the table away. "Start talking," he commanded.

"Rude much?"

"If I have to be." Crossing his arms, he narrowed his eyes. "Now out with it."

"It's—"

"Don't even dream of lying to me," he cut in, then circled a finger in the air for her to continue.

"I'm pregnant," she blurted.

Pregnant.

Disbelief exploded like a grenade in his brain. Of all the things Erica could say, Zack hadn't expected her to tell him she was pregnant. Her face reflected her discomfort with the conversation, and the longer he watched her in silence, the redder her face became. The entire time, her evasive gaze darted to his face and away.

She'd planned this!

How much of an idiot could one man be? When would he learn to take precautions and stop believing women who claimed to be on the pill? When would he stop being a dupe?

"...felt it was the antibiotics...stabbing..." she droned on.

Zack didn't hear any of her excuses. The roaring in his ears wouldn't allow it. Without a word, he stormed from the room, ignoring her yelp from behind him. What had she expected? Did she assume he would be all hearts and lemon donuts at the prospect of becoming a father? Perhaps he might have been had she gone about it the proper way.

He hadn't made it ten feet when the truth punched him in the face. This was *Erica*. She didn't have it in her to be dishonest or trick him with the intent of trapping him into marriage. Scrubbing his hands over his face, he inhaled deeply.

Christ, he was such a fool! Hadn't he set out to marry her?

He rushed back and stopped short when he saw the look on her bruised and battered face. Large hurt-filled eyes stared at him. Her bitter disappointment scraped along his nerve endings, and he was uncomfortable in his own skin.

"Erica, I'm sorry. I—"

"No worries. You don't have to be involved. Really, I'm fine on my own," she replied in a dull voice. Lying back, she closed her eyes. "If you don't mind, please tell everyone I'm tired and need some sleep. Let them know I appreciate them coming by. Thanks."

She rushed the halting speech, and her eagerness to have him gone was salt in his self-inflicted wound. But he wasn't leaving, and he certainly didn't intend for her to parent alone. As she remained stoic, he helplessly struggled to find an explanation to make things right.

The love he felt for her became greater in the face of her quiet dignity. All-encompassing. And it included the new life forming inside her.

"Please don't shut me out, babe. Surprise pregnancies appear to be my trigger. But it took all of ten seconds to remember you're, in no way, like Christie," he said. If there was a desperate quality to his voice, he refused to be ashamed of it. "It shouldn't have taken even that long. I love you, Erica. And I'll love our child."

He hovered beside her with bated breath, silently begging her to forgive him.

"It was a shock to me, too," she said in a soft voice. "You get to panic. I did."

The relief and joy he felt were a strange combination, and he smiled as he touched her abdomen.

"I'll be a great dad," he promised.

She placed her hand over his. "You already are."

Moisture built behind his lids and stung his eyes. Fuck. He didn't want to cry. When his brothers saw, they'd never let him live it down.

"When do you want to tell everyone?" he asked.

"I think you already did."

He glanced to where she pointed behind him, seeing the mix of her family and his.

Laughter and congratulations flowed freely. But one person didn't appear happy, and he hugged the wall, off to one side, away from the festive crowd. Zack crossed to Jacob and knelt down.

"What's wrong, lil man?"

"You and Erica."

"You don't want us to be together?"

Zack hadn't given any thought to his son's reaction, but he never would've dreamed Jacob would be upset.

"Are you going to send me to live with Grandpa again?" Jacob croaked. The pain in his solemn eyes slayed Zack.

"Oh, buddy." He led him to Erica's bedside. "You want to field this one, babe?"

She reached out, palm extended up. Hesitating only a second, Jacob placed his hand in hers. His young face showed caution and anything but thrilled.

"Jacob, neither I nor the new baby, when it comes, will *ever* take your place in your dad's heart." Erica's words were heart-breakingly sweet. "You're his firstborn and the apple of his eye, buddy."

"But you said because of my mom, he wouldn't love me as much as you."

"I didn't mean it." Tears flowed down her cheeks as she solemnly swore that he would be loved first and foremost, forever. "I promise you, nothing will ever change how your dad feels about you," she said. "Not me, not any brother or sister you may have. Nothing. You're his first priority, Jacob. I swear it."

Zack rested his hands on his son's shoulders and felt a small measure of the tension drain away. "Erica is telling the truth, bud. She said those things in hopes of saving you. Not to hurt you."

"How?"

She squeezed Jacob's hand and smiled lovingly at him. "My plan was to convince Christie your dad didn't care about you as much as me. I'd hoped she would hurt me instead of you," Erica told him. "She was a very sick woman and wanted to destroy everything your dad loves. You included. I wasn't letting that happen, sweetie."

"You don't hate me?"

The tentative question was like a sharp blade, carving the heart from Zack's chest.

"God, no!" she exclaimed.

"I can live with you guys?" Jacob asked with a choked sob.

The insecurity in his voice almost broke Zack. Erica met his eyes over Jacob's dark head wordlessly asking him if she could take the lead. He nodded.

"Well, I refuse to live there without you," she said, pulling Jacob closer. "Who else is going to teach your little sister or brother how to play Mindcraft?"

"Minecraft," all the Sharp males said in unison.

She grinned and winked at Jacob. "See? It has to be you." For a long moment, she watched him. "Do you mind if we become part of your family, too?"

Instead of an answer, Jacob leaped forward, slamming into Erica's midsection. She hissed her pain.

He gasped and started to straighten. "I'm sorry! I didn't mean—"

But she hauled him close for a tight hug, ignoring the apology and her personal discomfort. From his vantage point, Zack could see what it cost her. She paled and her lips thinned.

"I love you, Erica," Jacob told her.

"And I love you, sweet boy." She held him like that for as long as an eight-year-old boy would permit.

"Want someone to stay with you tonight?" Zack asked her a half hour later as everyone filed out to let her rest.

"You should see to Jacob. He's feeling vulnerable."

As he studied her face, he noticed the purple bruises had begun to fade to a sickly greenish-yellow. Although he hated the fact she'd suffered greatly through her ordeal, every mark on her was a testament to the fighter she was. The *winner* she was.

He smiled. "Is that a no?"

"I don't want to take you away from him."

"That's your only objection?"

"Of course!"

"Okay. I'm staying." Zack grinned at her disconcerted expression. "It was Jacob's suggestion."

"Have I told you how much I love your kid?" she asked with a wide smile.

"I love you, too, Erica."

They hadn't expected Jacob to be lingering inside the door or that he would overhear them. But her smile was blinding, and his beaming son's face told Zack all he needed to know about the three —or rather *four*—of them becoming a permanent family.

"I thought you left with your Uncle Dane," Zack said.

"I forgot my transformer."

"Ah, gotcha. Erica wants to know if you're cool with me staying here."

Mischievousness transformed Jacob's face, and he looked like a devilish sprite. "Uncle Dane said to tell you that he's got the hookers on speed dial, so it's all good."

"You tell your Uncle Dane that I want to have a few words with him," Erica ground out.

With a laugh, Zack ushered Jacob toward the door.

"Back soon, babe," he called over his shoulder.

EPILOGUE

E rica stared at her rounded belly reflected in the full-length mirror, poked it a few times, and let out a heartfelt sigh.

"It's not fair," she muttered.

"What isn't?"

She met her recent-wedded husband's admiring gaze in the reflection and jerked her shirt down. "That I haven't had pizza for a week and still haven't lost any weight."

"You had pizza two days ago, and that isn't how it works," he corrected, his voice and expression heavily laced with amusement.

"It's been a week, I tell ya!" she denied hotly.

He squinted his eyes and strode to where she stood pouting. Embracing her from behind, he drew her against his fit frame. He inched her shirt up over her protruding stomach and cradled her baby bump in his large hands.

"Okay. A, it's only been two days. B, you had donuts last night, or have you already forgotten we made love? And C, you're beautiful and not likely to lose weight while you're six months pregnant."

"Pfft. Well, I'd better burn calories while nursing or I'm done with this baby-making business."

"We'll start you on an exercise routine after our peanut is born. You'll lose the baby weight," he promised.

"But no running! I'm not down with that," she warned.

His laughter pleased her. Doubtless, he'd love her even if she was the size of a barn. Which, in her current state, wasn't far from the truth. Her train of thought derailed when Zack's hand slid under the band of her maternity pants and he touched her south of the border.

Her breath hitched the instant he found her sweet spot.

"Um, what are you doing? Charlie and your mom are bringing Jacob back any minute," she said.

"Okay, never again mention my mother when we're about to make sweet, sweet love." He nuzzled her neck, then put his lips to the shell of her ear. "Also, I just hung up with her. They're stopping for ice cream, so we have at least twenty minutes for me to show my hot wife how sexy she is."

"How horny you are, you mean," Erica replied dryly.

"That, too." Zack dropped to his knees in front of her and followed the trail of his fingers with his lips.

Unable to see him over her extended belly, she turned her head and watched him pleasure her in the mirror's reflection. She caught his eye *and* his smug grin, feeling a surge of warmth.

"I love you," she blurted as the feeling rocked her.

Zack sat back on his heels and met her teary-eyed gaze. His love shone back like the brightest beacon, right alongside his desire. Undaunted by her hormonal mood swings, he grinned. "I love you, too, babe. Now, let's get naked. Time's a-wasting."

She laughed as he hustled her to the bed.

BY THE TIME Jacob arrived home, they were fully clothed and lounging on the couch. Erica's legs were draped over Zack's lap as he massaged her aching feet.

"Mom! Dad! I'm home!"

Erica felt a hitch in her heartbeat whenever he called her Mom.

"I brought you donuts," Jacob sang out, entering the room.

Raising her voice to make sure he heard her, she said, "Have I told you how much I love our kid, Zack?"

Jacob threw back his head and laughed—a deep belly laugh so similar to his father's, she grinned.

Had he already thrown dirt on some girl's dress and made her cry? Or offered her a pencil on her first day and won her affection forever? He hadn't said, but Erica wouldn't be surprised. Jacob would love with all his being, like Zack.

"What are you thinking about that has you smiling so wide?" Zack asked, moving his ministrations up her calf, eliciting her moan.

"What *doesn't* have me smiling is the better question."

"Speak, woman, or I hold the donuts hostage."

"You wouldn't dare!"

"No holding the pregnant woman's donuts hostage," Connie scolded, entering the room on the tail end of his threat. Charlie followed on her heels.

"No, of course not." But Zack smirked, thereby assuring everyone he would.

"Connie," Erica called out. "Did I ever tell you Zack ruined my favorite dress the first day of scho—"

He surged forward and clamped a hand over her mouth. "She's lying, Mom!"

"Mm-hmm, why don't I believe you?" his mother asked wryly. "You'd better hope no one throws dirt at *your* daughter."

Eyes bugging out, Erica warned Connie with a wave of her hand. She had yet to tell Zack the results of the last ultrasound because he didn't want to know the baby's sex. At her urging, the doctor was quick to tell Erica as Zack left to set up their next appointment.

"Daughter?" He nearly dumped her on the floor as he jumped up. "We're having a girl?"

She nodded, biting her lip, accurately guessing how he'd take the news.

"We're having a girl!" He hauled her up off the couch and wrapped her in a bear hug. "A girl!"

"Is now a good time to show you the dress I picked up for her?" Connie asked, holding up a tiny replica of the outfit Erica had worn on her first day of school.

"Ohmygod! How did you find it?" Erica asked, amazed she had.

"It's exactly the same!" Zack exclaimed.

His mother laughed and held up a photo of a five-year-old Erica. "Mary sent the picture to me. She thought you might get a kick out of it."

"You had a copy of my dress made?" Erica's eyes sprung a leak, and she used Zack's sleeve to mop them up.

Damned hormones were making her a mess!

"A gift from your mother and me. She swears it was true love from your first day of school."

Erica and Zack shared a grin.

"It was," they said.

FROM THE AUTHOR

*Thanks for taking the time to read **Burning Resolution**! I hope you enjoyed reading Zack and Erica's story. I mean, who knew you could have that much fun with lemon donuts!*

The next story in the Stonebrooke series centers around Mason and Shonda. In case you haven't guessed, Mason is a bit of a grumpy alpha-hole. BUT, he does have a softer side as Shonda is about to find out.

Be sure to subscribe to my mailing list to learn about new releases. https://www.tmcromer.com/newsletter

*For fans who like to interact, my Facebook group entitles readers to "fan only" contests, as well as an exclusive first look at covers, excerpts and more. **Cromer's Carousers** is the most fun way to follow yet. I hope to see you there!*

Love & Lemon Drops,
T.M. Cromer
www.tmcromer.com

TURN THE PAGE FOR A LIST OF MY OTHER STORIES!

BOOKS BY T.M. CROMER

CONTEMPORARY & ROMANTIC SUSPENSE

The Fiore Vineyard Series:

PICTURE THIS

RETURN HOME

ONE WISH

The Holt Family Series:

GOODBYE TO YOU

THIS TIME YOU

INCLUDING YOU

A LIFE WITH YOU

The Stonebrooke Series:

BURNING RESOLUTION

HIDDEN RESOLUTION

PARANORMAL ROMANCE

The Sentinels of Magic Series:

THE AETHER

THE DEATH DEALER

THE SEER

The Thorne Witches Series:

SUMMER MAGIC

AUTUMN MAGIC

WINTER MAGIC

SPRING MAGIC

REKINDLED MAGIC

LONG LOST MAGIC

FOREVER MAGIC

ESSENTIAL MAGIC

MOONLIT MAGIC

ENCHANTED MAGIC

CELESTIAL MAGIC

EVERLASTING MAGIC

CAPTIVATING MAGIC

The Thorne Witches: Happily Ever Afters Series:

ENDURING MAGIC

BOUNDLESS MAGIC

The Unlucky Charms Series:

PINTS & POTIONS

WHISKEY & WITCHES

BEER & BROOMSTICKS

COCKTAILS & CAULDRONS

WINE & WARLOCKS

HIGHBALLS & HEXES

The Angels of Legend Series:

LUCIFER

GABRIEL

About the Author

T.M. Cromer is a multi award-winning, best-selling author, who loves to craft wildly entertaining stories designed to keep you glued to your seat, turning the pages to find out what the hell happens next. She specializes in kickass heroines and the men who adore them.

Genres she writes include paranormal romance and romantic suspense.

Want to stay up to date on what's happening in the world of T.M. Cromer? Subscribe to her newsletter, https://www.tmcromer.-com/newsletter, or text JOIN to 1-877-795-1526 to receive release news and promo alerts.

You can also join her VIP reader group on Facebook to chat with her, participate in polls, or just keep current on what's happening. Become a member today: http://www.facebook.com/groups/cromerscarousers!

FOLLOW T.M. CROMER:

facebook.com/tmcromer

instagram.com/tmcromer

tiktok.com/@tmcromer

bookbub.com/authors/t-m-cromer

pinterest.com/tmcromer

amazon.com/stores/T.M.-Cromer/author/B011QK3WXY

www.ingramcontent.com/pod-product-compliance
Lightning Source LLC
Chambersburg PA
CBHW072028220726
48293CB00016B/518